Ash

DAVID WALKER

Ash

Houghton Mifflin Company Boston

1976

/

Library of Congress Cataloging in Publication Data
Walker, David Harry, date
Ash. I. Title.
PZ3.W14666As [PR6045.A275] 813'.5'4 76-4480
ISBN 0-395-24345-9

Printed in the United States of America

C 10 9 8 7 6 5 4 3 2 1

To Willa and our sons

Author's Note

In the autumn of 1948 I wrote a first novel, *The Storm and the Silence*, about a man who killed and was chased across the highlands of Scotland. A while ago it occurred to me that a different man at a different time at a different place might have written that book, have lived through the writing of it. Hence the story of Nigel Ash.

Ash

1

Six sandpipers flew along the shore to alight among seaweed and puddles beyond a rock, small birds whose home moved with the meeting of land and sea, sedately busy as they dipped and dabbled.

The tide flooded faster now to dispossess the spotted sandpipers, which rose together to seek another feeding ground. Not so — they made a short foray to sea in clipped hesitant flight and swung back to perch on that bare rock.

Almost always there was disturbance on the water, a riffle of breeze, a contrary set of current, a commotion of waves, a boat's wake washing to the shore. But this evening the estuary was polished calm as the tide grew in it. Only at the water's edge was there stealthy movement to see and to hear, a lipping and a sippling, dry stone, wet stone, stone no longer.

The sandpipers were quite still on their rock, and he watched the sea creep up to them beyond the mudflats. It would be the first time that he had seen the tide flood across that clam-pocked mud without disturbance from wind or wave.

If the Fundy tide rose two inches a minute, which someone had told him, and if there were fifty yards of almost perfect flatness, then it would fairly romp across. Here it came, and the sandpipers would have no choice but to fly away. He was wrong again. They ran from the tide.

It moved fast, at a slow man's walking pace, darting here, hesitating there to fill a hollow, on again, the tide was marching. There was a pulse in it too, surging ripples chased one another, chasing the birds.

The sandpipers teetered and tottered and ran again. They

were enjoying it, fun to be hunted by the tide. Fun to be hunted? To be hunted, that was a memory, a clue, some hint of an idea.

About a minute he had guessed, and it had taken perhaps that length of time, whatever time might be. But time was visible here and now.

The mudflats were covered to the steep shores of the cove, and the six sandpipers flew away. They called quite loudly, and were gone from that place.

He left the promontory where he had been sitting, and walked to the cabin to get a drink and a cigarette. If he stuck to his ration, the booze was no trouble to him nowadays. but those damned cigarettes . . . When he had been ill he had coughed himself even out of smoking. But here he was, at them again.

They called it the log cabin, and it was of log construction, western cedar squared and tongued and grooved. That was the limit of its resemblance to a log cabin in the wilderness: It was a rich man's electrified summer cottage at the shore, and he was the rich man's brother.

He put the potatoes on to boil, the stew in the oven, and went outside again to sit in proper comfort in a long garden chair, feet up, a table for his whisky. Being chased, he thought. I know about that, and I could choose familiar country. But who being chased, and why?

He got no further than asking himself this important question when the labrador arrived. "Congo!" he said to the dog, who smiled with fangy pleasure, wagging his backside. Sometimes Congo paid visits to him alone, sometimes in human company. If the latter, he would exchange greetings and then dash back to ensure that the person still followed him through the woods.

"Heigh-ho," she called.

"Heigh-ho." He went to meet Lorna, who carried a basket. "Bringer of goodies," he said. "What is it this time?"

"A raspberry tart, not quite cool yet. Shall I put it in the fridge? Or in the oven, if you would rather?"

He decided for cold raspberry tart, and got her a drink, the same as his own, and they sat outside, sharing the table.

2

"Such a glorious day. What did you do?"

"I read in the morning, tried to think, snoozed after lunch, went for a walk, had a cup of tea. Just lately I've been watching the tide come in. I've never lived with the tide before."

"Haven't you? I would have thought that with all your travels . . ." She left the rest of it unsaid, an economy of hers.

"The tide makes sense of everything. Time is the tide was what I thought, brilliant really."

She considered that amusing, or droll, anyway acceptable. They did not talk quite easily, but the whisky helped.

"You look so much better since last week. Are you eating well now, Nigel?"

"Vastly," he said. "I feel new again. Or perhaps that's another first — perhaps I never felt new before."

"Perhaps you never let the world arrive before."

"True," he said. "I hadn't thought of that." He had met her half a dozen times in twenty years until this time, and had disliked her: Snooty, cool, disapproving, as boringly conventional a beauty as only Westmount could produce. How wrong I was, he thought, and he knew that she might be revising judgment of him. There were the thoughts, and always the feeling of man and woman. ". . . I wasn't listening, Lorna?"

"I asked about the writing."

"I had a sort of idea just now. I can see a possible story but not a man for it."

"Why not a man like you? Isn't that what most people do the first time?"

"I expect so," he said. "But I don't make one man."

She said nothing to that. An osprey came to fish the cove. It was two hours or so before high water, and the flounders would be in, bellying their way for clams. The osprey hovered at one place, and then another, dropped a little, hovered again, and closed its wings for the headlong dive. "Now!" she said. But a false alarm — the fish hawk leveled out and flew upriver to try elsewhere. "They used to be common," Lorna said. "Just one more thing." She was a passionate conservationist.

"What's your news?" he said, to steer that subject out of mind.

"Dan is flying down tomorrow, lovely to have him back."

"What in, where to?"

"In the Jet Galaxy to Flume Hill — that's a disused airport along the coast."

"I know it," he said. "I landed there in my flying days. It'll be good to see Dan," he added, liar. "What's young Bobby up to?"

"He went off on that motorbike, perhaps for a get-together with the gang to agree about the infamies of capitalism, perhaps to smoke pot in some bushes with Kim Anderson."

"I can think of better things to do with Kim Anderson in some bushes than smoke pot."

Lorna laughed. "You cheer me up sometimes." A pause. "I was wondering, Nigel . . ."

"Yes?"

"Well, this could turn out to be one of those weekends. Dan is the most patient man on earth, but Bobby needles him and accuses him and patronizes him until finally poor Dan climbs the wall, and that's another weekend. What I wonder is — could you ask Bobby down one evening, say on Saturday, to ease the pressure?"

"Of course. Extend a cordial invitation from me, and to his pals, if they bring the food. I can get some beer."

"No, we have lots. I'll drop some down tomorrow. Now I must go in case the young gentleman revolutionary elects to come home for five dollars' worth of steak at the plutocrat's expense."

"You sound bitter," he said.

"I am. He's such a good-hearted boy at sixes and sevens."

"Not to worry," he said. "Sure you won't have a top-up?"

"No, I can't. Come on, Congo." The black dog pranced about and Lorna stood. Her hair was an unusual color, not auburn, not fair blond — genuine? Some day, if he knew her well enough, he might ask. But he did not know her well enough.

4

She was looking at him, with something to say. "If you can't find the right fiction person for a novel, couldn't you leave that at the moment, and just write your memoirs? You may not be one man. Who is? But your different men could make a story."

"And make libel suits, or worse," he said, irritated. "Still worse — just think what his brother's fascinating memoirs could do to the President's image — *bad blood there, y'know.*"

"One minute you're so kind and understanding; the next you make slick phony cracks about Dan. Well, he's one man, even if you're not."

"*Who is one man? He's one man.* You should be consistent." His temper was stirring, but he forced it down. "Sorry, Lorna. I think I'm finding a bit of peace or truth or whatever you call it here somehow. But how could I if I kept reminding myself?"

"My stupidity," she said smiling. "I did mean well." She kissed him, just touched his cheek with her lips. "Not to worry, as you would say," and was gone.

He put her new potatoes to dry in the oven while he had another drink, and then he ate his supper. The cold raspberry tart was delicious. My God, she gave me a kiss, he thought, like the innocent her annoying innocence threatened improbably to make him.

The sun had set by the time he finished washing up. He went outside with Dan's binoculars to sit on that rock for a late look at what the shore-world happened to be doing. Gulls were climbing to set course for their roosting island. It was high water now, a biggish tide because the moon would soon be full. This is the best place on earth to live with tides, he thought.

Nothing much was happening at high water slack, a full and lovely time. Then a delightful thing did happen across the cove. A doe and her fawn stepped tentatively out to feed at the edge of the field below the woods.

The mother was watchful, stopping to listen and to scent. Once her big ears faced him directly, but she fed again. He knew the red deer of the Scottish Highlands, and he knew these white-tailed deer in Canada.

5

The dappled fawn went for milk, but its mother nudged it away. They played a small chasing game together, and dipped their heads again on the field across the cove below the woods, which would be perfect daytime shelter. And in those woods were old apple trees, loaded with fruit for later on, if men and dogs permitted the deer a later on.

The fawn was the color of its name, but the doe had no brown at all in her coat. She was gray, the pale gray of lichen on a rock. Was it an illusion of the fading light? He looked through binoculars, which hardened, intensified the gray image, no doubt about it. Indeed, her face was almost white.

So many new things were happening to him, and some of them were linked to memory, and so was this. Once long ago he had seen the White Stag on the hill. It was a great beast, known across fifty miles of the Highlands, a twelve pointer, a Royal with a noble spread, and its color, or its lack of color, was the same as this.

A breeze came now as the tide began to ebb. It was the lightest touch of wind from behind him, from the south, a change of weather on the way. Both heads jerked up, the white and the brown. They had caught his scent, and were there no longer.

Nigel Ash went in for a nightcap, and so to bed. It was his habit to read himself to sleepiness. But that night, alone at the cabin by the shore, he switched off the reading lamp and lay and thought. He thought: I know the place, and I know what might happen at that place. I still haven't found the man for that place. But not to worry, not to worry, not to worry, here sleep comes.

The rattle of the window woke him. Gusts shook it intermittently. That's the south wind, he thought, the rain wind, so they say. The sky was still clear, for the moon shone through curtain chinks from across the river. The moon had gone a long way round, so it must be four o'clock or so, and the window rattled. A jet-propelled log cabin shouldn't have a gimcrack window, he thought. I must draw the matter to the attention of my long-suffering brother.

6

But now — it was a sort of small miracle — now he had his man. And he thought: He is a man like me in some ways. He is a man with a bloody wicked temper. He is a man of some endurance. He is a man with some courage of the physical variety. He is a man who likes the birds and beasts and the hills and trees rather more than he likes the common run of the human race, and that is me. But there we part.

He is a true-blue chap, would never cheat, fib, plunder women, rob the kitty, bear false witness. In other words, he is a decent man of honest fault.

I even know a name for him because once I knew a man with just such qualities and quirks — and horrid vices too, no doubt, of which I never learned. But this is fiction, my first attempt, and it must be simple.

His name was Diamond, a good hard name. The Christian name I have forgotten, if I ever knew, no matter. I shall call him Tam. He is Tam Diamond.

It had come easily, inevitably, and he slept again.

IT HAD BEEN FINE WEATHER since he came here ten days ago, with often a west wind growing in the afternoon, sometimes no touch of wind at all.

He plugged the offending window with a wad of paper. It rattled no more, but rain blurred the fly-screen and slatted against glass, a reasonable sound. The view the other way was dismal, gray sea, gray cloud, wet seaweed, and the tide was coming back. "I'm going to beat you, Tide," he said. "I'm going to make a start before you get here." But one must plan. One did not get much further than one planned, as he had found out in his life.

Yet he had the man and he had the country. He had the beginning and he had the end. Already the end was real for him. Surely the rest was incidental building from that start to that finish. It would grow for him.

He stapled ten sheets together. Lorna had bought the yellow paper for him when he told her that he might try to write here. *What a good idea,* she said, probably meaning to be kept busy, off the bottle, out of mischief. His father had once suggested it to him. That was in a letter to a German prison: *Your descriptions of places and events are notably vivid. And you can bring people alive with economy. Would it not worthily occupy your time until this business is over?* But his time until that business was over had been occupied in vain attempts to get out of Colditz Camp.

Now he considered things a while, and then he started. It came easily. It was amazing.

In the autumn evenings the hills are a deep and murky blue; and the stranger will think: These are gentle hills, warmed by the west wind and by the mild sun. There is no violence here.

But to the Highlander that color tells a different story. "Murrky" he calls it, and the abrupt U and the hard-rolled R hint at the true character of the place; for the steep moors are not always peaceful.

See them when blizzards come from the north; or see the spates of springtime tumble down the gullies. Then you will know the harshness in the beauty. But then you will no longer be a stranger.

He made a few changes for the better word, reduced adjectives, and that was it, the land of his story. Not quite true, he thought. One remains a stranger. But never mind.

Nigel Ash wrote again.

The White Stag was resting. He lay below the crest of a hillock. The wind was at his back, and from this place he could watch downwind where danger lurked . . .

He wrote all morning while the south wind buffeted the cabin, and the rain went on. It may be bad, he thought, but it's flowing for me. I am flowing. There came scratches at the door. It was his friend Congo, unescorted and very wet.

He put more wood on the fire and opened a can of Habitant pea. He had two glasses of sherry while that heated. "Steaming labrador, you smell," he said. "But it was nice of you to come." He was dizzy in his mind with this new thing.

A bowl of soup, a corned-beef sandwich — good Fraybentos, awful white enriched — a triangle of Lorna's raspberry tart. "I know it's against your dietary rules," he said. "But this is launch day." Thick pea soup with bully in it was much to Congo's liking. "Would you like to go home now?" he asked when they had finished luncheon. But the dog lay by the fire, head between paws, in some contentment.

The rain was easing, and the wind had veered. The tide was ebbing, half way out. "I don't like you, Ebb," he said.

He read what he had written. It would have to do. There

was a blank now. Lost the flow, he thought. I shouldn't have stopped. But it grew back slowly.

He wrote of the old stalker and the headstrong youth who pursued a White Stag on an autumn afternoon. Yet the deer was his protagonist. I mustn't be, he thought, what is that clumsy word? I mustn't be anthropomorphic. But how can one help it, never having been a noble stag? He smiled to himself, and went on writing. He was near the end:

> Dusk was falling. Soft shadows lay about the hills. The White Stag would be safe when darkness came. He did not know that he was safe already, for the men were going home.
>
> They came closer. Their nailed boots sounded faintly on the road: clop, clop, clop. Then they passed behind the knoll.
>
> The old beast was uneasy. He rose, and stood with legs spread wide, nostrils thrust forward, head circling. Then the wind changed, and a wave of the man-stink struck him.
>
> The White Stag was king of the bare deer forest. He had mastered many things, but this fear he had never mastered. He turned and fled. The blue was murky on the hills. The ground was indistinct. The White Stag ran blindly.

Ash drew a line under it. It was half-past four, and he was tired. There was a rim of blue sky in the west, beyond table and window, beyond the drained shore and the estuary, above the hills of Maine. "A cup of tea," he said. "Oh, hullo, Congo. You still here?"

You had to make it yourself to get a decent cup of tea in this continent where the wishy-washy coffee was no better. "Come on, Congo. Home for you."

He did not take the jeep road through the woods, but the shorter path which was steep for a man who had recently been ill. He rested on a large damp boulder, and Congo came to sit beside him. "Your boss should be here by now," he said. Congo's boss, his brother Dan, was a write-off with dogs, barked at them like a sergeant-major. Dan was forty, eight years his junior.

10

He thought about the White Stag. In the eye of his mind he could see it galloping that last time. And he thought of the pale doe and her fawn. "Will the deer be here again tonight?" he wondered aloud, and Congo whined. He hoped that Congo had not understood.

This had been cleared land once, about eighty years ago. Cedar fencepoles and a shamble of stone walls still marked the edges of fields that never should have been; for in some places the soil had leached away to rock; in some an inch or so of earth supported juniper; in some the trees grew strongly. The forest was coming back, an inconsiderable forest, with some charm to it.

The wind had fallen, and the sky was clearing. It had been a good rain, and it left wet-smelling goodness. Congo stayed close to him until the path joined the old farm road which went by the lily pond and the swimming pool to climb to the house. Lorna called it the road, but it was grassed over, a narrow lawn winding between shrub borders.

Congo went for a drink of muddy water. That pond was full of goldfish, but one never saw them in the shallows that they made such a thorough job of roiling up. One took one's sister-in-law's word for it that, spring and fall, they always appeared like magic. She derived some pleasure from her obscurantist goldfish, one could tell.

He passed the deep pond, which had a rock bottom and a filter and was near-pellucid. The landscaping was all Lorna's, but the swimming pool was Dan's pet baby.

They might have seen him coming, or it might be chance. They were walking down together, hand in hand, but they disengaged. Congo galloped up to welcome Master.

"Hullo, Congo! Good Congo! That's enough now, Congo, down, sir!"

Congo had muddied his charcoal gray Bermuda shorts, the green stockings too, but not the matching shirt, nor the paisley silk scarf at Daniel's neck, all belted and trim, Canadian band-box, now slightly muddy. Why in God's name couldn't he wear old clothes? "Hullo, Dan," he said nicely.

"Nigel, it's good to see you." Dan put his hand out, so one had to shake. He never shook hands if he could help it, except in line of business. But shake hands with your brother? God again. "How are you feeling?" Dan asked with genuine kindness. That was him, both genuine and kindly.

"Much better, thank you."

"That's great. You look it too. Is the log cabin comfortable?"

"It's wonderful," he said. "It's the most soothing place I ever was at."

"That's great," Dan said again. "Stay as long as you like. We're glad to have you, aren't we, dear?"

"Of course, Dan," Lorna said. She was different with her Danny boy, rather subdued and dutiful. I bet he hasn't taken her to bed yet. It's Bermuda shorts time in the country in the afternoon, not tumble-time.

"I'll just have a quick look at the pool," Dan said. "And then the sun will be over the yardarm." He went on.

"Congo paid a call on me, and stayed all day."

"He was asking for a walk, and I was busy, so I said: *Go and see Nigel, if you like*, and off he shot. I didn't think you'd mind."

"Good company," he said. "Does he wander much, hunting, I mean?"

"I don't think so, ever. He just goes to a destination."

They followed her husband to the pond. "I made a start today."

"Did you?" she said. "Oh, did you?"

Dan knelt, counting drops of red liquid into a vial of water, shook the mixture and inspected it. "PH nine at least," he muttered, "and look at the algae on the walls. What's the bottom like, Lorna?"

"A little slimy, but only at the shallow end." Dan's swimming pond was fed by springs from the woods, and its bottom

12

was a smooth ledge of rock sloping from ground level to seven foot at the deeper end. It was a fluke of nature, of which Dan was proud, and reasonably so. He went now to the filter house, whence came a faint motor hum.

"It only takes a few minutes a day for chlorine and those things," she said, "and one hour a week to vacuum it, Bobby's single solitary job. *Sure, Mum, I'll do it right after lunch*, but he forgets. Or does he forget? And Dan is so patient with him. Sometimes I wish he'd blast the bloody hell, but Dan is right, of course."

Probably wrong, he thought. A rushing of water continued for a while in the woods beyond the filter. Then bubbles erupted from the pond, and Dan emerged. "You should have seen the filth," he said. "It can't have been backwashed since I left two weekends ago." He frowned. Dan was a handsome, square-jawed fellow, the jogging executive, jog before breakfast, walk to the office, so damned decent with his baffled frown, not cursing his offspring.

"I'll give it a big shot of chlorine now, vacuum tomorrow morning, backwash again on Sunday. By the time I leave it should be clearing."

"It looks pretty clear," said Nigel Ash. "Not perfect, I will say."

"Well, six o'clock, let's get that drink."

"Marvelous air," Dan said on the terrace. "Two whole days of clean air to breathe."

"Where have you been this week, Dan?" she asked.

"Let's see — Monday was Winnipeg and Vancouver, Tuesday Toronto, Wednesday in Montreal, Thursday New York, and here I am."

"All by your jet?" he asked.

"Yes. I suppose I spend a third of my days in it."

"You should learn to fly the thing. That would pass the time aloft."

"Aloft is where I get the work done." At forty Dan was president of the Laurentian Bank, director of umpteen blue-chip corporations, trustee and governor of this and that, highly respected, highly successful, and he deserved every bit of it, and what a perfect bore he was. "Do you find enough to do at the cabin?" He would not mean to be condescending.

"I find plenty of nothing to do, and I watch the world go by." Their inability to communicate, incomprehension of one another, never stayed long below. "Well, back to idleness," he said. His mind had worked as hard today as on any day in his botched-up life.

"If we're dining with the Skafes, I'd better put in that chlorine now. What time do they expect us?"

"Half-past seven, darling."

"Hang on, Nigel. I'll start down with you."

"Bobby says the gang would love to come tomorrow, and they'll bring the food. Would five be all right for me to take down some beer and things?"

"Five would be fine," he said. "Many thanks." If Lorna wanted to provide beer and things, why not? "About this so-called job I'm on — well, I'm not on it until I'm sure of it."

"Okay, but . . . okay," she said. Here came Dan with a pail of chlorine tablets. "About five, then," she said. "I'd better go and change. Goodnight."

He walked down with his brother, who had been brought to Canada by their mother in nineteen-forty, aged eleven. Millicent Ash was Canadian, and there were numerous sound reasons for removing herself and ewe-lamb from the Blitz. But their neighbors at home did not much enquire about the welfare of the Ashes who had opted out. Not Dan's fault, Ash thought, but what a prissy little beast he was.

Dan broadcast chlorine tablets in plopping showers about the pond. "A massive dose," he said. "But they'll be dissolved by morning. Now for that sign." The sign read: *No swimming. Danger. Chemicals.* "Young Bobby . . ." he began, and stopped himself.

"You know the birch glade this side of the cottage?"

"The log cabin, yes?"

14

"Would it be all right with you if I tidied that through a little, took out the alders and the useless stuff?"

"Yes, certainly. I'd be grateful, Nigel."

"I need a bit of exercise."

"Of course, but after pneumonia you shouldn't overdo it. Well, I must go."

"I hear a lot of big business is moving to Toronto."

"Not any business that I'm involved in."

"But if things get worse, will you pull out of Quebec?"

"Certainly not, and things won't. I have the utmost confidence in Quebec. Goodnight."

Needled him, Ash thought. Dan was lying, but it was a lie that must be told by any honorable bank president.

He had his second drink, reading what he had written. Would he call it "Chapter One," or "Prelude," perhaps? Not "Prelude," that was fancy, and one must be plain, absolutely plain and simple. He would leave this first part unnumbered and unnamed, and tomorrow would be "Chapter One, Tam Diamond."

After supper he sat on his rock. The wind had gone to the west, and the tide came choppily. A catbird mewed, another of his neighbors. But the neighbors that he waited for had not arrived. This breeze would keep his scent from them. The man-stink, he had called it crudely.

The sunset was coloring as they came onto the flat field beyond the cove. They were about a hundred yards· from him, becoming indistinct as darkness fell. But he watched on through binoculars. The bright sunset faded, and the moon was up. He would watch the deer for as long as they might stay. But they were here again, and that was all that mattered, and he must sleep before meeting Tam Diamond in the morning.

FIRST, THERE WAS THE MATTER OF MOVING from here and now to there and then, from a chair in a cottage by the Canadian shore to a garage in a small town at the beginnings of the Scottish Highlands. The time was some twenty years ago, soon after the Second War. But any remembered time and any typical place were easy about the country of one's bones.

The man was more difficult. True that one had to play God to that man, leading him on the way one knew that he would go. But one must also be that man. One was not Nigel Ash, a disbarred member of the upper-middle. One was Tam Diamond, a lorry driver from Glasgow, an ex-commando soldier, a city boy who loved the hills of storm and silence, a man true in heart and helpless in anger.

He does not pity himself. He is not to be pitied. I am Tam Diamond.

And so he began. It was abrupt. It was the sack, much less than Diamond deserved for knocking down and out an old man of sixty who had taken his lorry tools, stranding him with a puncture, and then had told him to get back to Glesky where he belonged.

The boss gave Diamond a choice: Either get out without a penny of his wages, which would go to the other man, or he would call in the police. The boss was a bastard, but a straight-like bastard.

Diamond got out. He walked away from that gray town, shedding bad memories of the place, but uneasy about the anger ever stalking him.

It was a fine morning in the month of March. The buds were

16

still small, and the thrushes sang for spring not far away, and Diamond was soon cheerful enough, striding on his journey. He had twenty miles to walk to the power scheme at Dulrannoch, where there would be a certain job for him, a first-class driver, the best worker always, the most reliable man, the most reliable man until . . .

It was the shadow of a cloud like the cloud that hid the sun. He stopped at the bridge where he must cross the river, and he watched a while, and he was lucky. A silver salmon jumped, and jumped again.

But there were miles to go. He climbed out of the valley of tall trees, changing quite soon to a different world of the heather and the bog, the rushing burn, the bare brown hills.

Diamond grew hungry. He had no food with him, and no money to buy it, but he thought that he remembered a cottage along this road. He came upon the roadmender, and he asked him whether there was a house farther up. It was his own house, the man said, looking Diamond over, neither friendly nor unfriendly, seeing a big decent-looking chap, fair in the hair and straight in the eye, and he said that the wife might spare a bite to eat. Diamond told him that he would work for it.

Ash got up for more coffee. He still felt dizzy if he moved too quickly. But that was momentary. A fishing boat was passing in the estuary. Its engine blattered coarsely, and it needed a coat or two of white paint. He saw it, but in absence. He was there, Diamond at the cottage door, waiting to meet the roadmender's wife whom he would kill.

Must I kill her? You want the grand woman, and she wants you, a sudden driving want between you, but at the brink she stops herself, has never been unfaithful to her man. Too late, you go to take her, and she hits you, and instantly the red rage breaks, she falls and strikes her head on the pointed brass knob of the coal scuttle. You do not mean to kill her, but she dies, she has to die. It is the horror kernel of the story.

Slowly now. Build slowly to the hateful thing. Split kindling for her in the shed, back to the good soup, slow talk together, sympathy together. Odd, he thought, how much I hate it, can't escape it. I must do it in due dreadful course to make the story.

He stopped for sherry, lunch, a stroll along the beach. The dinghy on the running line was high and dry at dead low water. Back to write again. He liked the woman, fine strong woman from the North, from Caithness, *a wild bare country, with the wind and no trees*, she said it for him, and he had to kill her, but not yet.

"Enough," he said at nearly five o'clock, late tea time, an extra cup for Lorna, she did say five. He put the cosy on the pot, but she came punctually in the jeep, alone.

"Oh, hullo," he said. "Fancy seeing you again."

"Fancy you," she said. Her smile told him that she was glad too. Every day it grew a little, it was kindly for him. He could not say to Lorna: "You look marvelous, you look like the woman I have to kill"; hardly a nice thing to say to one's sister-in-law.

They carried beer and things. "Bobby's gone on his motorbike for the lobsters." She glanced at his stapled sheets of yellow paper on the table, and then at him. "Writing all day?"

"More or less," he said. "More than less."

"It must be tiring."

"Yes," he said. "And painful, the bit I'm doing. I'm afraid I might lose it if I tried to explain."

"Please don't."

"You understand so well," he said. They took their cups of tea outside. "Sun or shade for you?"

"Shade, I think. We played golf this morning, and were at the pond all afternoon. I feel roasted toasted."

He put her chair under the crab apple tree, and sat beside her in the sun. "That reminds me," he said. " 'Ane, twa three, ma mither cotched a flea. She roastit it and she toastit it and she had it tae her tea.' "

"What a lovely mad rhyme. I've never been to Scotland. Do you still like it best of everywhere?"

"I don't know," he said in the hot August sun. But he was

18

thinking that soon he would be hunted, he would be on the run in Scotland in the wild month of March. "Why don't you get Dan to take you there sometime?"

"No," she said. "That's out. Dan will never go now. Surely you know that."

"Yes," he said. He had known that, but he had not intended a provoking question. He had been away in mind. His father had not tried to dissuade Millicent Ash from taking off to Canada in 1940. If she wanted to skip, then let her skip, and when she also skipped with alacrity into the bed of her future second husband, that was that. Hector Ash wrote her off, divorced her. He was contemptuous, not apparently embittered.

". . . Dan wrote several times," Lorna was saying. "But your father never answered. And when Dan tried again two years ago, and he was dying, he refused the letter, sent it back. Why would he hold it against Dan?"

"Father was like that. I was thinking just now that he wrote her off, and everything that went with her, and that meant Dan. He was arrogant and Calvinistic, not a prude, though. He could be damned amusing in his sardonic way. Father was a complicated man. My mother on the other hand is a simple sybarite and floozy. I expect they were both relieved to get out of it."

"Not the happiest of families," Lorna said. "Dan's father wouldn't acknowledge his existence, and you won't see your mother again."

"But I did," he said. "I did my very best until even the price of sponging off her became too high to be endured. That plush vulgarity amid the memorabilia of doting widowhood in Victoria, B.C., my God."

Lorna laughed. "I know," she said. "But she's very kind hearted. That's something good."

"So is treacle something good." She had not spoken before to him of his parents, and forthwith he must kill the subject, saying treacle. "Sorry," he said. "Stupid remark. I haven't quite shaken the story off yet." He thought of telling her about his visitors across the cove, and she would love to hear that, being as fond of wild creatures as he was himself, but the mother deer had brought the first flash of the story to his mind. Perhaps unlucky, keep it. "Let's do something different."

"What different?" she said, in sympathy again.

"Oh, anything. A quick toot in the dinghy? But that means more sun."

"It will be cool on the water. Yes, come on."

The boat was at the other side of the point, on the steeper shore. It came easily on the running line, but he puffed a bit.

Lorna sat amidships, facing the bow, and he put the outboard down. The kicker, he thought, good name from the North. It was a modest five horsepower Johnson. "Be nice now," he said, and it caught first time.

He headed west across the estuary, meeting small waves on his starboard bow, smack-smack, nice waves, and he watched her nice brown shoulders, nice brown arms, a hand on each thwart. It was his guess, from sly inadequate observation, that Lorna was nice brown all over. One could hardly say to her: "Lorna, is your bottom well and truly tanned? I don't mean: Does Daniel tan your bottom, but you know, the buff?" She might not like to be asked that sort of forward question; on the other hand she might, the best women sometimes do.

He laughed, and she heard that above the motor purr, quite a decent purr, it was. "Joke?" she said, turning, pleased.

"No joke," he said. "How old are you, Lorna?"

"I'm thirty-eight. How old are you?"

"I preceded you by ten," he said, and ran on for a minute or two until the shores were about equidistant, and he shut it off. The tide was making up the estuary, but the breeze was making down, so the dinghy drifted a little, drifted back.

The dinky red speedboat was at its mooring over there. On most fine evenings it went for a spin, more a thirty-mile-an-hour spin than a ten-mile-an-hour toot. He himself preferred the toot.

"Who is Bobby bringing?"

20

"Kim Anderson, Molly Becker's daughter. And Nelson, the younger of two Kelly brothers. Their father is a salmon man at the station, a super family, they are. Actually, Kim is Keith Kelly's steady, but he's been away in Labrador on a job. Someone called Jane Paully is the fourth, a rather droopy speechless girl from Minneapolis. And Uncle makes five. They're dying to meet Bobby's wicked uncle."

"Wicked," he said. He did not mind being called wicked uncle as long as it meant glamorous, good value, neither of which he was.

"It's good of you to have them, Nigel."

"At your expense," he said.

"At yours in the cause of peace. I would never have suggested it if I'd known you would be so tired."

"Not tired now," he said. "It's just that this thing begins to burn me up, and I mustn't hurry it. I must let it grow and happen together."

"You will," she said. "Now home to change for dinner. We're entertaining the carriage trade."

He ran for the shore. The woods and the fields sloped up, greener, he thought, after yesterday's rain. It was pretty, or better than that, but nothing spectacular. He eased in slowly, cut the motor, a bump, a slither, quite neatly done, and Lorna stepped on to the red rock. Sandstone conglomerate, he thought, another item in the back of memory's beyond. He tilted the motor, hitched to a loop in the running line, hauled the dinghy out a little, and followed her up.

She stopped by the big window. Her eye might have chanced in upon his yellow pages again because she said: "Will you want to type it as you go along?"

"Yes," he said. "Yes, that would be better."

"Can you type?"

"Dot and carry, yes."

"I can lend you my portable, if you like."

"Oh, could you? That would be great."

"Or I could even type for you. I have lots of spare time when

Dan's away." Lorna strolled on to the jeep, her back to him, darker back and paler hair.

But she who types must read, must judge, must reveal by some hint, might kill it for him. "I wouldn't say a word about it, not to you or anyone."

"It isn't that," he said. It was just that, but it was also this: "The thing is that if I type myself, I can still be polishing. I remember that years ago when I did a few short stories for *Collier's* magazine, long defunct, remember it?"

"We used to subscribe. I liked it much better than the stuffy old *Post*. But I don't remember "by Nigel Ash," and I would have noticed that name. What were the stories about?"

"Oh, this and that, the North, other places I had been. Not under my own name, though." They were under the name of Neil Arnott, which happened still to be the name on one of his passports. But it might be unwise of wicked uncle to intimate that to nephew's mother.

"What name?" Lorna said. "Do tell me."

"Secret," he said. He looked across the cove at the field where the after-grass and clover were certainly greener since yesterday, and he turned to her. "But I have a much better secret I would like to show you some evening if my luck holds out, just you, not another single soul, I hope."

"You weave tangled webs," she said with coolness.

"This isn't," he said. "This is the loveliest twin strand of gossamer for you to see, and I can't promise I can keep my promise. Goodnight, Lorna."

"Goodnight, Nigel." It was a noisy stout jeep, dwindling out of sight and sound.

When first we practice to deceive, he thought. Why *first?* He wished that he was true for her to see him true. "I wish I was Tam Diamond," he said aloud. "No, I do not, poor sod." He went to chill the beer and Coke for the younger generation.

4

IT WAS A FISHING BOAT OF USUAL APPEARANCE, high in the bow, broad in the beam, a cabin with a stovepipe, an open stern well. The differences were in gleaming paint, coiled ropes, the quiet engine. "Ahoy there, Uncle!"

"Ahoy," he said. "Just coming. I expected a party by land, not a landing party."

He rowed the short distance out. "Mrs. Becker, this is Uncle. George Petrie, Jane Paully, Nelson Kelly, and you've met Kim, Uncle."

"Hi, Kim," he said. "Hullo, everyone." Mrs. Becker was a plump handsome woman of Lorna's age, George Petrie was about the same. I wonder who you would be, Ash thought.

Nelson Kelly came aboard, and Bobby handed him down a Styrofoam box. "The lobsters, simply masses."

"You could tie up to the running line," he said to Petrie. "There's plenty of water at this tide. Or would you rather anchor?"

"No, no," said Mrs. Becker. "Thank you so much, but George and I have business to discuss over dinner at home."

"List to my gem composed at sea:

> Dame Cordon Bleu's Alaska Bake
> Doth purest bliss of business make."

Mrs. Becker shook with ample laughter. "George, you're hopeless."

"On the contrary, fair hostess and co-trustee, the poet's mouth is watering in gastronomic hope. Sorry, Mr. Ash. Doggerel

23

is my besetting sin, or one of them. Shall I come back about ten for you people, when moon and tide are high?"

"Is ten too late, Uncle?"

"Ten would be fine." The others came aboard, and the boat went astern and then swung to head downriver. "Is your house far from here?" Ash asked Kim Anderson, a dark girl, a slim version of her mother.

"About a mile," she said. "And Nelson lives between us and you."

"George Petrie — he seems a slightly wacky type."

"Seems," Nelson said. "He's a good guy, George, considering."

"A co-trustee?"

"Of the aquarium," Kim said.

"It's a super place, saltwater and fresh, oh, look, the osprey! Is it going to? I bet it doesn't." The osprey did dive, and surfaced to fly away with a flounder held fore and aft, but one had the feeling that Nelson Kelly had quite adroitly emphasized the osprey to close the aquarium topic.

The boys drank beer and the girls drank Coke, and Ash mixed himself martini. "Music?" he said. "We have Rock and we have Johnny Cash and we have good old Belafonte."

"Which would you like?" said Kim.

"I think good old Belafonte might go down easily with lobster."

They ate vastly, and he ate largely, and he felt positively happy or content, to be with young people was as easy a thing as he knew, it was because they liked him, of course, of course.

Nobody spoke much until after raspberries and cream, after "a little girl in Kingston Town," end of Belafonte. "Let's just talk," he said, putting his weight against further music now that the sun was nearly down. Across the cove and out of sight from here, the doe and her fawn might soon be feeding.

"Take this napalm, y'know," Bobby speaking. "Making disgusting huge profits from roasting women 'n kids alive with burning jelly. And there's that stuff, 2,4,5, or something,

24

y'know, they spray to kill the vegetation, and what they kill is the fetus in the womb. And, y'know, my father is a director of the company, would you believe it?"

"And my mother has shares in the company," Kim said. "But I guess that still leaves you one up, Bobby."

Bobby laughed and gazed adoringly.

"I guess I'm the one who's up or down," Nelson said. "My Dad doesn't have shares in anything, he's perpetually broke." Jane whatsername, yes, Paully, giggled and gazed adoringly. Bobby was mad about Kim and Jane was crazed for Nelson, and Nelson and Kim, the vital ones, were just plain pals; it was interesting, the chemistry of sex, and chemistry he supposed it was, he ought to know.

They talked on, or three of them talked, and Jane Paully gazed. Bobby's thoughts poured out in scrambled fashion, and Kim's much likewise, but when Nelson spoke, it was with care and lucidity. The capitalists had better watch out for him, Ash thought. What seemed dreary about them, as about all the young New Left, was that they invariably agreed with one another. Apartheid, napalm, 2,4,5T, discrimination, pulpmill pollution, all was polluted establishment corruption, unanimous consent.

"Do you agree, Uncle?"

"I agree about a lot of things you're against. What I don't know is what you're for, what you believe in."

The others looked at Nelson, who said to him: "We believe in what human beings could be."

He had lost that belief long ago. He supposed that he had begun to lose it when first he had stepped across shady brook, and could no longer believe in himself. He might say: *You cannot change the nature of the bloody human beings you believe in. Nobody ever has, and nobody ever will.* But he did not say it.

"I know it sounds naive, Mr. Ash. But it's a change, a new beginning." What a formidable square young face he had, belief burning so brightly, it did make you wonder.

25

"Uncle, you've been listening to us gassing, but you hardly speak."

"Uncle is a wise old owl," Kim said, lightly and kindly said. "Bobby says you've been everywhere and done everything on earth. Couldn't you tell us a story or something?"

"Ain't got no decent stories," he said.

"Indecent ones then, Uncle."

"Indecency tends to become indecent in the repetition."

"He's funny," Kim said. "As my mum would say, he can be quite amusing. I know what my mum is doing now. She's stuffing George Petrie just like he said. My mum loves men's stomachs more than anything. Well, she loves men, period."

The atmosphere was easy, stomachs indeed full, contented. After a while they went to wash up, and he sat alone, thinking of tomorrow, but he feared tomorrow. Then the boys had more beer and he had whisky, one extra it would be tonight, in training.

"You were a prisoner in the war, weren't you?"

"Yes," he said. "For three years. I was shot down over France."

"And you escaped?"

"I got out once or twice, but never to a frontier, copped again."

"Could you tell us about escaping?"

He saw back to that, a jumble of it, chased by night, shot at by night, hiding by day without water in hot harvest-time. But tomorrow, or soon, he was to be hunted again in the cold March weather. If he spoke about it, he might lose the writing of it. "Sorry," he said. "That isn't easy for me. I could talk about something else, don't know what."

"Did you fly again right after the war?"

"In the RAF, and later I came to Canada."

"How many hours altogether, Uncle?"

"A bit over nine thousand," he said.

"Gosh, that's a lot, let's see — that's a whole year in the air."

"Yes," he said. "One forty-eighth of my total so far. Some of

26

it was when the DEW line was being built, fairly hideous flying, that could be."

"Did you have many near squeaks, narrow shaves?"

Tell them. Why not tell them? It had never been reported.

"A few," he said. "Oddly enough, I think the narrowest was about forty miles north of where we're sitting. I was flying a Mink, a single-engined four place job on floats, and we were at five thousand, a safe enough altitude in a country of lakes, it should have been and wasn't. The engine cut out on me without any warning, and not a puddle in sight, so I simply glided, glided simply for the softest looking bit of forest, it was a stand of young balsam fir, quite pliable, a lot better than bare ground. Anyway, the treetops sheared off the floats, and that slowed us nicely, nosed over and in, and the next thing I remember was climbing out or falling out of the cabin just as it began to burn."

"Were you alone?"

"Yes," he said. "I was flying in to collect a couple of fishermen at a lake."

"Were you hurt?"

"I broke my left wrist, but I think that was getting out of the plane, not in the crash. Well, the wind was from the south, so I walked in that direction while my fire went northward, the woods were tinder. Fortunately it rained that night, and the fire petered out, and two days later I emerged from the forest primeval at a place called Anvil Lake."

"I know it," Bobby said. "We go fishing there sometimes. Were you none the worse, except for the broken wrist?"

"It was the end of May, and I was a good deal the worse for blackflies, otherwise okay."

His story was true except in two particulars. He had not been flying at five thousand feet to collect a fishing party. He had been hedge-hopping, tree-hopping above the Province of New Brunswick in the direction of the state of Maine to deliver fifty thousand in very well forged ten dollar bills. The plane had not gone on fire. He had set it on fire in order to incinerate an embarrassing cargo, burst open and scattered all round the cabin.

"Was it your own plane?"

"Unfortunately, yes, and I had no insurance." He was not selling the stuff, he was carrying the stuff, cash-down freight charges on delivery.

"How long ago was that, Uncle?"

"It was soon after the DEW line. That would be eleven years ago, before your father bought this place. So, not for the first or last time, I was on my uppers. But the wrist soon mended, and I flew that summer for one of the budworm spraying outfits, not the cleanest or safest form of fun. However, I made enough to take off for Australia."

But he was thinking that his dull story could have been quite wickedly exciting if he had told the truth. *You weave tangled webs*, Lorna had said that afternoon. Ineluctable webs. He had taken off for Australia because the forger people were after him about their undelivered merchandise. Somehow or other they did not believe the painful truth, and that made him lose his bloody temper. He beat two of them up, broke the knuckles of his other hand, and jetted safely to the Antipodes before they could come back for him.

"Do you still fly, Uncle?"

"No," he said. "I stopped after Australia."

"And you don't miss it?" Nelson asked.

"Sometimes, I don't know. Scared of it perhaps. Or scared of being scared of it."

It would have been true if he had said: The last time I flew was into Alice Springs from Darwin, half drunk, and I pranged the thing on a power line, got whole drunk for a change, and when I sobered up, I was palpitating terrified of flying. What a four-flusher I am, he thought, and a fat lot I care.

The moon was high at ten o'clock, cutting short shadows from tree and rock, but the shadows dimmed as patches of cirrus crossed the moon.

28

"The wind has gone southeast," Nelson said. "That means fog in the morning."

It was quiet here, no sounds at all on the Canadian side, a murmur of traffic across the river.

"George is coming," Bobby said. But it was a while before Ash heard the engine, and running lights showed outside the point. "Most of them make a hell of a racket," he said.

"Custom-built and super-silenced," Kim said. "It's my idea of a perfect boat, not like that other beast."

But she did not explain that other beast, and Nelson went over to pull in the dinghy.

The boat went astern, lost way, and the engine stopped. "It is I, Skipper Petrie, at your service." And he sang, loudly and tunefully: "Speed bonny boat like a bird on the wing,/Homeward, the little ones cry."

"George is in a very corny mood tonight," Kim said.

"He may be corny, but he's still a pig." It was Jane Paully's first verbal contribution of the evening.

"A pig?" Ash said.

"A cop," Bobby said. "Inspector George Petrie, R.C.M.P."

If you had experience, you could usually spot them, even the smoothest of smooth cops. It was the casual level eye, moving, pausing, moving, videotape. They could not quite hide from you, and it was as little likely that you could hide from them. Ash had wondered, and the other thing that he had wondered was whether he had seen George Petrie before.

"George is a bird photographer too," said Nelson. "A brilliant one, actually. That's why he's a trustee of the duckpond sanctuary and the aquarium with Kim's mother and my father and Mr. Skafe. Do you know him?"

"I've heard of Skafe."

Ash sat amidships to row them out, Kim and Bobby in the stern. "Do you ever go fishing, Uncle? Trout, I mean."

"Yes, I do. The water's too warm in August, though, surely."

"Not at Anvil Lake where you walked out that time. There

are good spring holes. We could take the Wagoneer and the canoe some evening if you like."

"I would like very much, say in two or three days' time." By then the deed would have been done, the killer become the fugitive.

"You shivered, Uncle."

"Night chills," he said. "Yes, let's do that, Bobby."

They climbed aboard at the stern of the boat. Petrie was tallish, broad in the shoulder, an athletic type, but his face was vaguely in contradiction, beaked nose, high cheekbones, serrated brow, interesting moonlit face. I may have seen you somewhere, Ash thought, and if I have seen you, you may have seen me. "I hope the dinner came up to expectation," he said.

"The dinner was fabulous. We had escargots, half a dozen garlicked beauties to appetize. Then a superb convocation of crabmeat and cantaloupe. And to conclude, the Baked Alaska. Unlike lesser cooks who tend to throw the dish at you, Kim's mother hints, even consults, in advance."

"Bedtime for me," he said. "Goodnight, everyone."

They all thanked him. "Thanks for a super evening," said the taciturn Miss Paully.

"I didn't contribute much," he said.

"Just yourself," Kim said. It was charmingly spoken, and he smiled, and so did George Petrie.

"One thing I wanted to ask, Mr. Ash. Have you seen any herons at your shore, Great Blue Herons?"

"One stands for hours at the next point upriver. I've never seen it catch anything. It simply stands, elongated graven image."

"Would I be intruding if I tried to get a telephoto shot, fish in the bill, the very act?"

"Do by all means," he said. "Over high water, it's usually there."

"Tomorrow would be my only chance," Petrie said.

Goodnight again, Goodnight. The sound of the boat faded round the point, and the dinghy rocked slowly in the wash. There had been no phosphorescence before, but as he rowed back, the water curled in liquid gleam at the tips of his oars.

If George Petrie, photographer, aspired to take a telephoto shot of a Great Blue Heron at the *moment suprême*, wiggling prey in beak, then Inspector Petrie might aspire to switch direction for a telephoto shot of a human subject. He might; he just might; not probable. But it would make sense for the potential subject to remain indoors. Not even the most brilliant photographer could take telescopic pictures from broad daylight through glass window into shady room.

They had done a splendid job of washing up and stacking, nothing for him to do except to check that the door to the garbage-can shelter was properly snibbed against raccoons, and it was.

And now, before bed, a quick look across the cove with the aid of moonlight and binoculars. The deer were not there tonight. The field below the woods was empty. But over to the left, beyond the point where the Great Blue Heron fished, or perhaps it rested, for all he knew — on the shore beyond that point something moved. The something became two men. One carried an object which the moon reflected this way. It was a large silver-plated flashlight or torch, the kind with a handle, the kind that threw a narrow beam a quarter of a mile or more. The other carried something over his right shoulder, and when he turned, Ash saw that it was a rifle, muzzle forward, held in the way that no good stalker holds his familiar tool.

He dropped the glasses to hang from his neck, cupped his hands, and shouted. "Ho!" a wordless bellow. The men froze for a moment; then turned and went quickly upriver, back the way they had come.

IT WAS A MIST RATHER THAN A FOG, closing one's visible world to fifty yards or so, quiet, agreeable, intimate. A gull cried occasionally somewhere.

"I like you, fog," he said, going back to his armchair here in the cabin in the fog. But it was there that he must be, in the hill cottage on a crisp March day.

"Christ, I hate it," he said. Having said that, he was gathering, he was coming to it now at last.

. . . She smiled, a small secret smile of kindness and compassion which came and hovered and was wiped away.

And she died. He saw her die. He saw the fingers of death move across her face, smoothing expression from it, taking the living color, leaving only stillness, unruffled, unhurried, with a splash of blood where his fingers had touched her cheek, and the dark mark of the bruise he had made.

More coffee. Another cigarette. Flame dying. A shot of butane gas, small things to do, and back to it. He was sailing, he was floating, that was the feeling, floating, writing fast now, coldly, hotly without hurry, the damned deed done.

It was his left ankle on the footstool that brought him back. The sun had come round the southern corner to toast his ankle, fog long gone, damp collars on rock, a wet line of seaweed on the sand confirmed that it was about an hour past high water.

"Got you, I do believe," a man said out there.

The heron emitted one harsh croak and flew away, lumbered into flight from the point across the cove. Oh yes, Petrie, about whom he had forgotten.

He was sitting in shade below the bluff, his back to a rock, before him camera, outsized lens and tripod.

"Hullo," Ash said, looking down. "Successful, I gather."

"I think so. It stood there for ever like a graven image, as you said; then finally action. This thing winds itself on. So one simply keeps pressing the tit."

"What kind of camera is it?"

"A Hasselbad, with the five hundred millimeter." Petrie rubbed his eyes. "Rather tiring," he said. "You have to watch and wait so long, and then be so darned quick." The corny aspect of George Petrie was absent. "I hope I didn't disturb you."

"Not at all. I never heard you until now."

"I arrived about half-past ten, when the fog was clearing. There's a good path all the way, although this lot is quite a load to lug. Sorry, alliteration not intended."

"I was just going to have a glass of sherry. Would you like some, or a gin and tonic? The boys finished up the beer."

"Gin and tonic would suit the climate. It's going to be hot again this afternoon, the dog days of summer."

"I know the expression, but why dog days?"

"Because they used to think that the spell of inert sultry weather there usually is at this time of year sent dogs round the bend. Might be something to it, I suppose. Burdensome high summer. I feel it myself."

They got their drinks, and if Petrie cased the joint, he gave no indication of that. "Let's sit outside, I've been closeted all morning. As a matter of fact, I'm trying to write a novel, first attempt."

"That's interesting. A good place to do it, I would think." Petrie said no more.

"They mentioned an aquarium and bird sanctuary. I gather that's why you're here."

"Yes. You see, Molly's late husband, Frank Becker, had planned and endowed the aquarium; but before building was begun, he ran his speedboat on to a rock in the bay and killed himself. The Kelly brothers were with him, and they jumped just in time, a near squeak."

"I was much taken with Nelson Kelly last evening."

"He's a great boy. And so is Keith in his totally different, artistic way."

"Some beast of a boat was mentioned, and the aquarium. But they seemed to cut those subjects short."

"Yes," Petrie said. "It was a complicated business." He picked up a stone beside his chair, a limber flick of his left wrist, it splashed far out, within a few inches of a floating bottle.

"You throw like a pitcher."

"I did use to pitch once upon a time. Well, there it is, best small aquarium in North America. You should have a look at it. But the bird sanctuary nearby is my pet baby, G. Petrie, duck trustee. I think that might interest you. Bobby says that you're a whiz about the natural world."

"Amateurishly — not a whiz at all. But I'm fond of it, yes."

"One escapes from a surcease of humanity," Petrie said. He was companionable, an appealing man, a cop. "I must go, late already for Molly's Cornish Hen in Aspic, what a cook. Then Ottawa tonight, worse luck."

"Are you stationed there?"

"Based there. I travel a bit, wandering minstrel, east and west. I envy you at your log cabin by the shore, a world to watch and a book to write. I might get down again around the end of the month. Will you have finished it by then?"

"I don't know," he said. "I really don't know. Just possibly."

"A most inept question. How could you time an intangible? But the best of luck with it, Mr. Ash, and many thanks." He shook hands gravely, shouldered his paraphernalia, and strode away at a lanky pace.

It occurred to Ash that the question as posed might be inept, but was a delicate way of finding out the probable duration of one's stay. Oh, forget it. He went inside for a quick bite, and back to work, and work it was, hard lovely labor.

34

Diamond shifted his position under the dark ledge on the hill. He curled his legs for warmth and wrapped the two coats tighter around him.

I wasn't so lucky, he thought. But I was a red-minded killer, hitting her in the face. A push or a hit, either could have done it. Yes, you can say that, but a hit's different. There's no good in fretting over what I've done, I must forget it. I must do all that's left to me, escape, get clean away. I'm over the bridge, no more for me to lose, no way of saving my neck if I'm nabbed. Or even if they didn't hang me, they'd put me away for a lifetime. And I'd be mad in a year, closed in the darkness of prison. That makes it easier a bit, knowing I'd rather be dead than let them take me.

Ash stopped at that, at half-past five. Sometime in the afternoon Lorna had telephoned on the house-to-cabin line to ask him for a drink because Dan was off to Montreal at seven, not a party, Nigel, so sorry to disturb you. It had been a welcome disturbance, soon forgotten, everything forgotten in Diamond getting away and up the hill.

It was a hot afternoon, the dog days, Petrie called them. It had rained two days ago, but already the woods were dry again, heavy with summer, and no birds moved. He shed Diamond as he climbed, thinking of mundane matters to speed the shedding, like the split-second or split-minute schedules of Dan's life. Leave the house at seven-0-two P.M., Flume Ridge at seven-thirty, an hour to Montreal, still seven-thirty Eastern Time, and into town by eight. But who am I now to scoff? he thought. I'm doing the same thing myself, a writing machine, more or less by the clock.

He heard voices at the swimming pool as he reached the fish pond and stopped to count water lilies in bloom. Lorna always counted the water lilies.

She was swimming without a cap, her hair sleeked back. Not many women of thirty-eight would soak their hair-dos.

"I make it twenty-nine pink, and two pure virgin white."

"Same here," she said. "It's a record, I think."

"What's a record?" They say *reckard*. I say *reckawrd*.

"The water lilies, Dan."

"Oh, I see. This is my brother Nigel, Mr. and Mrs. Skafe."

Not a party, she had said. But two hardly made a party. He went round the pond to meet the Skafes, who both stood up, polite of her, a well-preserved blonde in a pale blue dress, quite plain, but the pear-shaped diamond on her wedding finger gave the show away about where the elegant dress might come from.

Skafe himself was almost flat-stomached in his middle sixties, one would guess, lean and lined, a carved-out face, white hair, a laborer's wrinkled neck. So this was the legendary Husky Skafe, S. K. Skafe, number one Canadian tycoon who could put fifty Daniel Ashes in his pocket. *A great guy*, some said, not a great guy to cross, though, by the looks of him. Odd, thought Nigel Ash, this one and George Petrie, co-trustees, same sure thing about them, and they happen to be two people I could do without meeting.

"Help yourself, Nigel. I think all the usual is there."

"Thanks, Dan. Where's old Congo?"

"We shut him up. He's a bit of an insanitary nuisance at the pool." Dan dived, and swam down and back like a torpedo.

"Such a marvelous swimmer," said Mrs. Skafe loudly enough for Dan to hear. He swung himself up with one long muscled hoist to turn and sit on the concrete wall. Danny Boy was fighting fit.

The drinks were on a trolley cart with rubber wheels, everything in racks for safe transport to the cocktail hour by the swimming pool, a handy rig, Dan's own invention. Ash got his whisky and went to sit beside the Skafes.

"Do you spend the whole summer at Gallery?"

"I do," she said. "Husky comes and goes. He goes a lot more than he comes." She made a veritable pout, *muy feminino*, or was it *feminina?*

"Two weeks here, one week away is a bit more like it. You must beware of those little whoppers, Grace."

She giggled at her husband's quip. "Well, away too much. He's off again with Dan this evening."

36

"Dan is giving me a lift to Montreal."

"Talking of which, one last dip and I must get changed. We have to leave at seven, S. K."

"Under your orders, Dan."

Dan smiled, pleased to have the great man under orders, such a transparently decent chap, proud of his torso, not of his abilities. "There's a spare pair of trunks in the hut, Nigel, if you want a swim."

"When I've finished my drink," he said. "Or a splash. I never got much beyond the Congo-paddle."

The water was perfectly pellucid after Dan's ministrations. He called it the pool. Lorna called it the pond. She had been floating about in idle fashion, but she stood now and walked out at the shallow end. Her shape was all right in the black sheath of a bathing suit. You have the loveliest bottom in Christendom, he thought, transferring attention from the bottom to his brother's parting dive and crawl. His drink was halfway down, no hurry, never hurry, never, that poor sod Diamond on the hill, don't be sorry for him, I told you that. ". . . I beg your pardon, Mrs. Skafe?"

"I was just saying that you English people aren't great swimmers on the whole. It's the climate, I suppose."

"Yes," he said, letting it go about you English people.

"Dan says you've been ill," Skafe said. "Feeling better, I hope."

"I feel fine now, but I lost a bit of weight. That virus pneumonia takes a whack of you."

"A horrid thing, I nearly lost my Husky with it two years ago."

Ash was reaching the conclusion that if he was her Husky, his Mrs. Husky would drive him up the wall. Perhaps she did. Or perhaps he enjoyed being loved to pure distraction. *Mebbe ay'n mebbe hoochay*, they said in that country North of the English.

Dan dried his hair with with a purple towel. "It was good of you to have the kids last evening. Bobby said they had a super time, and they got you talking about a plane crash you had near here. I never knew about that."

"It was before you came to Gallery, Dan." What had possessed him to tell that story? The RAF Wing Commander had been Nigel Ash, but the pilot of the bashed up Mink had been Neil Arnott, as had the flyer in the North, and this man Skafe owned the biggest private outfit in Canada, Skafair. "I was lucky that time," he said. "Got away with a broken wrist."

"You were a fighter pilot, weren't you?" Skafe asked him with a certain diffidence or respect.

"Yes," he said. "Spitfires in the war, and Meteors and Vampires until I got out of the service. Then I flew in Canada, Australia, other places."

"Husky was a super pilot too."

"I was not a super pilot," he said testily. "I was a fair to average pilot until I lost my touch."

"Don't bark at me, Husky dear."

"Sorry, Grace."

"Would anyone like a top-up?".

Only Ash took more whisky, and Dan wheeled his trolley cart uphill.

"Just a quick one in and out," he said, and went to the changing hut. He had brown forearms and a ruddy face. The rest of him was pallid skinny.

"Blissful," he said, coming up from his belly flop.

Lorna laughed at the blissful or the belly flop, probably at both. It was good clean fun.

"I'm taking a grass widow's picnic to Paradise Island for lunch tomorrow," said Mrs. Skafe. "Lorna, would you like to come? And you, Mr. Ash?"

Lorna would like that very much.

"That's kind of you, Mrs. Skafe, but I'm afraid I can't." He was into the book now, why not say it, a good reason for a reclusive life? "Well, actually I'm on a writing job, trying my hand at a novel."

"But how thrilling! May I ask what it's about?"

"About Scotland, Mrs. Skafe," he said, having invited that annoying question.

"Oh, Scotland! I do adore Scotland so."

"Bonny Grace, I do adore thee so," said Simon Skafe.

"Ah, poo!" she said, she really said it.

"Five to seven, Dan's marching orders."

"I must run," Lorna said, and run she did, all the way up to the house.

Ash dressed and combed his hair and went to see them off.

Lorna kissed Dan in a no-holds-barred sort of fashion. They were indeed a handsome and devoted couple. "What about me?" said Simon Skafe. She smiled and kissed him on the cheek.

"Glad you're so much better, Nigel. See you weekend after next." Dan got into the back of the dark green Mercedes, the Skafes in front, and they drove away.

"Super car," Lorna said. "Super evening. Everything's super. Will you stay for non-super Sunday supper?"

"I don't mind if I do," he said, "Which is Scotch for I would adore it so."

"Grace is a bit much at times, but so nice really, and she simply plain worships him."

"Nice husband worship. I don't know how he stands it."

"I expect he likes it," Lorna said. "Most husbands do."

"I ain't no husband," said Nigel Ash. Once he had been a bloody awful husband to a non-worshiping wife.

She frowned. "Have a drink while I get the supper. Would scrambled eggs and bacon do?"

"Scrambled eggs and bacon would be super supper." She laughed at his super-repetitive bad joke. He could make Lorna laugh and he could annoy her.

"It really was," he said, after homemade bread and Camembert, after peaches and cream.

"It really was what?"

"Superlative."

"I'm trying to feed you up. You're awfully thin, I noticed at the pond."

"You're just about right, I noticed at the pond."

Lorna blushed, a faint tide of color came and went in her summer-brown face. "No, seriously. Have you put on any weight?"

"Five pounds, by the cabin machine."

"That's good," she said. Two humming birds were vying for the red nectar in the feeder, chasing, whirring back to the attack, chirping with fury. Now they grappled and fell to have a brief set-to on the lawn below the apple tree, to speed away in opposite directions. "Such bellicose mites," she said.

No more humming birds came. "Peace reigns," he said. "I could sit here for ever. But I should go back to early bed to sleep for tomorrow. The book's coming, Lorna, I think, I think."

"Oh, I'm glad," she said. "What about my typewriter? Do you need it yet?"

"Not until after tomorrow. But are you sure you can spare it?"

"Sure, certain," she said. "Won't you need white paper, and carbons too?"

"I suppose I will."

"I'll get some for you tomorrow, then. When would be a good time to come down?"

"Just about sunset, and bring field glasses. I might be able to show you that secret I mentioned. But probably you're busy."

"No," she said. "A boat picnic with Grace is quite enough social life for Monday. No respite from parties all weekend until now. But poor Dan works so hard he needs a change the few times he gets down here."

Poor Dan, poor poor Dan. Ash stood. "Will you come a bit of the way with me?"

"As far as the water lilies," Lorna said. "I like to see them closing up for night. Walk, Congo."

40

"This place is beautiful," he said. "Open within the woods. You've worked down wonderfully well from what the Lord provided."

"We're so lucky to have Jake," she said. Jake was their gardener, handyman, factotum.

"Where's Bobby this evening?"

"He took Kim to a movie, making hay while the sun shines. Or to mix my metaphors, I'm afraid Bobby's nose is going to be out of joint. Keith Kelly is coming home this week, and Kim is mad for him."

"I was amused last night about whose yen for who. It's a strange thing, isn't it?"

"Yes," Lorna said. "Passing strange it is. An uncle of mine fell hopelessly, passionately in love with a two-hundred pound female at the age of seventy-nine."

They both laughed in the evening. "It's good to have a laugh together," he said, but Lorna said nothing. Barn swallows circled, dipping to drink in flight from Dan's swimming pool.

Congo barked once at her, his head tilted, asking. "All right, Congo, you can go in now." The labrador swam one circuit or perimeter, and came out to shake himself. "Unlike the swallows, he won't drink chlorinated water. Congo likes the clean murky puddle."

"Amiable hound," Ash said, and Congo bared his fangs in a labrador grin.

Some of the water lilies had closed altogether, some not. "Bobby said they all loved it with you last evening."

"I enjoyed myself too," he said.

"You seem to hit it off with dogs and young people."

"Doggy, I guess," he said, sensing another thought behind her light comment, and there was:

"Dan was saying that he wished he had your touch with the teens."

"Dan is a good chap through and through," he said.

"Meaning you're not?"

41

"Meaning I'm not."

"You do puzzle me a bit," she said.

"Same here you," he said, and they laughed again.

"Goodnight, Nigel."

"Goodnight, Lorna."

Would she, or wouldn't she? But she smiled fleetingly, quite shyly, it was enchanting. Lorna called to Congo and went away.

6

ASH WOKE EARLY IN THE COOLNESS AND THE QUIET. He had to make the framework for the thing to come, and that concerned himself, the instrument. His experience in this matter was minute. But he had observed for thirty years or so, and he was convinced that the way to art of any kind was not by waiting for pretty inspiration when the spirit chose to move. The way was to live and work by rote.

Wake at seven, make a cup of tea, think briefly of Diamond's present circumstance and where he would be going, get up, put the coffee on, now forget about him, go for a quick walk in the immediate here, downriver or upriver, in the woods and back, have breakfast, get down to it at half-past eight, stop four hours later on the dot. The break for lunch meant a break in rhythm too, but it was a rest. Then he would go it until half-past four and teatime, stop for exercise, another hard walk or tidy Dan's woods a bit. A drink at six o'clock, plan in some detail for tomorrow, and think further ahead in Tam Diamond's journey. At half past six the working day would end, but have the man in mind again as sleep was coming, and so it would be until this job was finished.

It seemed a bit like slavery. It would be demented that if one did not learn to banish Diamond until the next appointment.

On this day he spent that day with him in a shallow cave high above the glen. The whole countryside would be alerted, and he was pinned here until darkness came.

Things happened in the present:

. . . The eagle came right down with talons forward ready to grip. But the white hare checked, jinked, and came on, and the eagle had to swing again.

The big bird stooped and missed a second time, and still the hare came up the hill, throwing its limbs forward and back with desperate urgency.

The hare came straight for the place where Diamond lay, bolting in beside him in a thudding scurry. And the eagle was coming again, certain this time of its quarry, for there were no deep places to hide.

Diamond raised his hand to cover his head, suddenly frightened of the outstretched talons. At the very last moment the bird saw him. The wings and the tail bit down into the air as if it were a solid thing to grip, and there was a roaring whistle of the wind. Then the eagle climbed above his head, up, up until it dwindled into the high blue sky.

The hare lay beside him without seeming to notice. The beautiful snowy coat was heaving, and the eyes circled in terror.

Diamond put his hand out and lifted the warm beast into his lap. It kicked once and then lay still. It was queer that, wasn't it? Perhaps the hares only had room for one fear at a time. Anyway it wasn't feared at him, this other thing that was being chased.

He'd never liked killing beasts. Would eat the meat but leave the killing to others. He didn't know why it was, a soft streak in him mebbe.

And this hare now. It was good meat. He could cook it if he found a safe place for a fire. Yes, kill it!

He moved his right hand to the neck, but checked his fingers. He would be knowing the feeling soon enough, the despair of being chased. No, he couldn't kill it, not when he'd seen it escape the eagle.

"Get away now, my wee hare," he said, and he laughed at himself for his daftness. He put the hare down and pushed it gently from him, urging it away before he could be tempted again to take its life. The hare hopped once and lay still, eyeing the sky. Then it moved off slowly, regardless of the man who had saved it . . .

And later a man and a young girl came up the hill. It was a keeper and his daughter going round the traps. They headed dangerously this way, speaking of where a fox might make its den, and Diamond had to climb still higher to escape them, lying clappit in wet snow as their voices grew and faded.

Things happened in the past. He remembered back to his

44

dad, drunk again on red biddy in the tenement in Glasgow, hitting his mum, a hullabaloo, and policemen came. The one with three strips on his arm was Sergeant Thoms. After they had taken Mum on a stretcher, and after Dad had been hustled off to the clink, the sergeant stayed a minute with Tam and his wee sister Janet. Sergeant Thoms was decent, not acting like a bobby.

That was a memory of a long time back, of man hitting woman, but his mother had been only bruised, as the woman yesterday might have been only bruised.

The present always here, the past to haunt the present, but the past to guide the future. There was an officer in the war, a human sort of chap, not like the stuck-up rest of them, the only chap who could rebuke Tam Diamond without his anger stirring.

The Officer said once: *First you've got to know what you want to do yourself. Then think of what the enemy wants to do, think what he expects you to do.*

I want to get clear away, clear across Scotland to where the big ships come and go. He, the enemy, he wants to catch me. Now what does he think I'll do? A lorry driver, used to picking up people on the way, used to quick moving from here to there, a city chap, impatient. He thinks I will have tried to hop a lift before even the alarm went up, or before the roads could be right watched. Roads, roads, roads is what he will think, knowing too what travel on foot is like in the month of March.

So on foot it will be, slowly by night along the valley sides, never hurry, taking mebbe a week to reach the west. But first I must get food.

Diamond waited all that second day. If he had had the sense to kill the hare, he might have been able to tease up a fire to cook the beast and put warmth in his stomach. But he had not, and the chills grew in him, and he had the trots.

As light faded, he ate the last of the bread, the margarine, the small hunk of meat that he had stolen from the cottage. Funny, it was the first time in his life that he had stolen.

45

Darkness came, and he could move at last. The main valley ran east to west, and he must go into that for food. But to get there, he had to cross this side glen, and there was only one place, by the roadbridge over the big burn or small river, too deep to wade.

Diamond crouched before the bridge. It was a crossing place where they might put a man. Sure enough, he moved, moonlight on the bastard's silver buttons.

Lobbing stones, it was an old trick, and it worked — one downstream of him, another farther, now on and to the right. The bobby went to investigate. He challenged: *Halt, who goes there?* Must have been a soldier in his time, had for a sucker now.

Diamond ran through on his rubber-soled commando boots to stop beyond, and the policeman clumped back to guard his bridge — a false alarm, he would be thinking, just a roe deer, it might have been.

He moved along the valleyside. These were the hill farms, poor bleak places, not what he wanted. He must find a richlike house down by the river, with plenty rations in the larder.

But the ploughed land, terrible heavy for walking, forced him up, and he was in amongst hill birches.

. . . It was the crazy way they grew that started the fancies in his mind. Those two that went up straight and turned in to meet; they weren't trees. It was the end of a house, secret in among the woods, suddenly quite real with a window below the roof and a lamp shining through. He stopped to look. Was it a house? But then the picture faded and he saw the two trees as they were, and the white stone which had been a lighted window.

He went on. Next it was a church, half seen from the corners of his tired eyes, with a fine steeple stretching up to the sky, and the cross above.

And what was that platform with two posts and a crossbar? Was that a rope that dangled? So they went on, the real dream pictures, kindly and horrible.

It was a relief to him to be out on the open grass again, to be lonely, but to be alone . . .

46

Ash stopped according to the rules at half-past four, made tea, had one of Lorna's cookies. A cookie in his native land was something different. These were crumbly biscuits, excellent.

All day he had been applying Ash to Diamond. One's stomach was the first to go, even in summer weather. And some other things came from Ash's experience — the hare, for instance. That happened to him when he was a boy. He killed it, though, of course, alas. Some came from a man's imagination. But the tired fancies of the night were real enough, the trees that made a house, the white stone a window, the church bell pealing. He still saw and heard them now.

Goodbye, Diamond, *auf wiederschauen*. He took bucksaw, axe and clippers to start tidying Dan's grove of birches. They were not twisted, stunted, like those of recollection, but straight-growing, a stand of young *betula papyrifera*, some still ruddy brown, some grown to be immaculately white. They made him think of Indians once upon a time, of canoes on this river before the east bank enjoyed an Anglicized German name, and the west bank a name from France, paleface plunderers.

He limbed up some trees, cut a fair lot of useless stuff like alder, spread it to rot on the forest floor, and he had worked up a decent sweat without feeling unduly tired, had a shower, and got a drink to encourage him to work out Diamond for tomorrow. "It's so damned remorseless what I have to do," he said.

That finished by the clock, he put the supper on and took his second drink outside. The evening was sultry, and a mass of cloud hung in the north, fading from black or indigo at the horizon up to an indeterminate meeting with blue sky. They were cumulonimbus, thunderheads, but the storm did not grow beyond a distant grumble; and in a while it disappeared, trouble over, simply vanished.

It was the season of the goldenrod, as pretty as the name, golden at the edge of every grassy place, in every clearing. The red speedboat came out for its spin. The owner or the skipper, whoever he might be, and it was a he, must be a habituated type. He followed his standard course, down the American side, across

47

toward Gallery Island and up this way. He passed with a merry spank, quite a tuneful snarl, turned at the red channel buoy, mystery neighbor, shot for home.

After supper Ash went out again, and a good thing happened. It was that rarity, a nighthawk evening. A few times each summer they would appear, sickle-winged birds in wayward flight, hunting whatever insect hatch it might be. North, east, west, over city, over river, over forest, and once in Panama, he remembered, it would of a sudden be a nighthawk evening, the sky full of them and their small nasal cries, and as suddenly devoid of them.

The nighthawks helped to pass this waiting time. It was good feasting, not caprice, that brought them here and took them from here. But their visitations seemed as capricious as did their flight.

Life is waiting, he thought. Life is waiting for the worse, or life is waiting for the better. Or life is simply waiting, as a peasant waits at Delhi station, as a pilot waits to pick up his charter. It was such waiting that had prompted Neil Arnott to write a few short stories years ago.

This waiting was for the better, for the worse if she did not come. But as the sun sank to meet the hills, the jeep approached. It was a farm vehicle, not licensed. It had a winch for logging, a trailer hitch, a power take-off to saw lumber, a blade assembly to plough snow in winter. It was the sort of tough utilitarian job that Nigel Ash admired.

"Did the nighthawks come your way?"

"Yes," he said. "The first I've seen here."

"Gray darting ghosts," she said. "I love them."

He carried the things in. "It's electric," she said about the typewriter.

"That's a bit beyond my form."

"Easy," she said. "Let's plug it in . . . And if you want to cross out or to underline, you just press that key harder."

"Handy," he said. "Real handy. How much were the paper and carbons?"

48

"Fifteen-sixty altogether," Lorna said.

He found the money. "Thank you," he said. "I have a good many things to thank you for."

"My pleasure. You're entirely welcome, I'm sure." She made a light small joke of it to cover awkwardness, and he felt the same.

But outside it was different, with things to see and to share. The tide was at half-flood, and the mudflats were covered, a sheen of sunset on the water. "A school of herring," she said. "Yes, Nigel, look!"

It was no more than a difference, an added silver in that sheen, moving in to shore, swinging out again, a school of herring in linked rhythm.

"I never saw that before," he said. "There are more changes and more new things to see than any place I was ever at."

"And the great tides to remind us," Lorna said.

A wind came from the north, a fresh cool wind to carry scent away, to drown quiet human talk across the cove.

"Life is waiting, I was thinking before you came, for better things or worse or simply waiting."

"Watching too," she said. "I wait upon your secret, watching."

"If we watch in vain, I'll have to tell you."

"Don't tell me, wait."

Night had fallen on the river, and the full moon had risen beyond the forest, and they did not watch and wait in vain. The doe stepped out at her wonted place, facing downwind where danger would most likely be. She looked and listened east to the woods, west to the river, south to this cove, and her nose would be sentry for the north. She might have called to her fawn: *Come, child, all is well*, but that was too quiet a sound to be heard. They fed together.

Lorna drew in breath, and put her glasses up. "Almost white," she said. "Or is that the moon?" She dropped her left hand to rest on the arm of the folding chair beside him.

"Almost white," he said, happy that Lorna should share his

49

secret, and, with or without meaningful intent, he made his right hand spare and laid it on her left hand, which turned for the meeting, but briefly, a moment's rise of tide, and her hand said thank you, and she took her hand away.

The deer did not stay long that night. Two dogs came hunting up the wind, a high yelping and a deeper bay, moving through the woods between shore and house. But the movement stopped; the barking became frenzied. "That's okay," he said. "They're into a porcupine."

The deer had gone. "To be hunted always," she said. "To be alert even when you sleep. A human being would go crazy."

"Yes," he said. There was the difference of anticipated fear. But would Diamond go crazy? One told oneself: *forget him.* Possible until a topic became relevant to his plight. "I don't know," he said. "When you're chased, I think you do become inured to that."

"You did in Germany?"

"Yes. And it was a fellow-feeling. I remember a mouse that came up to me, a roe deer feeding ten feet away."

"Perhaps you could tell me some day."

"I could try," he said. He was wary of the telling, not in this instance because of skeleton in cupboard, but because of losing what he told. The larger-voiced dog was silent now. It might be wrestling with its shot of quills. The other yapped on. The doe and her well-grown fawn would not be in much danger from a couple of dogs. A pack would be another thing. "Is there much jacking here, Lorna?"

"Jake says that what with that, and skidoos in the winter when they're yarded up, the deer population is down by half, or worse."

He told her about the two men on Saturday night after Bobby and Co. had left.

"They must have driven down our back road. There's no other way to the shore."

"Why driven?"

"Because they would need a truck or a car to get the body out. You know how steep it is."

50

"Can't you bar the road?"

"There is a gate, but I expect it's still open since haying time. I'll get Jake to padlock it. But I wish you'd told me sooner, Nigel." Displeased with him, she sounded.

"I warned them off quite effectively."

"I doubt it, if they're the same people as last fall. We didn't post the land against hunters. We just barred the road, and they tore down the barrier, and jacked a buck at midnight on that same field—hence the new gate. I asked Jake if he knew who they were, and I'm sure he did, but all he would say was: *There's a few real ugly guys around, Mrs. Ash,* clammed up on me.

"That's par for the course with country people anywhere." I might sound Jake out myself, he thought.

"It was so lovely seeing them. Thank you for sharing your secret with me."

"My pleasure," he quoted her. "You're entirely welcome, I'm sure." The full moon had risen high enough to shine over their shoulders upon them here. "Mammoth moon," he said. "Would you like a quick one for the moon-touched road?"

"Quick, yes," she said, without a please. It was rather good.

The wind had dropped, and the tide lapped still higher, and the dogs were silent, perhaps gone home to be booted by hard master, to be tortured by kindly master with the tweezers.

"Some people are coming to dinner on Wednesday. Dan phoned about this man, Jeremy Prentice, a business friend, they're passing through. Would you make a fourth?"

With one Jeremy Prentice? Decidedly not. "Forgive me, Lorna," he said carefully. "But I'm in my shell, and I think a life of absolute routine is the only way to do this job."

"You can't live it twenty-four hours a day," she said.

"I don't," he said. "I'm not living it now with you."

"You do seem a trifle reclusive, though."

"Yes," he said to that loaded remark, if only slightly loaded. "The fact is that if I go out to dinner I drink too much, can't afford to drink too much at the moment."

"Don't, then," Lorna said with asperity. But in a minute she said: "Sorry. I didn't mean to be schoolmarmish."

"That's okay," he said. "Anything you say is quite okay by me."

"Bobby was wondering about a fishing expedition you were going to make. Shall I tell him that isn't on?"

"The bottle and the canoe don't mix. I would like to go for an hour or two. Let's see: Write tomorrow, and then a typing marathon to bring me up to date. Perhaps Friday evening, if that would suit him. Will you come too?"

"No," she said. "He wants to have you to himself. Boring old Mum would be *de trop*." Lorna stood.

"Such a crashing old bore Mum is," he said.

"Thank you again for showing me. Goodnight."

"Goodnight, Lorna."

"It's so peaceful here," she said, not moving yet.

He put a hand on each of her shoulders in the silk blouse, Italian with a bold moonlight design, and they smiled at one another in peace. They kissed one another, their bodies together, ephemeral peace, and her head lay a moment in the hollow of his shoulder. "Oh, hell," she said, it was quite explosive and quite amusing, quite.

The jeep had a small leak in its silencer or muffler, depending on where you come from. *Oh, hell*, they start as a pinhole, and inevitably grow until the thing roars like the White Stag in the rut. He had such disorderly fanciful notions. But his body had confessed to hers, and her body had confessed to his. *I want you*, it was beautifully simple, carnal, friendly too.

7

SEE ME WITHIN FIVE MINUTES, *or I shall be talking to your wife.*
Whose wife? Mrs. Ash, Arnott, Diamond, Prentice, Prentice.
The starboard engine was on fire, still twenty minutes out from
Camford Point, burning heat above the white desert of the
Arctic, and his fingers closed on the white neck of the hare.

He woke up sweating from the nightmare jumble, tiny self,
a pinpoint in that desert. But it went away, and he thought
back to the reality of the Prentice thing, Jeremy Prentice, once
general manager of Arctic Construction, who was dining with
Lorna on Wednesday.

He was on the wagon in those days, Neil Arnott, a veteran
pilot among the windy DEW line riffraff, flying a twin Muskox
from Edmonton via Yellowknife to camps along the western
Arctic. Being an observant chap, he noticed that Prentice made
more frequent and more protracted visits to Camford Point
than to the other main stations in his charge, and he soon found
out why.

With firm evidence as potential insurance, he set up his supply line. The consumption of canned milk in the cowless teetotal
North was large, and a few bogus cases of Carnation on each
trip a drop in a creamy bucket. It was a thoroughly professional
job. The rum cost four-fifty a bottle, and he paid nine-fifty to the
purchaser and packer, who also derived a resale value from dis-
placed Carnation. Neil Arnott flew it North, was paid twenty
dollars a bottle cash by selected storemen, who sold it for twenty-
five or more. Thus, Arnott was making a hundred and twenty-
five odd on every dozen of blackstrap rum transported.

It was a good racket while it lasted but, like other rackets, it

lasted a mite too long; and only because they made the rudi-
mentary mistake of raiding the supply before they raided the
source of supply did he happen to get away with it. He had a
retailer at each of four main camps, and all had been caught
with booze, and one of them had it in for him.

Back at Edmonton, he went to the head office of Arctic Construction, and asked to see Mr. Prentice, who was in conference,
his secretary said, and would not be available as he was leaving
for the North at noon. So Arnott wrote the note: *See me within
five minutes or I shall be talking to your wife,* sealed the envelope and said: *Please ask Mr. Prentice to read this at once.*

Shown in, he came to the point: *I presume she knows your
writing. Here is a photostat.* It was a revealing note to his boy
friend at Camford Point, the clerk in the camp office, which the
big boss so democratically shared on his visits there. *Not very
wise to commit yourself to paper.*

No, said Prentice. Surprisingly, he kept his cool. Or not so
surprisingly. He had a reputation for being unflappable in
crisis. *What do you want?*

*I want all charges against these men withdrawn . . . And I
want the investigation of the booze racket stopped immediately.*

Does the booze racket stop immediately?

*It has already stopped. As soon as you do what I say, I will
give you the original of that. I never break my word.*

Your word, you unprincipled bastard.

Don't provoke me, Prentice.

All right. He really was a good tough man except for his
funny failing. *Get out.*

Neil Arnott flew for two more weeks in order to be sure that
his instructions had been obeyed, gave Prentice the original, and
left the job. What with legitimate earnings, equaled by the
booze money, he had enough to buy the Mink which he would
prang in the woods of New Brunswick that next spring.

Not one of my prettier efforts, Ash thought now. My only
blackmail venture, more or less. An irony of the affair had been
that when Prentice was away from Edmonton, and Arnott was

54

there between flights, he and Rachel Prentice had much enjoyed one another's company. Another reason for not going to dinner on Wednesday.

He watched the moon dipping to the hills of Maine, thinking that if he had come to this writing long ago, his life might at least have had some purpose, made some sense.

And he thought: But now it does have purpose and make sense. I am going somewhere without finagle. When did I last go anywhere without finagle?

An owl was calling in the woods. He supposed that it would be an owl, although it did not hoot or rasp like the owls he knew. The cry was melancholy, brief, a trill, an ululation, lonely sound.

He closed his eyes for sleep, but sleep stayed far away. Not one intent, but two, he thought. And both are beautifully clear, parallel lines that meet somewhere. I shall write my book, good or bad, I will write it. I shall get Lorna into my brother's log cabin bed, and she will love it. *Oh, hell,* she thinks of it already, denying it, no doubt, may even be thinking of it now as dawn is coming. Come then, woman.

He slept peacefully enough until he woke precisely at seven o'clock. It was always so in sobriety.

Ash changed his mind that morning. He had intended to write on until Diamond had broken into the widow's house for food. But the typewriter, the paper, the carbons were here. Why not type up as far as he had gone, bring what was still a scrawl to form and substance? Perhaps codify was the word, not quite, but it would do. For an unprincipled bastard, he was quite principled and puristical about the English language.

Lorna's Smith-Corona was a little wizard of the electronic age. It did those speedy automatic things that she had mentioned, but it was trigger happy. If you so much as tender-touched the wrong key, the wizard obeyed orders. He got better at it, though, and the better he got at it, the more he loathed it.

Writing was drudgery, could even be pleasant in full flow. Typing was dim slavery. "Thank God that's over," he said

55

at six, having been slave to it all day. It was not over; it was not half done.

He got his drink and read what he had typed. "It is alive," he said. "It happened, didn't it?" Funny peculiar to have invented something that really happened, and would happen. *One must be that man,* he had told himself at the beginning. It was very much alive for him, but only for him?

Ash walked uphill. A minor drawback about turbulent peaceful life by the sea: One climbed from it, or one walked beside it, choice of directions limited. Then always one returned to it, which reminded him of something that he could not remember.

There were voices at the swimming pond, young people's talk and laughter. The path to Jake Tovey's house branched off before that, winding through a cedar glade of good straight growth, thinned enough to allow regeneration on the forest floor. *Cedar's goddam tricky,* Jake had said. *Shallow-rooted, see? Take out too much useless split-headed stuff, and the next big wind you lose the lot.*

He crossed the brook that was the outflow from the pond, but it was dried up now, and he climbed again through untouched forest. *Mr. Ash, he likes the woods all tidy, but Mrs., she's with me that you gotta leave 'em cover where to live in, about half and half's the way I see it.*

The porcupine paid no heed to him. It was an old porcupine, doing an efficient job of chewing up a young white spruce. "Unlovely creature," he said. "Why in God's name did the Lord make you?" It was a conundrum, to which the fashionable answer was that God made the sluggish porcupine so that a lost man need not starve in the woods, but he thought that somewhat less than likely.

The path went up the side of the field where Jake's Jersey cow was chewing the cud, and to Jake's haphazard garden, and to Jake himself in one of two rustic seats, a table between them. He wore half-glasses, and was sewing.

"I didn't know you were a seamstress, Jake, or a seamster, is it?"

"Needlepoint, Mr. Ash. I took it up two winters back when I was laid away with the rheumatiz. Kinda soothes a fella. This one's a chair cover for the wife."

"I like the design." It was impressionistic, a splash of colors, green, blue, red and gold, with sharp touches of white and black. "Did you do it yourself?"

"Well, sorta half. I got the notion from a picture book of them new-fangled artists Mrs. Ash give us at Christmas time, that and patchwork quilts I was thinkin' of some, and I painted it on with the acryllic. Well, how's things down your way?"

"Fine, thanks, Jake."

"You sure look different to that washed-up fella at the station."

Jake had met him, brought him, ensconced him at the cabin, which Mabel Tovey had cleaned and stocked. By the time Lorna and Bobby arrived by car a day or two later, Jake had shown him all over the place, mostly by jeep, sometimes by easy convalescent stroll. He and his wife had the diffident kindness of solid country people anywhere. Solid, he thought. I never was that. ". . . What, Jake?"

"You'll do a lot of readin', I suppose."

"To begin with, I did. Not so much now, except in the evenings. As a matter of fact, I'm writing a story."

"A true story, or made-up like?"

"Made-up," he said. "But it seems to be getting true for me."

"Thinkin' of a story to write, I couldn't never do that. It's only my hands that works for me in a kind of a way, not too darned good." His broad fingers wielded the needle with precision, the same small double tug for tension, the same deft twist to unspin the wool, next stitch.

"No difference, Jake. There's more than hands in your design."

"Well, that's right too. But with a story it's different. With

57

a story there must be in back of it a lot of things you've bin and done yourself."

"That's true," he said. "Too many damned stupid things."

Jake chuckled. "Well, you done 'em."

"Not only stupid," he said. He had detected lately in himself a most uncharacteristic and inexplicable urge to confess his sins. Now stop it. "I made a start on tidying the birch grove by the cabin."

"I seen that this noon when I was down for a visit with you, but I heard the rattle of the machine. You go it good and quick, I was thinking."

"Bad and quick," he said. "I came for a visit too, but also to ask if you happen to have a bush-scythe I could borrow. I need one to whack out the brambles, choke cherries, that kind of stuff."

"Oh, sure. Let's see — it's in the toolshed or the workshop, and there's a stone some place. Help yourself, Mr. Ash, or will I bring 'em down?"

"I'll find 'em thanks." That would be a good excuse to take him home by Lorna's way. The big house was only a couple of hundred yards from here, hidden by woods. He sat beside Jake in the shade of Jake's fine old ash. Strictly speaking, it would be Ash's fine old ash, not Jake's. Ash beneath ash, he thought inanely. " 'Oak before ash, we'll have a splash,' " he said. " 'Ash before oak, we'll have a soak.' Which tree leafs out first, it's a saying at home. Whether any truth, I wouldn't know."

"There's usually somethin' to them old sayings." Jake tucked the end of his wool into the back of the canvas, cut it off with scissors, threaded another double strand, and began again.

Ash came tentatively to the prime reason for this call. "Did Lorna tell you about the men I saw at the shore the other night?"

"Mrs. Ash was sayin' that. I locked the gate today. Won't stop nobody who means business, though. The woods there are small stuff, they could cut a way around in half an hour."

"She said that a buck was jacked on that field last fall."

58

"Right," Jake said. "That's why we put in the gate."

"Did you catch them at it?"

Jake turned to look at him over his glasses. "No, Mr. Ash," he said. "It mightn't've bin too healthy to catch them at it."

"Is that a favorite place for deer?"

"Sure is," Jake said. "There's the old orchard I was telling you about, but farther up it's a crossing-place too between the woods. The deer don't like moving close along the shore, got no escape route to one side, see? They like to follow it, but a ways in from it. You seen any deer around, Mr. Ash?"

"I've seen tracks," he said. "Up from the shore, just as you say." It seemed improbable that stout Jake might also be a jacker, but one never knew. One knew only that deer meat was delicious deer meat, however obtained. "Talking of health," he said, "I don't particularly fancy the idea of bullets flying round my head at night. If you happened to know who it might be, I could have a word."

"That mightn't be too healthy neither," Jake said, continuing to stitch. The black wall of cloud was again in the north, and lightning flickered faintly, thunder just audible on another sultry evening. "Too late," he said. "I don't believe it'll come tonight. Mebbe tomorrow we'll get a storm to clear the air and give the place a soak like you was speakin' of. The woods is goddam dry again."

A car had turned off the highway, and was coming along Jake's lane. It was an ancient vehicle, down at the backside and pouring smoke. "Shack people," Jake said. "You can spot 'em a mile off before you can smell 'em. But who?" The jalopy stopped at the turning place, and a man got out. "Oh, jeepers. It's that Dibble bastard."

The man came over, hands in pockets. He walked with the shack people's invariably shambling gait. He wore a peaked cap that once had advertised somebody's paint, a woods-shirt with a can of beer in each breast pocket, slacks tucked into half-laced boots. The hair was a matted tangle down to his shoulders, a week unshaven or a week's growth of beard, perhaps he took the scissors to it on occasion. All in all, the Dibble bastard was a prototype of the breed, and they were a shiftless breed apart. But the pale eyes were curiously hot and still, not to be disregarded. "He's bad stuff," Jake muttered, continuing with his needlepoint, but as the man came near, he put down the canvas and said: "Well, Randy, what can I do for you?"

Dibble swayed a little, transferring hands from pockets to hips. Beyond him, sallow faces of varying ages watched from the car. "We was goin' down to the Commons to pick blueberries, and sudden round the corner there's this gate."

"There's a sign at the top. *Road closed to vehicles*. Didn't you see it, Randy?"

"Sure I seen it."

"Why didn't you leave the car and walk? Pick all the berries you want."

"Walk!" Dibble spat. "There's a right of way to the Commons is what. Every August month since I bin a kid we've drove down for berries."

"No right of way," Jake said equably. "Ask a lawyer."

"Ask a fuckin' lawyer!" Dibble took out a can of beer, pulled off the strip cap and threw it on Jake's lawn.

Jake drew in breath, but said nothing.

Dibble took a long swig. "You wanna pick blueberries, there's a fuckin' roadblock. Dig a mess of clams, some govment bastard warns ya off. That's what we fuckin' get for tryin' to feed our kids."

"The clams are red-poisoned, you know that, Randy." It was noticeable how Jake Tovey's grammar, syntax or what-have-you, tightened up in conversation with this Randy Dibble. The antipathy was inbred, mutual, profound; but Jake was wary of him. "You want that your kids eat poison clams?"

"Poison the poor man and his kids. That would suit you'n the rich arseholes you suck just fine. Look at you, sewin' like a fuckin' woman." Dibble spat again. Not still sober, not yet drunk, a man with hate.

60

"That's enough," Ash said. He lifted his forefinger. "That will be all from you."

"Who in fuck would you be, Mister?"

He considered the question. *Bad stuff*, Jake had said, and bad stuff he evidently was. Better keep them out of it. "Diamond is the name," he said. He felt the small old stir at the back of his neck, long time no feel. "And I don't think I like you very much."

The man stared at him with hot still eyes, a madness in them. "Come on, Randy!" a woman called from the car.

"And I don't like you, fuckin' Englishman." He drained the last of the beer, and threw the can on the grass.

"Pick it up," Ash said, standing.

"Aw, shit!" Dibble rocked on the balls of his feet, fists up, a tough customer, reflexes slowed. "Pick it up yer fuckin' self."

It happened to him just as it happened to Tam Diamond, snap, it happened. He feinted with his left and gave his right brutally to the solar plexus. The air gasped out, and Dibble was on hands and knees for breath. When his panting had begun to ease, Ash said: "Now pick it up."

Dibble picked up the beer can, and went.

"Jeeze, you hit 'im," Jake said. "I wouldn't fancy bein' on the wrong end of that one. I guess it's the first time anybody fixed Randy good."

"I lost my temper, I'm afraid," Ash said. And he was afraid, as always afterward, cooling from the ungoverned, the ungovernable. "It's been the same all my life," he confessed to stout solid Jake, back at his needlepoint. "You're sewin' again like a fuckin' woman," he said to forget about it.

Jake thought that very funny. "There's a tribe o' them Dibbles. And a worthless lotta trash they are, no more morals'n monkeys. But Randy's the only real ugly one. He's bad enough sober. With the beer in him he's a crazy man. Well, you seen it." Jake cleared his throat. "I'm not just too happy," he said.

"You mean he'll try to get his own back?"

"Some way, he will, unless he's given a good scare off. Mebbe I'll ask the Mounties to pay a quiet call. That's a thing they're smart at. They just mosey in and say they wouldn't like to hear of any Dibbles makin' any kind of trouble."

"Suppose he complains about being assaulted by a man named Diamond?"

"He won't. Assault is not a word Randy likes, not after doing six months for it. I noticed you said Diamond. Is that a name of yours too?"

"No, Jake. I thought I would keep Ash out of it."

"A sound idea, Mr. Ash."

"Diamond is the name of the man in the book I'm writing. He has a little temper trouble too."

"Funny," Jake said. "You never seem like that to me until I saw it for just that second. You seem a good-natured jokey sort of guy."

"I've been happy here," he said. "I've been thinking I found something here. And perhaps I have, but I was reminded just now that the nature of the beast remains."

"I was saying to Mabel last night — I was saying I'd never know you and Mr. Ash were brothers. He's a good man, Mr. Ash, fair and decent and generous, nobody could be used better than Mr. Ash uses me. But I guess I just feel he's on a visit from the city, waitin' to get back to where it's real. But you sorta belong here. Mrs. Ash, she belongs in the place too."

"Yes," he said. "Well, I must be going, Jake. Sorry about that trouble."

"It might be the best thing you could've done. Or again it mightn't."

"Shall we keep it to ourselves? I think it would only bother Lorna if she heard."

"Not a peep," Jake said. "And if there's one thing sure, the Dibbles'll keep mum. Come again, Mr. Ash. And good luck at the story. With that punch of yours, it should be a knock-out."

62

He walked over to Dan's house in the hope of seeing Lorna. I thought I was doing well, he thought. And perhaps I was, and perhaps I will. What the hell does it matter? Forget about it.

His father had belonged to the arrogant school of *Never explain*. To which Nigel Ash in some measure also subscribed. And, like his father, he belonged to the school of *What's done is done, water under the bridge, spilt milk,* and so on.

JAKE'S TOOLSHED AND WORKSHOP WERE SOMEWHAT CHAOTIC. But the scythe with the short brush blade was a prominent object. The sharpening stone involved a search through farm equipment, wedges, broken axes, paint cans, garden tools, the lot. Paradoxical, he thought about the neat-handed man, untidy handyman.

Her station wagon was not at the house. Thrice damn, she would be out, but he called: "Heigh-ho."

"Oh, hi!"

He carried the scythe round to the terrace, where she was reading a *New Yorker*. Such a jolt of pleasure to see her again, to see her this time in a yellow dress, moderately mini, long legs tucked round one another in the way they have, and she smiled. "That menacing implement," she said. "Do put it down."

"Sorry," he said, laying it on the lawn. "I wouldn't want to scythe you."

"Have a drink. It's on the sideboard. No mine's all right, thanks."

He went for that, meeting Congo in the coolness of the house. They did have good things. They had lovely things. How trying it must be to have to arbitrate good taste. *No, Dan dear, honestly, it simply won't do in here.* It simply won't do for me in here, dictator to the decent chap. In artistic matters democracy could not prevail.

"These stories," she said, closing the *New Yorker*. "So well written, but they don't exactly go anywhere much."

"Like life," he said. "Stories of mood, I wish I could write them. But action is my thing, I think, if anything."

"Yes, I would expect action to be your thing."

"I was thinking just now about humanity — that paradox might be a redeeming grace."

"Explain a bit."

"Oh well, the unexpected opposites."

"What a strange thought for you to have." She smiled to herself or him. "It's been so humid hot all day. I do wish we could have a storm."

"Tomorrow, Jake thinks. I was up asking him if I could borrow the scythe."

"Did you write today again?"

"No, I changed my mind, and typed all ghastly day. Pure purgatory," he angled carefully. "No reflection on your machine." She might offer again, and if she liked what he was writing, she would be drawn closer. If she disliked it, or thought little of it, quite the opposite. It was a gamble. ". . . Sorry, Lorna, I didn't hear."

"You're always off somewhere."

"Not so very far away."

"I said: Are you typed up to date?"

"Not even half."

"And you can't do it straight onto the typewriter?"

"No. My mind won't work that way."

"I did offer," Lorna said. "I enjoy typing, actually."

"It would be a marvelous saving of time. I would be making use of you again, though."

"Altruist."

He did not mind that she saw through him. He rather welcomed it.

"One technical point — can I read your writing? You'd better dash me off a sample."

"There was an ancient beak at school who hated my guts, I can't imagine why. He said: *In a man of sixty, Ash, your hand might be held tolerable. In a whippersnapper of fifteen, it is atrocious — Thank you, Sir. I look forward to my hand being held less atrocious at your time of life.* Six on the bottom from the grunting Dean."

"Who was the grunting Dean."

"The headmaster, stupid." She was delighted with him.

Paper provided, his own pen ready, he said: "My mind has gone a total blank. It's like when dim people expect you to write something funny in their visitors' book."

"I know," she said. "A quotation, anything will do." He was much in favor at the moment.

He wrote: *Dear Lorna, Shall I compare thee to a summer's day? Thou art more lovely and more temperate, yours sincerely,* and he signed it. "Here," he said. "With the compliments of William S."

Lorna frowned, reading, and said quietly: "More lovely and more temperate, what godly things he wrote." She glanced at him. "I see what the ancient beak meant about your hand. Are there many corrections, changes in the manuscript?"

"Here and there," he said. "But on the whole it seems to move fairly straight ahead."

"I think I can manage, then." She looked at the paper again. *"Yours sincerely, Neil Arnott.* Who's Neil Arnott?"

In all his years of dual identity — usually Neil Arnott in Canada, usually Nigel Ash elsewhere — he had never made that mistake, confused the two. The difference was only in names, but the difference was complete. He had learned to be as surely, instinctively, spontaneously Neil Arnott as he was Nigel Ash, no hesitancy at the hotel front desk, nor anywhere in anything. He was the one . . . He was the other, never yet caught out. And now this damned intoxicating woman had made him betray himself. "Just a name I made up for fun," he said. He felt the blood draining, and shook his head. "I still seem to get these dizzy spells. Better now."

Her face was kindly, concerned, and yet inscrutable. "I think you're driving yourself too hard too soon," she said.

A single humming bird was at the feeder in the tree, a mist of wings, a whirring. When it had slaked its thirst, it moved to a nearby twig and perched, absorbing nectar energy. "Motionless elf," he said. "No other small bird sits like a sphinx in daylight hours." Rest over, the humming bird buzzed off.

"I'm going to the summer theater at eight. I could pick the things up now, and read your manuscript before I go to bed."

"Why not come after the theater? That would give me time to improve legibility."

But short shrift to that gambit: "No. Either now or tomorrow morning."

"Okay," he said. "I'll get the jeep."

The barn swallows were teaching their young to fly, and they dive-bombed the intruder with aggressive twittering. "You do always just miss," he reminded himself and them. Or they always had so far in his experience. Congo jumped the tailgate, and he put the scythe in with him.

"Down to the sea," he said en route. "There's something in the Bible, can't remember."

" 'They that go down to the sea in ships, that do business in great waters, these see the works of the Lord, and his wonders in the deep.' "

"Do you feel the Lord about you, Lorna?"

"Sometimes I think so," she said. "Do you?"

"I never did. Perhaps I begin to." He had to stop for a rabbit, a snowshoe hare in its brown summer coat, a cousin of Diamond's hare in its white winter coat. It sat up on its back legs. They were almost fearless, bemused at this mating season. "Run, Rabbit, run," he said without acknowledgment to Mr. Updike. It lolloped unhurriedly away.

"The coolness down here is so lovely," she said.

"So temperate," he said. "Like lovely Lorna."

"I'm neither," she said. "And would you please not be facetious, Nigel Ash? Or is it Neil Arnott with a dizzy spell?"

He said nothing to that, picking up the typewriter after its overnight stay, and she the manuscript and papers. "May I read the typed part first?" she said. "That would clue me up."

"Please do." He did not say that he feared her artistic judgment, yet longed for it. He was not the aforementioned deity.

He stood beside the jeep. Her fingers moved to the starter key, but he said: "There's something I should explain," and she put her hand back on the steering wheel.

"Yes?"

"You remember I told you that I'd written a few short stories once?"

"For *Collier's*, yes, and your nom de plume was secret."

"My nom de plume was Neil Arnott. But there's slightly more to it than that — I was living as Neil Arnott then."

"Oh, I see. Why on earth?"

"Because once things were a bit sticky, and I needed a change of name. Quite useful, it proved to be."

"So I suppose this is another deadly secret."

"You could call it that. Known only to you and me, I hope."

She had been looking straight ahead, but now she turned and said angrily: "Why must I be the sole recipient of your dingy little secrets? Is this another of the webs you love to weave?"

"No," he said. "And I'm sorry, Lorna. It was a damned stupid slip."

"Always to dissemble, always to strut a phony part — how tedious that must be."

"I used to quite enjoy it, as a sort of game. Not any longer. Now I agree with you."

"Well, that's nice."

"Don't sit there, saying smugly: *Well, that's nice.* It's all your fault."

"My fault? How could it be? I don't mean to hurt you, Nigel."

"I know," he said. "I know, I know. Let's call it an unwitting hex, you bamboozle me. No other woman ever has." And unaccountably, or most accountably, his eyes were blurred, and they said goodnight, and she drove away with Congo.

No other man ever has, she thought. I know what I should

68

do. I should get kind Dan to give him his marching orders. Or I should go away and leave him to type his own damned book. Or I should say at dinner tomorrow: *In your time in the North, Mr. Prentice, did you ever run across a pilot called Neil Arnott?* He didn't deceive me about that. The arch dissembler cannot quite dissemble. But I will type it, and I will like it, the other thing that is burning him up.

Nigel, the debonair crook, I'm sure he is; Nigel, the hot-headed killer, he has that look; Nigel, who loves the world, if not humanity; Nigel, the sardonic warm enigma; Nigel, with two fires kindling in him, and I am one. Sooner or later, unless I stop it and I won't, we are going to burn ourselves up together, ashes to ashes, what a ghastly pun. He looked at me on the terrace and he said: *I wouldn't want to scythe you.*

⑨

HE DID A DAN FOR HIS CONSTITUTIONAL, jogged a hundred, walked a hundred, jogged and walked a mile or so, and managed twenty press-ups on the cabin broadloom, no dizziness at all. "You would be proud of me, Danny Boy," he said in the shower. He was a proper S.O.B. about little brother he would so admire to cuckold.

He cheered himself with dishonorable thought, being apprehensive. Fried egg on the buttered half, now Chiver's Olde English on the other, but he jumped to the summons: Buz-buz-buz-buzzz-buz, VE, I have a message for you, how would she have learned the Morse code?

"Hullo."

"Oh, good morning, Nigel." She often began with a diffident *oh*. "Well, I've read it all and I do have a few things to ask, mostly single words, if you haven't started writing already."

"No," he said. "Not until half-past. Go ahead, Lorna."

"He's under the ledge, and he thinks: *There's no good in fretting over what I've done, I must forget it. I must do all that's left to me, escape, get clean away.* I can't read that word. Is it *clean* away or *clear* away?"

"I wrote clean away. But I wonder. Clear, clean, more clear than clean. Yes, let's make it clear away. Good point."

"And then there's another one, when the hare comes running from the eagle. I'm sure it's stupid of me, but did you write with *desperate* urgency, or was it *disparate* urgency, you know, discombobulated?"

"Desperate," he said. "I suppose the other might just be pos-

70

sible, but we're in Diamond's mind. He's never heard of disparate."

"That was clueless of me." She had a few more words, and then: "The capitals aren't quite consistent. In your own typing, for instance, it's sometimes the White Stag, capitals, sometimes in lower case."

"That's my fault. I meant capitals to personify the beast."

"And your punctuation, it varies a bit."

"I punctuate by feel, for rhythm, emphasis. No changes, please."

"Okay," she said, small chuckle. "I wouldn't dare."

"You're so good to do this." Would she say anything, or would she?"

"I won't be able to type very much today because of these people coming to dinner."

"Oh, yes," he said. These Prentice people.

"But by tomorrow evening I should be up to date. Then will you have another one for me?"

"I think so, Lorna, hope so."

Silence, but he heard her light breathing in the house on the hill at the other end of the buried line. "Write well, Nigel," she said, and hung up.

She had told him, hadn't she?

"Whoopee!" he said, happy old schoolboy. He took his toast and marmalade out to the day, which was going to be a scorcher. "I love you, Loon," he said. He did too. He dearly loved the risible loon. It dived to fish, on business bent, and so was he.

. . . Diamond stood in the moon-shadowed room, listening. The house was silent, with a deadness quite different from the living silence of the open night.

The warmth was the most surprising thing, the blissful warmth which stole upon his legs and arms and over his cold face. The fevered lightness, the nagging pain in his stomach, the burden of his tired legs, all were stilled. And the thought of sleep, the overpowering need to go over to that basket chair in the corner.

He took a step toward the chair and then remembered. He shook his head, shaking the weakness from him. There was food to get, quickly, and out to the cold night again . . .

Diamond went from the kitchen to a pantry, and then he caught the smell of food. The larder was very dark but he lit matches to see a cooked chicken, sausages, a slab of margarine, back to the kitchen with them.

. . . He was just outside the door when his foot touched the mouse-trap. It went off with a sharp smack. He cursed under his breath and stiffened again. But the house was still charged with silence. Folks never wake when the mouse is taken in the trap, he thought, and he was comforted by that.

Diamond put the food on the kitchen table. Then he took the bird in his hands and sank his teeth across the pointed breastbone, tearing the good meat off, hardly chewing it. Like an animal, he thought, lusting for it like an animal.

He had heard no movement, but the light came on, and a woman faced him. She wore a shapeless boilersuitlike thing, zipped to the neck. She was a calm young woman, with fear in her face but calm, and bonny too, to hell with bonny women. She told him to relax. It was the voice of command, the way the Officer used to speak, and instinctively he did relax a little. Where was her man? She had no man, she said. If she had a man, would she be the one to come downstairs?

But a child cried in the house, a feverish crying of distress, and she said that her small son was sick, she must go to him.

The phone, where was it? In the sitting room, she said. Diamond went to guard against tricks. It was a comfortable room, a thick carpet on the floor, a rich woman's house. A photograph of a dark chap with a rugged face, her man, that might be. The child was quiet again, and soon she came back.

It was then that he heard footsteps on gravel. Told on him! Sold him to the police! Diamond seized the first thing to hand, a stone ornament to hit her.

72

Go and hide, you fool!

He hid while she spoke at the door. It was the local Sergeant of police, who had seen the light in the house and, Diamond not being caught yet, he had just come to check.

Everything's all right, she said, explaining about the sick bairn's nightmares, and the man went away.

". . . Why did you do it?" she asked suddenly.

The question took a moment to sink in. So she knew! He hadn't believed she could know; but it wasn't much of a surprise that she did. She had saved him, and he was sure now that she was his friend, a friend in the middle of the whole bad dream of it.

"I never meant to do it," he said. The tears welled up in his eyes. He felt them trickling down his face and hanging in the stubble of his chin. Him greeting!

"It was the anger again," he went on. "It gripped me and I hit her; but she was killed against the coal scuttle." He looked up to meet her eyes. "I'm no steady," he said. "I canna stop myself when it takes me."

"If you didn't mean to do it, if you didn't really do it," she said slowly, "why don't you give yourself up?"

"I'll never do that," he said fiercely. "It's no the rope I fear. It's being in a cell, shut away from the bonny hills, from the storm and the silence."

She smiled then, for the first time.

"You speak like a poet," she said. That was a queer thing for her to say.

"I must away," he said.

Diamond swayed a little, for the sleep was singing in his head. There was something he had to ask her. The places could come and go, the ledge among the rocks, the bridge, and the hill birches. And the uncertain endless dream could go on. It was all vague and shadowy, something that was happening and had never happened. But here was one thing that he must know.

"Why did you do it?" he asked, not meaning to use the words that she had used.

She looked at him for a moment, and then away, over to the picture of the man. She kept her eyes on it.

"John was a prisoner," she said, speaking in a flat steady voice as if it were all some story she had heard about a stranger. "He was in Germany for three years. Then he escaped and for a month he walked

73

by night. He must have felt like you. They shot him on the Swiss frontier."

She stood up then. The story was over.

"Did you never weep?" Asked Tam Diamond, just saying what had come into his mind.

"I never wept," she said.

She followed him along to the kitchen. He put the food into the bag and into his pockets, not asking her for it.

He turned at the window. "I'll not forget," he said.

She was watching him, but nothing showed in her thin bonny face. "Goodbye," she said and switched off the light.

Diamond climbed out of the window . . .

The cold smacked him in the face, painful and reviving. He moved to the west but soon his way was barred by a young plantation stretching far up the valley side. It was prickly spruce, unthinned, impassable, and he turned down to cross the dangerous road, to follow the line of the river beyond.

It was a low-lying field which the big river would flood in spate, but river and road narrowed soon again to meet below the broken slope, and he had no choice, he would have to risk the road.

". . . Who are you?" said a voice from behind the bright torch. It was the voice of authority again. Ten to one it was a bobby.

"Am I right for Dunmore?" asked Diamond. He put a silly smile on his face as he went across the road, swaying as if he was a wee wee thing tipsy, hands loose at his sides, getting his words out all the way: "Missed the last bus, and I've to be there for work the morn. It's a cold walk on a nicht like this." He was doing it well.

"You stop there!" said the man behind the light. His voice rose at the end as if he suddenly knew his danger.

Diamond jumped at the light with his left hand forward. He smacked the thing from the man's hand. Then he swung his right fist with all the weight of his body behind it. It only took a moment after that. He could just see the face; a left hook and a right uppercut as good as ever he done in the ring. It was the last one did the trick, right on the jaw.

Diamond knelt beside him. He still wasn't sure it was a policeman. He felt the shoulder. Yes, it was. Then his foot touched the

74

torch, sending it off with a clatter on the hard road. He groped for it and pushed up the switch. It was still working.

The chap was out cold. A young chap, big and heavy, no strips on his arms. Couldn't be the Sergeant, then. But the Sergeant wouldn't be such a bloody half-wit as to let that happen to him.

Diamond heaved the unconscious man over the bank on the lower side of the road. Then he got on the bicycle.

. . . He'd done it now all right, telling them where he was. And hitting a policeman! That was the way of getting them on the job. The bloody bastards in blue! They forgot about their hours of work when one of their own kind was hit. The scare would die down, and the ordinary folk would forget, but never the police. They'd never forget Tam Diamond now.

Diamond lost his head then. He knew that too, but there was nothing he could do about it. He pedaled madly, driving his legs until they were afire with pain, until he sobbed aloud at each breath.

It was the steep hill which brought him to his senses, but it nearly killed him first. He had to get off and stagger the last bit to the top.

He stopped at the crest. There was just one good thing. If he could hide the bike so they wouldn't find it, then they might think he was far away. It was the best hope, far better than riding on as he'd been going to do when he was daft back there.

He coasted downhill and soon he found such a place, where the river bank was abrupt, the water deep. He dropped the bicycle over, out of sight. No one would find it there. That was one lucky thing.

Soon, as night was fading, and sleet began to fall, another lucky thing happened for him. He came on a cart track and followed it to a cluster of old sheds.

The two small sheds were locked, but the big one was open, with a space for a door. Diamond went inside. There were farm implements in there, a plough, two harrows, a potato lifter, all rusty and neglected. At the other end some straw was lying about the bottom of a chute; a ladder was standing too, set into a square hole in the ceiling.

Diamond wiped his boots dry in the straw. Then he climbed the ladder. It was what he'd expected, a straw loft.

He slumped down on the floor. Then he forced himself to eat one of the legs of chicken. It was dry and sour to him, but he had to get something into his aching belly. He drank the last of the water from the bottle.

Then he burrowed into the straw, and pulled and wrestled with the coarse stuff until it was all round him, making a soft bed below and a prickly blanket over his face.

. . . He sailed away on the warm sea, on the drowsy silver sea, on the silvery sea of sleep . . .

Ash stopped by regulation at half-past four, made his cup of tea and took it out. He had been sharing Diamond's pain, exhaustion, hunger, fear, the cold that was burning fever, cold — all that in a day of heat, the thermometer read ninety-four, and Jake's storm was coming.

How had Jake known that the storm would come today? An informed guess, probably. The condition gathers in unchanging weather. Eventually it comes.

He watched the thunderheads build in the north. They did not, as on the other afternoon, shade vaguely into blue sky. They were almost as sharply etched as Himalayan snows — Kanchenjunga from Darjeeling — white peaks, dark depths. But those mountains were inert. These mountains grew in motion.

She had said about Shakespeare's sonnet that he wrote godly things, *more lovely and more temperate.* The mountains of the sky were godly things, by no means temperate.

The storm came fast. It had a will. It came. The sun was covered now, and the vivid contrast of white summit, black abyss had gone. It bore down, a plumbeous blank wall alive with light, thunder booming, tearing, rippling, multiple bombardment.

A flock of herring gulls fled downriver, crying. Far up the estuary he saw the lash of wind on water, but here no wind stirred yet.

Lightning and thunder flashed and crashed across half the

sky, and it was twilight at low water, damp mudflats mauve, macabre, the lightning flickered in reflection.

All things were new beside the shore, and this sepulchral flush was new. A doom light, Nigel thought.

The wind and rain raced here together. He saw the sharp line of them racing to him on the river. The seagulls had fled before the storm. He fled to shelter from the storm.

It was a noisy shelter. One could not but think of Jove's mounting thunderbolts, that kind of thing. The lightning sizzled, and the God-awful crash came with it. He did not much fear thunderstorms, but one of that was quite enough. He was sure that he had heard the lightning sizzle.

But the storm passed soon, to grumble in the south, perhaps to spend itself beyond the islands. The wind fell, the downpour eased, the daylight had come back. He went out, avoiding puddles in the rock. The sun shone again, and the air was miraculously clean and clear across the cove, across the river, placid as a pond.

A strong smell of smoke came from the immediate woods. After an inch or two of rain, a forest fire seemed improbable. But one never knew in this mad world. One must investigate.

Having survived the storm bone-dry, if somewhat shaken by one fearful bolt, he got himself soaked, top to toe, from long grass and dripping tree, and he found the source of smoke.

It was the tallest tree in his vicinity, distant about its own height from the cabin, what they called a pasture spruce, a tree that had grown in open land, with side branches thick as a man's thigh. He always looked at it en passant, thinking ugly beast.

The lightning shaft had sheared many of its uncouth limbs off. The shearing was quite surgically done, the tangle of the sheared a shambles. They smoked and spluttered harmlessly, would soon go out. The lightning's spiral gouge from crown to foot also smouldered and would soon go out, leaving a scar that he who ran might read.

Ash thought about man the master of the universe. Lorna

had meant a similar thing the other evening, sitting with him at the shore.

  . . . *There are more changes and more new things to see than any place I was ever at.*

  And the great tides to remind us, Lorna said.

10

"THIS IS A GREAT PLACE," BOBBY SAID. "Just in line between the anvil and that white rock, a bit out from the reeds." He dropped the stone that served for anchor. "We'll get one here, bet my bottom dollar."

But no trout moved at that spring hole, nor at two reputed others farther down the lake, each worth Bobby's bottom dollar. "Hopeless. Y'know what I think, Uncle?"

"Divulge," he said.

"I think the lake's been dynamited. It's easy, y'know, all you need is a stick of the stuff and a detonator and a fuse, and wham!"

"What about a canoe to collect the corpses?"

"Look at us in a canoe."

"We drove here. It's too far to portage, and no other car has been in this year."

"I hadn't noticed," Bobby said, deflated. He was a clueless, friendly, annoying youth. "What say supper, Uncle?"

"What say just drift it once, then supper?"

"Drifting's no good, but we can try, I guess."

They paddled to the head of the narrow lake. From this northern end one could see the anvil of the name, vaguely reminiscent of a blacksmith's anvil, a bald projection above the low cliff. The other shore was almost flat, with woods rising gradually from the water's edge.

"It's deep below the anvil," Bobby said. "I tried once with a weight, let all the line out, and never did reach bottom."

The true wind was from the west, clouds crossing that way, but here the breeze funneled down the lake, enough to make a riffle on an overcast dry evening, good fishing weather. They drifted broadside near the reeds, and nothing happened. Bobby cast badly and too fast. He was a thrasher. Take time, Ash thought, but he did not say it. Now the light wind died, and they were motionless, black cliff, black water over there, but near to them the many shades of green. No trout were rising anywhere. "It's hopeless, Uncle, let's have supper."

But Ash had seen a possible place, where a small brook came in, making a channel through the reeds. "Just hold us at that," he said, false casting for more line. It was a long cast into a narrow space, and he dropped the Parmachene lightly, neatly, below fast water, and nothing happened. "Two schools of thought," he said. "Dull day, bright fly — dull day, dark fly. Let's try the latter."

He changed the Parmachene Belle for the Dark Montrealer, and cast again. It was harder this time, for the breeze had come back, and he had to put a long roll on his line across the wind, a satisfying skill, still more satisfying when the trout gobbled it. It was a speckled trout of a pound or more.

That revived Bobby's enthusiasm, and they drifted the rest without success.

"You make it look easy, Uncle. How did you learn to cast like that?"

"Practice, Bobby. It's timing, and a trick or two to cope with the wind. The hill loch at home could be difficult."

"Was it like this?"

"No," he said, paddling in the bow. "It was a bare place on the hill. The reeds were much the same, though." He saw that loch, the boathouse, the white wild cotton and the bog, the peat hags and the sphagnum moss. It was the place, or a place like it, to which Tam Diamond would find his way, be driven on his way.

"What is Scotland like? I can't quite see it."

"Drab cities, good country, ghastly slums, solid people a bit self-righteous, this and that, the opposites. We had the river and the lowland farms, the hill farms and the bare deer forest. We were lucky."

"All gone now?"

80

"I kept one cottage. I had to sell Glenash when your grandfather died."

"I guess that must have been hard, even if I'm against inheriting property."

You won't be for long, he thought. In five years' time you will have finished at McGill, and you will be on the sure and certain road of assimilation into your father's world. There are not so many flies on patient Daniel Ash. And as for having to sell Glenash for death duties — I could very well have kept it on if I had been prepared to be a working farmer-laird, unimaginable fate. With a good wife, unimaginable?

"I would love to go to Scotland."

"You must come and stay sometime."

"Gosh, could I?"

They beached the canoe at the head of the lake beside the main inlet brook. A flask of whisky for him, ice for him, beer for Bobby, fried chicken crisp and brown, homemade rolls still warm, garlic butter and Oka cheese, fresh peaches. "Your old mum is a champion provider."

"Yeah," Bobby said, skinning his third downy peach. "It's what she likes doing, though."

"For the blessings that we receive, may the Lord make us truly thankful to Mum."

Bobby laughed, but there was puzzlement. "Are you religious, Uncle?"

"Not noticeably. I thought grace was in order because of your somewhat graceless comment." He went to the water's edge to rinse peaches etcetera off his hands.

"Mum's great," Bobby conceded. "But I don't know what's got into her lately. Take this morning, y'know. Well, I was supposed to help her with some things for some church sale, but I went to sleep again. I was out late last night. I needed the sleep."

"What time did you surface eventually?"

"Around noon, I guess. Well, you should have heard the bawling out she gave me, like some crazy woman."

"Did you provoke the lady, apart from sleeping in?"

"I guess I did say something about giving stuff to her old church sale just being a way of putting on the charity dog. Then she got really mad and gave me all that little rich boy crap."

"Not my favorite word. But you were out late last night so your bloody beauty sleep was more important than doing a job. If that isn't being a little rich boy, I wouldn't know what is."

"I thought you were different," Bobby said. "I guess that's why she was so keen on us going fishing. *Give Bobby a pep talk.*"

"No word exchanged," he said.

"Didn't you sleep late when you were young?"

"Not allowed to, Bobby."

"The good old days."

"Much easier days," he said.

"Why, Uncle?" He was less resentful.

"We had almost everything that you have except a television set. We still accepted rules, an ordained way of life that nobody believes in now, and I can't say I wonder."

"Just easier for rich people, though, wasn't it?"

"Yes," he said. "The poor were far worse off. Happier, perhaps."

Two ravens flew across the lake, an old bird croaking encouragement to the young one that followed, still unkempt of feather. "Flying lessons," he said. "They have a special call. I always enjoy watching them."

"Mum pointed that out to me the other day at home. You and Mum like all the same things, don't you, Uncle?"

"I wouldn't say quite all," he said. "She's a woman you know."

"I meant that too," Bobby said.

If he meant that too, he might mean quite a lot. Ash finished his cigarette, and packed the picnic basket. The sun had come out, but the lake was in shadow. It shone only on the slope of the forest to the left, a drench of sun-touched green, and the

82

name for the richest might be viridian. So many Canadian lakes, he thought, seeing a potpourri, a kaleidoscope of them — lakes in the barren lands, each with a pair of whistling swans; lakes at the stunted limit of trees; lakes in the rocky shield; Great Bear Lake, enormous, blue; Great Slave Lake, enormous, dim; high mountain lakes, and swampy puddles; lakes with a skim of ice; lakes in white winter; lakes breaking up; lakes open at last. "I suppose I must have seen a million," said Nigel Ash.

"A million what?"

"A million goddam lakes," he said. "Well, what's the program now?"

"Fish some more?" said Bobby. "All we've got so far is your breakfast. Do you have the right time?"

"Twenty to eight."

"They'll just be starting the clam bake." Bobby picked up a stone, threw it as hard as he could, and grunted.

"I thought the clams had a bug or something."

"Not at Paradise Island. They took the boat."

He remembered Lorna's comment, and Bobby had brought the subject up. "A pity you didn't go," he said. "We could easily have fished some other evening."

"What's the use of going? When Keith Kelly's around, Kim won't even look at me. What chance do I have with a guy like that, spouting poetry at her? Oh, sure, he's a brilliant guy, and he's got her panting for him."

"She's got ants in her moonlit pants for him," he said. "Not to worry, Bobby."

"Ants in her moonlit pants, that's funny."

"Hardly original," he said.

"Well, its hardly what my Dad would say in a thousand years. Dad would say: *Young man, you must learn to take the knocks in life.*"

"So you must," he said. "And I wish you wouldn't make cracks about your father. He's a good decent man worth ten of me."

"Ten times as perfect," Bobby said. "Dad goes to church and

prays for the world and gets director's fees for making napalm."

He was going to say: *for Christ's sake grow up,* or some such exasperated comment, but the poor boy was in tears. So Ash endured the tortured sobs of seventeen, not unmindful, as ever, of his own interest. Bobby's hostility could right soon cool Mum's friendly feelings. And he sang, he had quite a decent kailyard voice, he sang:

> I love a lassie
> A bonnie Hielan lassie
> She's as sweet as the heather in the dell.
> She's as sweet as the heather, the bonnie purple heather.
> Is Mary my Scots bluebell.

"We're all in the same fuckin' old canoe," he said, reminded inanely of Randy Dibble.

"We were saying," Bobby said, recovered from tears and laughter. "We were saying the other night, you never seem old to us."

Well, that was gratifying, and it kept him in the hero's seat. "Is the book nearly finished, Uncle?"

"God, no," he said. "Half done almost, I would think."

"I asked Mum what it was about, but she wouldn't give. She said: *Ask Nigel, if you want to risk getting your head bitten off.*"

"It's about a man who hits a woman, kills her, doesn't mean to, and he's being chased across the Scottish Highlands." How banal that sounded.

"What happens in the end?"

"I can't say what I haven't written yet, what hasn't happened yet."

"I bet it's more real to you than sitting here."

"Dunno," he said. "Don't know nothin'. Ah, reality, what is thy name?" Time and reality, he thought, those kissing cousins. But this time and this reality were not the lake, were not Tam Diamond. They were Lorna looking at him, Oh, goddammit. "I tell you what, Bobby," he said. "If you don't mind

84

fishing alone, I think I'll go walkabout a bit, perhaps climb to the anvil's nose. Can you manage to load the canoe alone?"

"Oh, sure," Bobby said. "I'll pick you up round there. Watch you don't fall off, though, Uncle."

Ash took his rod down and put it in the Wagoneer, and went walkabout. With four-wheel drive the head of the lake was still just accessible, but the logging road, down which he had come from his plane crash a dozen years or so ago, was grown over and barred by fallen trees.

He walked back along the wheel tracks they had made, six inch ruts in swampy ground. There must be beaver at work somewhere farther up these days. He saw deer tracks, moose tracks, the elongated fingers of raccoons, and the fresh marks of a bobcat, yes, veritably so. He had seen many bobcat tracks, but only once in all his time, that long-legged burly cat itself in freedom, russet among the browns and greens, glimpsed and vanished, the most elusive creature of the woods.

The swale ended, and he came to cranberry land, firm and springy underfoot. It was about here that he had met the survey party that other time. They were college boys blazing compass lines through the bush, and a man with a broken wrist, hardly able to see, provided an excellent excuse for all three of them to escape blackflies for an hour or two to drive him to a doctor. For their benefit, and the doctor's, he was a prospector who had run foul of a mother bear with her cub, broke the wrist in flight. When he fell, she lost interest, let him go, lucky, eh?

Ahead now, and to his left, was the rise to the anvil, which hid the lake from here. He climbed that way, eating a few red cranberries, not very appetizing, eating one juniper berry for the taste of gin, or for no reasonable reason. Then the low vegetation petered out, and he was on a bare gray slope with shallow fissures here and there, but in general smooth as a bald man's scalp. It was an unusual formation, not particularly rare. Either soil had never accumulated on this rocky slope, or its thin coat of soil had been burnt off in a forest fire. The latter might be the likelihood, for on the top of the inconsiderable hill there was one wire birch, a solitary twisted tree, like those trees which had pestered Tam Diamond's imagination.

It was to think about Tam Diamond that he had come here, for this fishing expedition, so popular in Lorna's book, had deprived him of his evening planning time.

He passed the tree in its quite sizeable hollow on the crest, and went down to the anvil, the Neanderthal brow, sliding on his backside for the last few feet, and he dangled legs. Bobby was flogging the springhole opposite.

"Heigh-ho," Ash called.

"Got one, Uncle. Hi!" His voice floated about. There would be an echo from the cliff below.

Heights did not particularly bother him, but he was no mountain goat. So he thought better of that typical bravado, and withdrew to sit safely and quite snugly, his back to the birch tree, able to think.

He sat there, letting it come to him. The point at issue was: Should the whole story carry through in Diamond's mind and person? In a way that was the simpler, truer thing to do. But now that he had to face the question, he knew that the answer could not be that. There are two sides to every question, he thought wisely. The hounds are hunting. The hare is running. That was simple too, but it was not a sound reason for switching briefly to the hounds. The sound reason was that he must link the cradle of the end and the beginning. There was no other way.

He thought about that for a while, changing himself from the pursued to the pursuer. There was the swift hot pursuit, coming up to the belly of a JU88. There was the slow cold pursuit, coming up with him at last at a lake not unlike the one Ash sat above. You are the enemy, one juddering squirt, I execute you, clean and impersonal, even sorry. You are my partner, and we were lucky, we panned a few thousand dollars' worth, and not only did you make off with it, but you contrived a deadfall at the cabin door to clobber me. I follow you, I execute you, no regret whatever, then or since.

He wondered what Lorna would say if he told her that true story. He knew the measure of his affliction — that he did want to tell her that, tell her everything, the whole shoddy lot, not all so shoddy, quite amusing.

But he heard an engine start. The sound came from the wrong direction, south, impossible, no roads or tracks that way. He stood to see that it was the Wagoneer with the canoe on top. "The echoes bounce at Anvil Lake," he said. What did echoes do but bounce?

He went down to wait for Bobby, who rushed the swamp, going deeper this time, whacked the crankcase or whatever on a rock, but came on to harder ground. "I got two, Uncle," he said, "same size as yours. That makes one for each of us."

"Oh good," Ash said. "I think we'd better check your under-pinnings. That was a hell of a crack. No oil leaks," he said after inspection, "but the right spring bolts are flattened back."

"Oh, well, it's insured," Bobby said.

"I rather doubt if the insurance covers bashing boulders." Ash thought that enough of little rich boy was enough for one evening. There were no shades of Lorna in him. But perhaps the opposites of Dan were in him, if that meant anything.

"That was great, Uncle, thanks for coming."

"Thanks for taking me, Bobby, I enjoyed it."

11

ON ONE AUTUMN DAY THE LAIRD'S SON ROBERT and McNaughton, the old stalker, had failed to kill the White Stag.

On a dim March day in the valley below those hills, Inspector Thoms of the Glasgow C.I.D. pursued a different quarry. At first it was his opinion that once Diamond had the constable's bicycle he would get on it and go, ride clear out of that countryside. But McNaughton, who tended to know everything, and usually did, thought that a fanatical man like Diamond, his mind made up to move on foot by night, would soon hide the bicycle and would continue in the way that he had chosen. And McNaughton was right. He found the machine under the steep river bank.

As the night was nearly spent when Diamond hid it, he could not be far away. Now the Inspector sought advice about their familiar country. Where best to intercept him? Diamond had started toward the West, and the West was home to him. There were no boats to enable him to cross the big river. And so, unless he climbed to the high bare hills in the South, he was pinned to this wooded valleyside. But could he climb out of it?

There was already snow on the ground above a thousand feet, and a blizzard warning for tonight. Yes, he could climb, but without special clothing, which he did not have, he could not survive in those high places, so fiendish in wild weather.

Thoms had fifteen men. Two would be posted on the open moor to intercept Diamond should he swing high to evade the line. The remainder, with McNaughton and Robert Graham, would cover the river bank, the road, the few openings in thick woods.

88

His terse orders given, the Inspector talked in the fading day about the man they hunted. It was a small coincidence that this Diamond had been the boy seen by Sergeant Thoms in a Glasgow tenement, his father drunk. The name was unusual enough to stay in memory, and there was the police photograph taken a year ago when Diamond had done thirty days for assault.

"He must have been eight or nine. I can see his fair hair now, with a touch of red in it, and the pale blue eyes. Well, you often see bonny bairns, but I don't think I ever saw another like him. He had an honest face, a bit proud, and he looked ashamed. "I'm Tam Diamond," he said, and he held his head up as if he wanted to say: This is a bad thing that's happened, but we're as good as you are.

"It's queer that a laddie's face should have stayed with me all these years. But you don't often see a face like that in the slums, what you might call a hot, carved-out do-or-die face, the kind that stays the same from childhood to the grave. After that I used to see him whiles in the street."

Inspector Thoms sighed, "That was the same Tam Diamond . . ."

Until now Ash had taken the story on, or it had taken him on, steadily and inexorably. But the change to the enemy's viewpoint was difficult. His Hyde was his Jekyll, his Jekyll his Hyde, and both were climbing on his back.

"It's only a story, dammit," he said. "Only a story that never happened." But it was happening.

Wake, dress, walk, eat, write, drink, eat, write, work physically, drink, plan, eat and read and sleep. He could no longer dismiss Diamond until the next appointment. As August went on through the small tides of the waning moon, the man was near him always. Nigel Ash almost never woke in the night; but when morning came again, the distorted dreams would straighten. It was not Detective Inspector Diamond on the job. It was not Lorna hiding with him in a cave. It was him in the log cabin, and alone, gulls crying at the shore.

Quite often in mid-morning there would be a single tentative scratch at the door, Congo come to pay a call, to lie in the same place, black dog on small brown rug, not a stir until half past-twelve and sherry time. "I know you think of the midday snack," he said one day. "But I really do believe you like me for myself." It was gratifying, not surprising. He was at home in doggy land, and Congo a companionable comfort.

His new human characters were not. One had to meet them, then get to know them. They were only subordinate in the thing, but they must be real, that wretched adjective again. There was a memory of Diamond's officer, killed in war — all right. There was Ella, a small country girl, met once in boyhood — certainly all right. There was the stalker, austere, opinionated, a stereotype, but so they often did become in late years. There was the young Laird, a somewhat callow youth, like Bobby but subject to other mores in easier times in a different place — oh, well. There was the Inspector, a good tough cop, what he had to be. And there was Anne, the widow in the house, desirable young woman — yes.

All these Ash had to come to know. In Diamond's absence it went slowly, and Lorna typed ahead of him. In Diamond's presence he sometimes wrote fast enough to keep up with her. Another chapter done, he would give her a buzz on the telephone. *Won't you come down this evening? — Sorry, Nigel, I have to go out. Could you bring it up about six? — I think you're wary of me after sunset,* he said once. *That's not impossible.* She laughed, and hung up. It was between them, in abeyance at this burdened time.

He saw Jake once or twice. He saw Lorna often briefly in daylight hours. He took evening toots by dinghy. He went out once with Mrs. Becker and the young people. Of that will-o-the-wisp policeman, Petrie, there was no word. Otherwise, he stayed at home, if home it might be called, prison de luxe.

This evening — it was a Thursday, and Dan due again tomorrow — he had finished a chapter with the hounds. There remained one chapter still to be written with the hare, possibly two. He telephoned Lorna, who said she would be in, and he put the stapled sheets into an envelope and went outside.

The tide was still low, but coming in. As the dead of the moon

90

drew near, each successive highwater mark moved farther up the beach, not a clean rim of seaweed, but a messy conglomeration of that with plastic bottles, cans, sawmill tailings, a single cast-off shoe in excellent condition, an oil-blackened dead herring gull, nylon netting, unmentionables. What a dim rich continent of waste. "You name it," he said. "We garbage it."

But his attention was drawn from sordid cast-offs to birds of autumn. They were a flock of black-bellied plovers, calling cheerfully as they flew upriver to settle on the mudflats. The northwest wind had brought heat in the afternoon, but these last mornings there had been an invigorating nip, small hint that dog days were over and autumn on its way; and the birds of passage another sign of that.

He heard voices, and turned, not expecting visitors, nor wanting them. They were Keith Kelly and Kim, coming along the shore. He had met the elder Kelly on the boat that evening, some evening or other. It was not hard to know why the tall artistic boy and the voluptuous vivacious girl were matched together. As Bobby had said, what chance did he have with a guy like that around. A charming thing about them, though, was that in public they behaved quite casually to one another, no touchings, no lingering looks. One simply knew that they were linked.

"Hullo, you two," he said. "I'm glad to see you." And he was. "But can you wait a bit? I said I would take this chapter up to Lorna."

"Don't bother about us, sir. We only dropped by."

"No, no," he said. "Do stay. I'll be back in an hour and a bit or so. There's booze in the cupboard and beer in the fridge. Make yourselves at home. Can you endure one another's company until I get back, or would that question border on the rhetorical?"

They laughed. "It's fun with you," Kim said. "You're sly."

"Old dog of that ilk," he said. "Help yourselves, then."

"The book," Keith said. "Is it marching again?"

"Plodding," he said. "And there is no story until the story's done. I see the end so clearly, and I mustn't hurry to it. Left plod, right plod, along the bloody tunnel."

"Plod along the tunnel or hurry down the drain," Keith said. "How right you are."

The plover rose now, swinging to fly before the wind. "The plover and the wind," Keith said, watching them. "I wonder."

"See you later," he said, and walked fast uphill, feeling slightly story-ridden, but strong in body, no aches and pains, no rests for puff.

Lorna was not on the terrace, so he went round to the front door and called: "Fair amanuensis, where art thou, dear?"

"In the living room." She sounded, and then looked, less than pleased at being thus addressed. "Why the alien corn?"

"Stir-crazy," he said. "If you know the feeling."

"Bobby-crazy, I know the feeling. That blasted pond, his single solitary job, I told you. I must have asked him five times today."

"It's none of my business, but why doesn't Dan give him plain unvarnished bloody hell?"

"Because Dan can't," she said. "But why don't you? You're the big hero uncle, always trying to be popular. Why don't you give him plain unvarnished bloody hell?"

"Where is he?"

"Sulking in his room."

"All right. On with the popularity contest."

"I didn't mean that."

"Don't say it, then." He put his chapter on the table, and left Lorna, who was spitting mad. He liked her more than ever, spitting mad.

"You there, Bobby? Open up."

He went in, shut the door, and let him have it, a blitz technique, a skill of a sort, innate in a few, acquired by some, brazen, uninhibited, rebuke without insult, Jehovah's thunder to a conclusion of encouragement: "I know things aren't easy for you at the moment. But if you have a job to do, for Christ's sake get on with it, and stop being sorry for yourself. You have the makings of a man in you. Get on with that too."

It was brutal. It was what you had to do. In a while Bobby turned away to look down at the swimming pond. "Okay, Uncle," he said. And he said, "I wish you were my father. So does Mum, I'll bet."

Lorna was reading the chapter, a pencil in hand, but she looked up. "The reverberations shook the house. You certainly can dish it out. What did he say?"

"He just said: *Okay, Uncle.*"

"Was that all?"

"I told you, dammit."

"I'd better finish this. Could you get us a drink?"

She had several questions about his chapter. ". . . These ones are harder to read, more crossings-out."

"I know," he said. "It goes easier with the man himself."

"I can do this by tomorrow. But the weekend is a write-off, I mean a type-off." She smiled a little, and frowned, not quite her kind of small joke. "Then on Tuesday I'm driving Bobby to stay with my sister in the Eastern Townships until he goes back to school. They're good cousin friends, and he's always been fond of one of the girls. She might stand in for Kim a little."

"Oh, yes," he said, half taking that in. "I can't thank you enough for everything." His right eyelid began to flutter. It had done that off and on since yesterday. He put his finger up to stop the tic.

"It's hard for you to say, I know. But can you give me a clue about how much after this one?"

"One chapter, or two," he said. "And then — and then the end to meet with the beginning."

"Yes," she said. She still had not spoken one word about the book, marvelous good woman. The flutter had stopped, so he took his finger down. She was watching him. "There's something in your face that wasn't there before. Humility, I think. Or perhaps it's the other way round. Perhaps you don't hide behind that swashbuckling air I never liked."

"Could be a bit of both," he said. The tic began, flutter, flutter, and he covered it.

"You look well again, but your mind is so tired."

"Does that show?"

"Why does your eyelid tremble? Why are you not quite here now in this room?"

"Away up the glen, we say in Scotland."

"Will you go back to Scotland when the book is finished?"

"I don't know," he said. "I suppose that depends upon whether anyone in Britain or the U.S. will want to publish it."

"Certainties don't depend upon."

She had spoken at last, and it dismayed him. "There's no story until the story's done," he said for the second time that afternoon.

"You wouldn't think of taking a few days off? There will still be a week before Labor Day."

"No," he said. "I must keep on." A weekend with Dan? A weekend thinking of her with Dan? A chance encounter with someone who knew him as his alter ego? If he stopped, he might lose the story, have a heart attack, blow off steam by getting drunk. "If I stopped, it might go dead on me. I might even go dead on it."

"You have to, I know." But her glance was speculative. There were so many shadows, changes in her face. "Let's have another drink and another subject, slightly linked. There's someone I want you to tell me about."

He got the drinks. "Someone," he said. "I suppose you mean that bloody man, Neil Arnott."

"How did he happen? I'm dying to know."

"He didn't happen suddenly. Things grew until one day he had to happen. But I'd better go back a bit. I spent my three years in Germany trying to escape. That sounds glamorous, the sort of devil-may-care school boy derring-do so long exploited by those phony Colditz people, they'll be cashing in

94

on it to their deathbeds. In fact the preparations for escape were meticulous, zest to it, but no glamour to it, and no thought of glamour. We learned a dozen incidental skills like picking Yale locks, like diverting the goon's attention for the one split second necessary to relieve him of his saw, and so on. Most of all we learned to plan and watch and wait. We were young and intelligent and patient. By the time we came out of prison we were the best trained and most gifted criminals extant, albeit of a legitimate variety, and almost everyone reverted to the paths of virtue.

"Well, I found post-war Britain very boring, no spice to it, a lot of cushy people sorry for themselves — do you know that the first day I got home I walked past a trash basket full of thrown-out loaves, that sort of thing. Then I began to get ideas, dropped a hint here and there, and I was in."

"In what?" she said, leaning forward, captive audience.

"In with the right connections. After I converted to jets, I was evaluating the German ones, and that meant a bit of to and fro, and it meant a nice bit on the side or in my cockpit, conveying black market penicillin to the needy."

"Oh," she said, expressionless. "Go on."

"It began as a sort of game, or really an extension of a cautious slightly risky game at which I had become quite expert, and a squadron leader of impeccable credentials with the right wartime gongs can be a handy courier to the underworld. Start him small, test him, find him reliable and crafty, use him.

"So when I was sent over to demonstrate the SF6, a long-range nightfighter job, my contact handed me a small sealed package, told me what to do with it, said what I would get for safe delivery — they paid very well, one never had to bargain — and off I hopped by Iceland and Goose to Montreal.

"After I had done my flying stuff next morning at St. Hubert, I changed out of uniform, went into the city, telephoned from a callbox, and was told where to go.

"Well, to cut a long story short . . ."

"Please don't cut it short."

"But I have to — Keith and Kim are waiting for me at the cabin."

"Keith and Kim alone at our cabin?" She did not seem to like that much. "Why?"

"Just a call," he said. "I was leaving as they arrived. Shall I continue, or are you bored?"

Lorna laughed. "Bored?" she said. "How could I be?"

"To summarize, then — I gave him the parcel, trouser pocket size. He inspected the seals with a jeweler's glass, then opened up the wrapper. It was an Altoid tin, the original curiously strong peps, and in it, all sparkling, nestled in cottonwool, were five fabulous pear-cut diamonds, which he duly examined one by one.

"*Very fine,* he said. He was a funny little man, exceedingly polite. He opened a wall safe, put them in it, and handed me an envelope. *Please count,* he said. *Five thousand dollars. The bills are good, I do assure you.*"

"They were hundreds, moderately used, and of course not in sequence. So I thanked him, and he thanked me, and we parted with mutual esteem.

"I headed up toward the Cafe Michel where I was due to renew last night's acquaintance with a smashing Canadian Air Force girl for lunch, and I was thinking that so much of the ready was a difficulty. A bearer draft on London would have made more sense. So naturally I kept a wary eye, and I soon suspected and then confirmed that a chap was tailing me on St. Catherine Street. It could be his man following to get his money back. On the other hand, it could be a cop.

"If the latter, it was fairly obvious that even a squadron leader with impeccable credentials would be hard put to it to explain away five thousand smackers in his pocket. So I shook the man easily enough in Eaton's store, went to a Laurentian Bank nearby, opened a savings account with two hundred dollars, kept two hundred, which I changed into smaller stuff, and put the rest into a safety deposit box, and that was how Neil M. Arnott first saw the light of day."

96

"At the Laurentian Bank?"

"The very same. Dan had just started with them in Winnipeg."

"Why do you have to tell me that?"

"Because you asked how Arnott happened, and I'm telling you."

"You do rather draw me in," she said.

"I went on to Ottawa that time, and then to the West, and home. Nobody questioned me, although one Station Adjutant did drop the word that some plainclothes man had made delicate inquiries about my movements. I had got away with it once, but I had a hunch that the Squadron Leader might be of interest if he tried anything again. Anyway, when I got back, I asked my contact for a British passport in the name of Neil Methuen Arnott, a forged birth certificate was the only thing they needed, easy. And the next time I came back that year was as a civilian commercial pilot, landed immigrant. Five years later Neil Arnott took out Canadian citizenship and got a passport. Meanwhile Ash retired from the service and kept his British one. Sounds complicated but really very simple, and they were lax in those days."

He stood. "Lorna, I must go."

"Will you tell me more sometime?"

"I'll tell you anything you like, and you won't like it when you hear it."

She looked straightly and deeply at him. "I might," she said. "That's just the trouble."

"Come as far as the pond with me."

She put the manuscript and the typed chapter into her brown envelope, crumpled a bit by now, and gave it to him. She kept the carbon copies as insurance against fire or whatever.

They walked side by side with Congo in attendance. The evening wind was cooler. "Look," she said, pointing at a few crimson leaves. "The wild pear begins to turn."

"And the plover are at the shore. Tell me, Lorna — why do you object to Keith and Kim being alone at the cabin?"

"Because I'm a prude," she said. "I never was any squadron leader's smashing lay after a leisurely lunch at the Café Michel."

"H'mm," he said. "A pity, that, I mean for the squadron leader."

"Oh, dear," she said. "What a prude am I." The swimming pond was loaded with Bobby's tardy dose of chlorine tablets. The filter hummed faintly over there. "He forgot Dan's notice," she said. "I'd better put it up. No, Congo, you can't go in this evening."

The ritual count at the lily pond. "Twenty-three," she said. "They're on the dwindle too. Are the deer there still?" Disjointed conversation.

"I thought they had gone. But they were out again last evening. The fawn looks almost as big as its mother now. Lorna!"

"Yes, Nigel?"

"When I've done the last chapter with Diamond, will you type it for me . . . ?"

"Of course I will, idiot."

"I hadn't finished. Will you bring it down to me at deer time?"

"I don't know," she said. "Perhaps I will. All I know is that I dread this weekend." She put her fair head into the hollow of his shoulder. "Go now," she said. "Please go." But she held him to her. "We were happy until you came."

Bobby was running down the grass road from the house, rounding the curve of her shrub border to face directly here. He stopped short, hesitated a second, and vanished into the woods beside him.

"Bothersome," Ash said.

"That's the understatement of the year."

He did not explain, kissed her cheek, and went. Bobby knew now, but how and why had he guessed before? *You and Mum like all the same things, don't you, Uncle? — I wouldn't say quite all. She's a woman you know. — I meant that too.* And what had he said this afternoon? A funny-peculiar world, son wanting mother and uncle to shack up.

We will, he thought. When I finish with Diamond, we will, we will. And what will that do to her, to them? *We were happy until you came.* Nigel Ash had never denied himself, had always taken what he wanted. It was somewhat less than likely that he would deny himself this apogee of all the wants of all his life. And the moon will be in apogee, he thought. But first the job.

He passed the spruce tree which had recently been riven by lightning stroke, but Kim's voice beyond the cabin stopped him in his tracks. "Just to think we might have been making lovely love all this time on old Nigel's couch, he as good as told us to, and what do you have to do, mean beast, but go into a poem huddle."

"There's a time for everything, as that wise old codger wrote."

"Say it again for me, darling."

> Lean, wind, lean,
> For summer has been.
> Cry, plover, fly,
> For the year must die.

Ash withdrew a distance on his rubber soles, silent Indian flitting through the woods, childish, he knew, but he often thought of the ever forgotten Indian.

And he thought of something else, of this summer in New York City, feeling very unwell in the back of a taxicab. *It's all screwin'* said the driver, a loquacious type. *That's all there is to it, Mister, screwin'. — You might be right at that.* End of conversation.

But the beautiful thing — that it was not. This boy in love had written his small poem to the dying year. And he still had his story to finish. Yes, truly, unto everything a season.

He announced his arrival with a tactful heigh-ho, lest they should be making up for time lost to poetry. "Sorry I'm so late," he said.

Later, when they had walked downriver, he went to look for the deer. My talismen, he thought of them now. But they were not there, and soon it was too dark on a moonless night to see across the cove.

His mind had played truant from Tam Diamond for an hour or two. But the man came back to him in the dark — fevered, exhausted, desperate. He sat a while, and the west wind grew chilly. As he stood to go over the knoll to the cabin, a light came on upriver. It was at the shore, where he had seen two men before by moonlight. But this time the searchlight beam cut a narrow swathe across the field, swinging this way to the edge of the cove and back. But there was nothing on that field, hardly to be wondered at when the wind blew human scent directly toward the place they searched. The light swung away again upriver, silhouetting two men against the path it lit for them. The light soon disappeared, and Ash went in.

12

THE PERCOLATOR WAS A MARVEL. You loaded it, you plugged it in, and almost at once the gurgle and the gasp, short gurgles and long gasps for a few minutes, such a contented electric beast, muttering occasionally thereafter for decent coffee all the morning.

Having started that, he cut up through the woods, wet after a shower last night, walking fast by the paths he now knew well, and to the back road. There had been no car tracks as far as the padlocked gate. As Jake had said, anyone with a bucksaw and an axe could cut a way round it in half an hour, and nobody had. Last night's visitation might have been a reconnaissance on foot. He climbed the gate, went down over the steep hill, and then left the road to swing more easily downriver to home. There were fresh tracks at the crossing place of the deer above the cove.

He was not a naturalist in the true sense. He was a watcher who felt the world with him and about him.

Patches of mist lay on the river this morning, and the tide would soon be high, and he was already with Tam Diamond as he ate his breakfast, poor cold sod up there to be with again.

. . . Then the whistle blew. It was a long piercing blast, sounding clear in the wild confusion of the night. Voices came up from below, and torches flickered. Diamond saw them out of the corner of his eye, but he paid no heed. The man was still coming fast, growling and panting.

Diamond dropped his knife. He used both hands against the boulders. It was a heavy one that went home. He heard it thud and crack.

The man groaned and was still a moment. He began to move again, scrabbling on the snow-covered hillside, but he made no progress now.

"I'll get you," he panted. "I'll get you, you murdering bugger," and still he struggled down there. That was a brave man. That was a brave enemy you could hate.

"You'll never get me!" Diamond shouted back. His voice was loud and strong, strange to himself, like a voice not heard since long ago. But the strength of it gave strength to his body.

He climbed through the breach in the wall and he went down in a slither past the cursing man, on along the side of the hill toward the West, stepping surely through the snow. For that moment he was strong again.

That was the end of Friday's writing. He had his cup of tea like some lonely old woman in Maida Vale or you name it somewhere. Dan would be back this evening, met at Flume Ridge by his good and faithful wife.

He abhorred the prospect — inevitable sometime — of meeting his big little brother, of saying ever so nicely and sincerely: Thank you for letting me live all these weeks at your lovely seaside cabin, entirely free with innumerable perks. Thank you for letting me begin to find myself at last, but that you would not understand. Thank you for letting me become raving mad about your wife, but that would hardly do.

Funny thing, you know, he thought. Lorna vanishes when I'm writing. Nothing exists then but the me that is Tam Diamond, and the ambivalent me that is after him.

He rather wished that somebody young would come along to cheer him up, alone and troubled in the afternoon. But nobody came, and now he must go and get a bloody good sweat in Dan's grove of birches. That eyelid fluttered all the time.

He went out with his binoculars. There was always something different, usually something new, and this time it was a seal, regarding him gravely from out there, no question whatever, whiskered, doggy, motionless, the black face was considering Nigel Melville Ash, the human zoo. "Good afternoon, Seal," he said, and went to get on with forestry.

102

He had almost finished it now, the slash spread on the ground to rot, the birches like a company of irregular white soldiers, bad simile, but it gave the feeling.

Who should arrive but Jake, come to borrow back the bush scythe. Mrs. Ash, she was wanting him to clear out some brush first thing in the morning; and no, he couldn't stay for a beer, the wife would be after him, late already to his supper. "You done a good job, Mr. Ash," he said.

"Look, Jake, for Christ's sake can't you call me Nigel?"

Jake guffawed. "Well, for Chrissake so I could, Mr. Ash. So long, then, Nigel." He departed.

Ash gathered the other tools, sweat achieved, the eyelid tic mercifully in abeyance, and he went back to the cabin. An oven bird was calling somewhere. *Teacher, Teacher,* they always said. "A voice in the woods," Peterson described it well.

She had asked him about that call the other day when they were having a brief walk together. *I did know,* she said, *but I keep forgetting them.* And she said: *It's sort of sad, I think, that so few Canadians, one in a hundred, know anything, care anything about the natural world. Did you always love it, Nigel? — I've lived in the country almost all my life,* he said. *But I don't think I cared much about it until I lost my freedom for a while. — Yes, your freedom,* she said, another quietness together.

He slept right through that night, with his dreams of the story upside-down. It was such a relief to be awake, things straightened out for trouble. But he had to change sides in the hunt again this morning.

The last boulder that Diamond rolled downhill broke the leg of Sergeant McGillivray. Inspector Thoms sent for two policemen to look after the injured man.

. . . Where's the next place we can stop him?"

"The next place is the hill road two miles on," said McNaughton without hesitation.

"Come on then," said Thoms. "I'll leave my car for McGillivray. Take him carefully."

They followed their own tracks fast downhill, picking up the men as they went. It was then that the snow began. It fell in big wet flakes, driven flat by the wind.

They piled into the police van and drove along to the West. The snow was falling heavily, piling itself in a soft crust against the windscreen. The wiper labored in its slow sucking rhythm.

"The hill road goes almost due south," Robert explained, "with the burn on the west side of it all the way. The burn will be big now. He'll never cross that. If we line the road we're bound to get him."

They waited again.

. . . It was McNaughton's whisper, a faint murmur in the wind. "Something in front." Robert had heard nothing. He strained his ears and his eyes, trying to see into the blank painful wall of snow.

Then he heard a noise. It was a muffled thud, and a groan afterward, the wheezing eery sound of pain dragged from a man. The others heard it too. "Let him come on," breathed the Inspector.

The wind rose still higher, and the snow slapped hard on Robert's face. They waited a long time. Half an hour? Nearly that it must have been, but no figure loomed out of the darkness, nothing came to them but the hard wind-lashed fingers of the snow . . .

Saturday teatime. "Oh God, I'm tired," Ash said. And he meant God too. He always felt, and never spoke of, a god in things, a god in the mountain and in the stream, in the child and in the flower, although a god in the cobra was something of a problem.

But now he knelt down at the bed, and with each hand he covered his eyelids, the still one, the restless one, and he prayed: "Oh, God," he said. "Please give me strength to do this right. Amen." He had not done such a thing for these many years. And a small voice mocked him, accused him: *Hypocrite.*

The kettle boiled, and he had his cup of tea, and a slice of Lorna's homemade bread with Lorna's potted shrimp, and he lit a cigarette, and that buzzer sounded, buzz-buzz, house to shore.

"Hullo."

"Dan here, Nigel."

"Oh, hullo, Dan, glad you're back."

"Late last evening. And so am I glad, let me tell you. I would have given you a shout earlier but I didn't want to interrupt your muse. Lorna and I wondered — would we be disturbing you if we dropped down now for half an hour? Do please say."

"No, no, I've finished for the day. I'd love to see you."

My sacred bloody muse, he thought, getting the best tray out, the glasses, bottles, ice. Did Dan drink martinis? Couldn't remember. There were a few papers to tidy, Lorna's Webster to stow away, but in general the place was shipshape. If one lived alone, either one lived moderately neat, or one slummed it in a shambles.

Then he changed his old workshirt for a striped one, put on a tie, and brushed his hair. "The aquiline author has a thatch of iron gray," he said. Lately, he conducted more conversations with himself than was concomitant with strict sanity, whatever that might be — but not many about his personal appearance, which he avoided looking at as much as possible.

Dan alone would be all right. Dan simply bored him, then annoyed him, poles apart. It was the thought of them together. He had a quick modest drink, half and half, for courage, and rinsed and dried the glass for deception. And he wondered why it was that in movies and on television ninety percent of drinks were whisky taken neat. They sloshed and sozzled interminably straight.

He put on his tweed jacket and went to meet the strollers. These evenings it was jacket weather except in the balmy sun.

". . . Keeps him busy is the main thing," Dan was saying as he encountered them round the corner just beyond the birch glade. He should have coughed or called ahead or sung a snatch to announce himself.

But he might not have been the subject of that comment. Dan smiled instantly and gladly and held out his hand for the shake, not a knuckle-squeezer, firm and brief. "Nigel," he said. "You look a different man."

"You look well yourself." And so he did, bronzed and fit. Surely he must have a sun lamp. Well, why not? It was not Bermuda shorts this time. It was a linen jacket with a dapper check, green trousers, suede shoes. Well, why not again? The woodland paths were dry and smooth. One must wear something.

"Hi, Lorna," he said.

"Hullo, Nigel." She was carrying a brown envelope. Her plain dress was of that color which is a shade, a fade from navy blue, perhaps the loveliest of all colors, and certainly on her, and over her shoulders, casually cloakwise, a yellow cardigan. "It's been such a glorious day. But I suppose you haven't had much fun from it."

"So, so," he said. "Not exactly a riot."

"I hear you've been writing all day every day."

"No, Dan," he said. "I keep office hours more or less. Time off for exercise, evenings free. Routine seems to be the way to do it."

"A lot of self-discipline," Dan said. "Making up a story — I wouldn't have a clue." He spoke with humility, even respect, no doubt baffled about his wayward brother turned the servant of routine.

"It's a sort of a refuge, not self-discipline."

Dan did not notice the improvements to his birch glade, but he stopped at the spruce that had been struck by lightning. "Oh, I say. What on earth happened to this fir tree?"

"Lightning," Ash said. "I was in the cabin. The wrath of God, it sounded like, no other description."

"If only that energy could be harnessed."

"Harnessed," Lorna muttered.

They went inside. Dan had a martini on the rocks, the precise two ounces of gin, the thimble of vermouth, the sliver of lemon. He and Lorna had whiskey as usual. "I brought your chapter down," she said, laying envelope on table.

"Oh, thank you," he said. "Dan, I can't tell you what a wonderful help Lorna has been, typing for me."

"She says she enjoys it, don't you, dear?"

"Yes," Lorna said. "Besides, a perennial grass widow must do something." She was more beautiful than ever, but the mood seemed hardly sunny.

106

"And you keep the cabin spick and span. Have you been quite comfortable?"

"Marvelous, Dan. It's the perfect place for the job I'm trying to do."

"I'm glad. Perhaps it will be the famous place where Nigel Ash wrote his best seller. Have you a title for it?"

"No, Dan," he said. "Not yet." Annoying, well-intentioned, dammit.

"Couldn't we go outside. Why waste a lovely evening?"

Lorna went first, and he stood aside for Dan, and Dan stood aside for him. His booze, Dan's cabin. "A nice point of etiquette," he said, yielding, and Dan laughed. They were almost hitting it off, extraordinary.

"Marvelous air," Dan said, breathing deep. Probably he always said that. Most people did when they came from the city. The west wind brought a rumor of traffic across in Maine, and some vessel rumbled far down the estuary. "Do you watch TV much?"

"No," he said. There was a good small color set in the cabin. "At first I used to look at the Cronkite news, but I've had my fill of Vietnam. They go on about it, and on about it *ad nauseam*."

"I know," Dan said. "They have an obsessive thing, our neighbors."

"They have an obsessive thing about defoliating the countryside and bombing the defenseless peasants."

"That's war, Lorna. But about news — the CBC is quite good — at eleven here, I think."

"That's after my bedtime. Where have you been lately, Dan?"

"This week Toronto and Chicago, and then two days in Washington."

"And the next thing is London over Labor Day," said Lorna. "It gets madder and madder."

"I know, honey. It's been a hard summer, and I'm sorry. But with the economy booming the way it is, I just can't help it."

"I know, Dan," she said. The tide was flooding, but had not covered the mudflats yet. "What are those, Nigel?"

107

He had been watching three plover-sized birds across the cove. "Ruddy Turnstones," he said. "Want to have a look?" He handed over the binoculars. The rumble grew louder downriver.

"It was an energy conference in Washington," Dan said. "And interestingly enough, one of the subjects discussed was harnessing these Fundy tides. It's an old idea, of course, from the FDR days, and still not economically viable. Do you know about it, Nigel?"

"Only that this big bay empties and fills through two or three narrow channels, twenty-four feet average down and up twice a day. That's all I know. It's an interesting idea."

Dan talked clearly and well for a few minutes about the problems of tidal power, of the waste of energy necessitated by having to pump to head ponds which would provide flow at high- and low-water slack, of peak period power, of the changes in water temperature, marine environment, human condition. Dan knew his stuff. "If only the tides didn't change fifty minutes a day, the thing would be a natural."

"An unnatural," Lorna said, watching Ruddy Turnstones. The diesel rumble had grown to be a tug towing an oil barge on a long line. It passed slowly and noisily.

"It would be clean, though, Lorna," said Nigel Ash. "Better than that oil barge. Better than nuclear wastes with a half-life of a hundred thousand years or something. Better than strip-mining."

"All part of the same thing," she said. "And that comes oddly from you, the great tide lover."

It seemed that he was unpopular too. "Oh well," he said.

"But why this lust for energy? Why, why, why?"

"Our free world depends on it, dear. To survive, we must grow."

"To perish, we must grow. *The growth economy*, that sacred cow. Why can't we stop right where we are?"

"Because we can't," Dan said. "We simply cannot."

"You mean the world is out of control?"

108

"Perhaps," Dan said. "I'm beginning to think that just might be. There was a fellow at the conference, no Johnny-head-in-the-air either, Harry Gilpin, one of the most able industrialists in North America. What he envisaged ahead was frightening."

Somehow or other, or so it seemed this evening, Dan had suffered a sea-change. Or have I changed too? Ash thought. It was bearable so long as he disliked his brother. If he came to like him, it would not be bearable.

He got replenishments for Lorna and himself, and Dan made his other martini. Two, he would have, no more, you could bet on it. "Lorna's a bit upset about this Labor Day business," he confided. "But what can I do?" Ash could think of nothing to say to that.

They sat out there again. The tide, which he and Lorna enjoyed so much, crept up to its march across the mudflats. One minute damp land, the next an infant sea.

"Will you be long still with the book, do you think?"

. "Ten days, two weeks might do it, Dan. Would I be a nuisance if I stayed here that much longer?"

"Of course not. We love having you, don't we, Lorna?"

"Oh yes," she said. "Besides, you must finish the job. There's no heat in the cabin except a fire. But that should be all right for quite a while."

"Don't worry," he said. "I promise not to be the English-man who came to dinner and stayed the winter."

Lorna laughed at that old Canadian joke, rather a tired joke by now. She must want something to laugh at.

"What will you do then, Nigel?"

"I know a publishing chap in Boston. Actually, we were in one prison camp together. I think I might take it to him for a first reading, see what he says. Then London, see what they say. Then I think home to the cottage for the winter." Ash did not say that, before doing any of these things, it was necessary that he should pay a brief visit to Montreal.

"I do hope it works for you," Dan said. And he quite evi-

109

dently, entirely sincerely, did hope that. "Well, honey, we must go. I'm taking my bride out dancing, Nigel."

"Bride of nineteen years," she said. "It makes me squirm when you call me that." With which Nigel heartily agreed. They talked of their brides at their golden weddings.

"Wife, then," said Dan. "Many thanks, Nigel, and good luck with it." He put his arm round Lorna's waist, and then his hand lay on the curve of her bottom, and she moved away. Uxorious bastard, take his bride dancing, get her in the mood.

Ash went in and to the whiskey bottle, and he sloshed some in and swigged it down neat, like on television, in the movies.

13

THE SUN HAD GONE DOWN, and that meant half-past eight or so. But nice sitting in the gloaming, don't let's put a light on. "One more," he said. "And then I should eat something."

The ice was finished, but that did not matter much. What mattered were the glasses, the good spring water and the whiskey. He considered that. The bottle had started the evening full. His first quick one, and then two each for him and Lorna would have taken it down perhaps a quarter. There was still a fair smidgen in the bottom, not too bad, in fact very very good, one felt so happy. He took about half of it and added water. No more of that vulgar swigging neat. One should drink like a proper gentleman. He lit his umpteenth cigarette. "I don't like you," he said to the evidence in the ashtray.

It was almost dark now, so he put on one standard lamp and drew the curtains across the big window, not wanting to be looked in upon by all and sundry. "Time to eat," he said. "It's fatal not to eat." But one did not have much appetite.

He took the ashtray to the kitchen, pressed down with his toe and the lid popped open, and he poured the offensive stubs into the plastic liner bag, really most hygienic. An eggnog was the easiest, most soothing sustenance known to man. Crack Jake's brown egg into a wide glass, swizzle it, add pepper and salt, fill up with milk, and that was an eggnog, back to the comfort of the living room. A fortified eggnog would be better still, so he sipped to make room, and poured the rest of the whisky in. "Goodbye to you," he said.

Supper went down smoothly, and then he felt a little queasy, but that soon passed. He had drunk too much, no good pretending, and he was still quite sober, and he walked the edge of the carpet straight as a die to prove it. "I know what I'll do," he said. "I'll go and see if my friends are there."

Every action suited every word, or suited every decision, would be precise. He took the big flashlight, part of the cabin inventory. It had two switches, left for forward beam, right for a red flasher, traffic warning, slightly superfluous down here, one might think.

He opened the door very quietly, because their hearing was just as acute as their sense of smell, and left it open, enough light from the cabin to guide him up the bluff. It was pretty dark there, but he found his observation rock without a stumble, sat and aimed in a generally correct direction. The wind had backed into the southwest. That might mean bad weather, and it might mean that they would get his scent unless he was quick about it.

He switched on, much too low, it lit the water, up now, weaving a bit, but he got it right in time to see the white flag of a deer disappear into the cedars that lined the field. He was almost sure. He was not quite sure. Being a stickler for accurate observation, one could not be dead certain, and one might as well admit that the white-tailed deer could have been a figment of one's whiskyfield imagination.

He stood and shone it into the cove. It was highwater slack, *le moment suprême*. Yes, that would be right, with a new moon coming up on Monday. *You're the great tide-lover*, she said in her bad mood earlier. She had dreaded this weekend, and then she raised hell about Dan being in London over Labor Day. She's a woman, y'know, he thought. Feels like a quarrel, makes one.

He felt somewhat less blissful, lighting his way home. It was wearing off. So he took the corpse to the drink cupboard and swopped it for one of the two virgin bottles. Much better. Very much better. Let's see what's on the telly.

There was a shooting program, with the good guys murdering

112

the bad guys. He did not like that particularly. On the only other sharp channel, three owlish gents sat at a table, being questioned by a panel of show-biz celebrities, who were excruciatingly funny each in turn, and there was a jolly master of ceremonies, or referee. Now it was time to vote for One, Two or Three. Will the real someone or other please stand up.

But the three of them drifted into being six, and he got there in time to switch it off before the genuine smirking two stood to reveal themselves.

"Now I really am looped," he said, sitting again. It was a long long time since he had last been well and truly looped. "The real Nigel Ash," he said. "I don't believe the poor bugger could stand up, let's face it, not without a stagger."

But there was no need. Whisky, glass and water were at hand. I took on too much, he thought. Too much took me on. One thing alone would have been all right. He poured a small drink, but more went in than he intended, extra water to make up for it. He was sad, so sad, crying now, a grown man blubbing, shameful thing. "Poor old chap," he said, and he went to sleep.

They were dancing together, joined together from top to thigh, and the tune was slow, a tango thing. *Are you in the mood? — Yes, Nigel darling, I'm in the mood, but my husband must come first, you know.*

He was awake, and feeling bloody awful sick, but he made it to the bathroom where he was sick and sick and sick, all finished, got rid of it, felt better, but a fearful thirst. He quenched that with a long drink of water at twenty past two by the clock on the stove.

"I'm sober again," he said, and he was, not cold but quite. That last drink before he had gone to sleep was still half-full. He needed it and he drank it.

But one must go to bed and have a good night's rest. He undressed with excellent precision, jacket on the back of the chair, tie on it, trousers folded neatly on it, socks on top, even shoes lined up.

113

Blue silk pajamas, what a seductive luxury in this day and age, bought them in Hong King. It was raining and quite chilly, so he did the sensible thing, left the west window wide, shut the south one, and opened the east window through in the bathroom. He had a look at himself *en passant*. Funny thing, his eyelid was twitching to beat the band, but he couldn't feel it.

He pulled down the bedroom blinds and closed the curtains to keep out the day when day would arrive. Then he took a nightcap to bed with him. A whippoorwill was calling not far away in the woods somewhere, nice whippoorwill, monotony. "I am the Nighthawk," he said wittily. "And you are my cousin Whippoorwill who never stops." Soon he went to sleep.

It was exceedingly boring to wake again at a quarter to five by his watch on the bedside table, that damned whippoorwill still going strong. If I could find you, Whippoorwill, and I know I can't, I would shoot you dead through the barrel of Dan's small rifle-gun. It stood in his clothes cupboard, never used it, an under and over Belgian job. Jake's idea that he should have it. *Them darn' porcupines, Mr. Ash.* He did not like to confess to Jake that he tried to draw the line even at shooting porcupines. "At shooting anything," he said. "Until it's a question of you or me. It's you or me, Whippoorwill, please stop, I warn you."

Extraordinary thing, the whippoorwill obeyed him, no more monotony to drive a harmless chap right up the wall or to the shotgun.

His stomach felt a bit uncertain, not bad really, but as a precautionary measure he fetched the washing-up basin and put it by his bed. Then he had one last nightcap, one for the road, a morning cap, and he was soundly deep asleep until after eleven, that would be morning, wouldn't it, yes, light outside, that would be morning.

He managed the milk with both hands, and the whiskey too, but it was touch and go, spilt whiskey. His hand was steadier after a swallow or two, and back to bed. "Where's Tam Diamond now?" he said. "Who the hell is Tam Daimond?"

*

Voices outside, young men's voices, a girl's voice. "He's probably just having a snooze." Kim speaking.

"But the living room's closed up too."

"Perhaps he went away last night."

"He was here. Mum and Dad came down to see him. He could have had a heart attack or something."

Loud knocks. "What is it?" he said.

"Are you okay, Uncle?"

"I'm fine," he said. "Just go away." He heard his own voice not sounding very fine. And then he heard the front door open, and footsteps to his bedroom door, when Bobby opened, and some light came in with him.

"Oh, Gosh!"

"Don't *Oh Gosh* me. Bugger off."

He reached down for the bottle, couldn't find it, put on the bedside lamp to find it, but no bottle, only the basin he had been sick into. That was disgusting, would never do, so he dragged it after him to the bathroom, emptied it down the W.C., even managed to rinse the basin out, much better. He drank two glasses of water for his awful thirst and back to bed, and through the west window he heard: "I'll go and ask old Pugsley. Come on, then, girls. Borrow the bike, Bobby?"

"Sure thing, Nelson."

The thud of running feet outside, but now from the living room. "What should we do, Keith, take the stuff away?"

"Wait till Nelson gets back. He won't be long."

"Bobby!"

"Yes, Uncle?" Bobby's round face in the doorway, Keith Kelly behind him.

"What time is it?"

"Half-past six."

Half-past six in the evening, it must be, the sun shone through a crack. "Half-past six is drinktime. Get me a quick one, would you, Bobby, half and half?"

"But you can't have any more."

"I must, he said. Just one. I must."

"I'll get it," said Keith Kelly, bless him. Bobby came in and past the bed, and opened the south window wide.

"Don't let the bloody light in."

"I'm letting the bloody stink out," Bobby said unkindly.

Here was Keith with the drink, quite a decent slug on the bedside table. "Thank you so much," he said. He reached for it, but he couldn't, he simply couldn't.

"I'll hold it for you," Bobby said. He held it like for baby in the highchair, and Ash sipped it down gratefully, much more quickly than baby could.

"What happened, Uncle?"

"Too much happened, I guess," he said. "So sorry, boys."

They both smiled at him. They were not unkind. They were very kind indeed, and the good whiskey was soothing him through and through. "Keith," he said. "You wrote a poem here at the cabin. Could you say it for me?"

> Lean, wind, lean,
> For summer has been.
> Cry, plover, fly,
> For the year must die.

"It's only a small thing."

"With a small diamond of shimplicity," he said, which seemed to please Keith very much. "Anything else?"

Keith shook his head. "What poets do you like?"

"Oh, I dunno," he said. "Old-fashioned really, but Auden too, and some of Frost, but he's old-fashioned most of it." His speech was woozy. "I do apologize, not talking straight. What's that thing of Frost's about the deep dark woods?"

> The woods are lovely, dark and deep.
> And I have promises to keep.
> And miles to go before I sleep.

"Lovely," he said. "I broke 'em." They laughed, amused by him, sorry for him, both young faces said.

116

"Tell me another one."

"Do you know this of Auden's from "The Christmas Oratorio"?

JOSEPH: How then am I to know,
Father, that you are just?
Give me one reason.

GABRIEL: No.

JOSEPH: All I ask is one
Important and elegant proof
That what my love had done
Was really at your will
And that your will is love.

GABRIEL: No, you must believe,
Be silent, and sit still.

"Thank you," he said. "It isn't easy."

But a motorbike came popping down the woods, woods lovely dark and deep. Enter Nelson, dynamic youth. "I saw old Pugsley."

"Who's old Pugsley?"

"The doctor, sir."

The drunken sod objected strongly to being addressed as Sir, but he couldn't say it.

"He asked how long you'd been drinking, so I said twenty-four hours, correct?"

"Correct," he said. "If it's still Sunday."

"Still Sunday, and he asked how much. I didn't know."

"There's some of the second bottle left, I think."

"A quarter, yes," said Keith.

"He asked if you drank habitually, and I said yes, but not a lot. Correct, sir?"

"Correct," Ash said.

"He was awfully decent about it, sort of human. He says: Taper off this evening, take two of the Seconals, and a third if you wake up in the night. He gave them to me."

"But I don't hold with sleeping pills."

Nelson ignored him, and continued: "You've got to get some food in you, take a bit of exercise so you can sleep, drink all the water and orange juice you can, take a strong laxative, I've got that too; and then you have to go on the water wagon for forty-eight hours at least, get it right out of your system. He says if you don't, he'll put you in the hospital."

"No, he bloody well won't."

"It's either or," said Nelson, implacable, square-jawed bastard. "And we're going to stay and see you do."

"I'll have to go now," Bobby said. "Mum will be back from the airport, and I said I'd be in for supper. She'll get into one of her stews if I'm not."

"Okay, Bobby," said Keith. "We'll stay."

"You won't tell her, Bobby, will you?"

Bobby stared at him, or even glared at him. "I will tell her unless you promise me to stop tonight. Do you promise? Yes or no?"

"Oh, God," he said. "All right, I promise."

"That's great," Bobby said. "Not to worry, Uncle." He patted him on the shoulder. Not to worry, weakling uncle. Strong Bobby, wonders never cease. "I'll be down tomorrow to say goodbye."

Say goodbye tomorrow? The motor bike popped off.

"Tonight the promise starts, I promise. Now I need a drink."

"Later," Nelson said. "After we've taken a little walk."

"You'll need some clothes. Why not just put your pants on top? Here — legs out of bed, we'll help you." Keith was no dreamy poet, bad as his brother. Added to his silk pajamas were trousers, socks, shoes and jacket, no good protesting, dressed him like some tailor's dummy, took an arm each, and the world swam round.

He managed not to be sick until they had manhandled him to the open air. " 'The red rock wilderness shall be my dwelling place' ", he quoted appropriately from someone or other. Then he was being hustled along the sandy beach below high water mark — to the red rocks at one end, to the red rocks at the other,

118

back and forward, to and fro, interminably, it was appalling. "Cruelty to animals," he said, but that only made them more sadistic.

The dinky speedboat was out for its spin, shot downriver, shot across, shot up here and shot for home. "Does it most evenings, always alone, always same course, can't think what in aid of."

"We see him too. He never waves if you're in a boat. Must be some screwball from Vacationland." That was the tall officer on his right.

"He could be just timing himself, trying to break his own record." That was the square officer on his left.

"That's it. What a sensible bugger you are."

The forced march went on forever until he said, "I'm pooped, boys. I really am." Then they had mercy, took him in and gave him a drink in his chair in the living room. My writing chair, he thought from a distance. That hideous walk had done him good.

He managed to down one scrambled egg, not easy with the spoon, but he managed it himself, and he managed a little vanilla ice cream. He sat quite still to let it settle. Darkness was coming on Sunday evening, yes, Sunday evening. It's a Sunday for Tam Diamond too, he thought. "I must get right," he said.

"That's the ticket," Keith said.

"Why are you so good to me? I mean I hardly know you."

"Because we think you're something rather special."

"Special," he said. "Oh, Christ."

They were being so good to him that he should show some interest, although, truth to tell, he had none at all, but he asked. Keith was taking Honors English at Dalhousie, and Nelson first-year Biology at Queen's, he thought that was it, forgetting already.

". . . What, Keith?"

"I said: Did you have a best time in your life?"

He considered vaguely. "Sounds odd, but I think prison was

119

a best time. A life within life, simple, golden purpose, hungry too, common enemy a help. See what I mean?"

"I think I do."

"Just lately was good too. Got complicated, though."

They did not ask him about those complications. He liked them but he wished he could be rid of them. One brilliant way of doing that, what an inspiration, would be to pretend he was a queer, make a drunken pass. But for one thing it was a notion monstrous to him, spared that, thank God. For another, they would beat him up, a dangerous Jehovah in these Kellys.

"You've been awfully kind to me," he said. "I'll be perfectly all right now alone."

"We've decided to spend the night," Nelson said.

"But your family will be worried."

"I told Mum we were camping out. We often do."

"You haven't eaten anything," he said. "There's ham in the fridge, I think, and beer perhaps." There was beer if he hadn't finished that up for his thirst, but he thought he hadn't.

"Thank you, sir. We'll eat as soon as you go to bed."

"I wish you wouldn't call me sir," he said. "It's embarrassing under the circs." He took advantage of their mild amusement to wander his eyes across the whiskey bottle, enough for a decent one still, but his damned jailers caught him at it.

"I'll just tidy the bed," said Keith. He shut the door behind him, was away quite a while, tidying bed and hunting for non-existent bottles, you could bet on that, but he had not quite reached the stage of taking it to bed with him.

"Old Pugsley said: *Swallow the pills, and have one last good drink with lots of water, and that's the end of it.*"

"Okay," he said. Quite soon he began to feel sleepy, and he tottered off to be helped by Nelson with his trousers, and then to the bathroom, took the laxative, did his teeth, now into bed. Keith brought him another long glass. "Half orange, half water," he said. "But you must finish the whiskey now."

He obeyed orders, and Keith took that glass away. "If you

120

wake up in the night," said Nelson. "Sing out and I'll bring you the other pill."

"Okay," he said. Good nights exchanged. He switched off his lamp, with some thought about how wonderful the young were, could be, not yet polluted. He sailed off on the sea of sleep.

14

IT WAS THE PAIN IN HIS BELLY THAT WOKE HIM UP, or it was the knife in his head, or it was both. The stomachache was caused by one of some doctor's medicaments, and quickly cured. The headache came from those ill-assorted crutches, alcohol and barbiturates, he admitted that, he knew it well. Three aspirins might help, it was so hellish, they could not hinder much, as if that mattered. He went back to bed, resting his head against his knees drawn up.

Nelson at the door. "I brought you some orange juice. May I come in?" But he came in without permission. "It's after eleven. You had a terrific sleep, right round the clock and then some."

"Yes," he said. God, he felt awful. "I don't want that pap. Put a slug of gin in it for me, would you?"

"Nothing doing, sorry."

"Just one is all I need."

"But you promised last night."

"I don't remember last night. What's a promise if you can't remember it?"

"That's why Doctor Pugsley told me to take the drink away, and we did. He said it would be about a day before you got your strength back. A short jag, normally a moderate drinker, par for the course, he said. He's a wise old codger, you would like him."

Nelson stood with his hands on his hips, amiable and adamant. No good arguing with him, and no good arguing with what the wise old codger said, it was all too true.

Buzz-buzz, the house to shore. "Oh God! Tell her I've got a chill or something."

"That was Bobby," Nelson said, returning. "His mother's gone out, so he just phoned to ask if you were okay."

"Anything but okay. What did you tell him?"

"I said you were fine, just woken up."

"Is Keith here?"

"He went to get a shave."

His headache was a little less wicked. He held the glass in both hands and gulped at orange juice. "A shave," he said. "I'd better start with that."

He lathered the stubble on his puce complexion, and accomplished it without a single nick, advertisement for the safety of the Wilkinson Bonded System. Then cold water to rinse it off, Murine for albino eyes. "The pit of despond," he mumbled, getting dressed. "Or was it slough? Same thing, and I've got to climb out, got to, got to."

He went for a walk above the tide still flooding, and already very high. Something about them frogmarching him along this self-same beach. When he came back, Nelson had brunch ready — cornflakes, green pea soup from Campbell's can, a Velveeta sandwich, bland fare advocated by the wise old Pugsley.

"I wondered — would you like to see the aquarium this afternoon?"

"Crowds of people," he said. "I can't stand crowds at the best of times."

"No, it's closed today. They've been changing fish, and they like to give them time to settle down. I can get the key from my father. There won't be anyone else there."

"Have to do something, I suppose," he said. He did not mean to be ungrateful to his dogged custodian. "You must have other things. Why waste your time on a bloody write-off like me?"

"No other things," Nelson said. "And let's not be maudlin." It was a cheerful rocket or rebuke. "Do you know the way?"

"Yes," he said. "Follow the shore past your house and Mrs. Becker's. I've walked most of it."

"Okay, then. I'll go for the key and meet you there in about an hour."

Fine as the aquarium was, and knowledgeable a guide as Nelson proved to be, he loathed his visit. On this day all things were to be endured, and sympathies were blunted by self-pity. But since World War Two he could not tolerate zoos, except perhaps of the Whipsnade kind. And large fish in small aquariums were not much different. True that one did not pity cold moronic killers like the sharks, but one disliked their vain, circular, unending quest for freedom. "It's fat boy Groper I'm sorry for," he said.

Nelson, aspiring marine biologist, smiled politely at his bizarre remark. But Keith, who had joined them, said: "Hear, hear."

If one had felt better, the bird sanctuary would have been an improvement, because the ducks were free to fly in and out, with only a perimeter of tall mesh fence to discourage marauders, but he couldn't care less about quacking ducks. "Is this your first visit?"

"Yes," he said. As usual, there was a good reason for that. He had flown various parties of scientists in the North, and at least three of them had been stationed here, probably still were. "That chap George Petrie," he said. "The photographer-policeman, is he coming down again?"

"Kim says they have a trustees' meeting early in September."

The afternoon was wearing on, and the dawn of recovery was breaking, one might say. He still felt ghastly, but less ghastly.

They walked with him to below their house, which lay some distance inland of the path. "Thank you and apologize is the best that I can do," he said.

"No need," Keith said. "Pissed up, you were good boozy value."

"Just one favor — could you send us a copy of the book when it's published?"

124

"If and when, Nelson, I certainly could. *Au revoir*, then, boys."

He walked back to his boozeless cabin. He did not question that old Pugsley had been right about that. It made the climb possible, so long, so hard.

This evening to get through, the third and last of Pugsley's knock-out pills to make him sleep, tomorrow to fill in, feeling better, even plan it. "On Wednesday I must begin," Ash said.

He was sitting in or on the long garden chair, looking at a *New Yorker*, with Coca Cola for encouragement beside him, when he heard the throaty whine of the jeep approaching in low gear. He put glass and magazine inside and fled for thick undergrowth. One glimpse of his incarmined face, and she would know.

But it was Bobby in the jeep, with Congo. Bobby had found him drunk in bed, yes, he remembered that hideosity. One must come out and pay the piper.

Congo galloped over to pay respects, but sniffed him and withdrew, fastidious hound.

"Hullo, Bobby," he said.

"Hullo, Uncle. I just came down for a sec to say goodbye."

"Oh yes," he said. "You're off in the morning, aren't you?"

"Mum says to tell you she'll be back on Thursday evening, and if you have anything for her to type, could you just leave it at the house?"

"Right," he said. "Please thank her for me."

"And she says to say: Good luck with it. That goes for me too."

Again strangled thanks. "Does your mother know about my fall from grace?"

Bobby shook his head. "She doesn't know a thing."

"Good friends, you people have been to me."

"That's what friends are for," Bobby said, trite perhaps, but his stature enlarged, his uncle's diminished as was proper. "I don't wonder you blew off steam, with all the pressure."

Did he say *pressure* or *pressures?* Indeterminate. But Bobby knew anyway. He had guessed long before he saw them at the pond, her head resting in the hollow of his shoulder, by no means indeterminate.

"How are you feeling now?"

"Poorly," he said. "Better poorly. I'll be all right tomorrow."

Bobby smiled at him. "That's great," he said.

"I'm afraid there isn't any beer to offer you."

"I couldn't stay, Uncle, anyway. I'm not half-packed yet, so I must rush."

"Goodbye then, Bobby, and the best of luck."

"Goodbye, Uncle. Could you write to me sometime?"

"I will, and I'll expect you at the cottage in Scotland. You can have the attic. Or if I'm away, you can bring a fair cook and have the lot."

"Now I know you're better," Bobby said.

After another night of deep drugged sleep he was firmly on the mend. He went to see Jake, and found him weeding in the vegetable garden, complaining about the goddam coons were into his corn. They weeded together for an hour or two.

When he got back to lunch, he found his bottles all in place, and he was on the wagon until tomorrow, no doubts about it, little bother about it. On Tuesday afternoon he climbed toward the meeting that he feared, the crucial meeting with Tam Diamond.

. . . He picked himself up and struggled on. It was a road he was following, a narrow road which wound up the hill. He had seen the tumbling blackness of the river, barring him from the west; and he had looked to the east into the teeth of the blizzard, wavering in his resolve, thinking, Should I turn back now? But he had not wavered long. The determination was still strong in him.

So now he was climbing again. It was an endless trudging through the snow, a raising of weary legs and a scuffling, no longer painful.

He was not alone. A voice spoke to him often, soothing him, encouraging him, saying, You are still strong, you are a tiger in your strength. Guard it, Tam! Keep into the left here, hug the hillside, take what shelter you can. Forget the black water on your right. I will not let you wander there.

126

This is a good dream this coldness, this dream of frozen feet and burning chest. It is the cold milk on the hot porridge, one too hot, one too cold, but good together.

Remember the green fields of spring, and the color of young leaves bursting from the bud. That will come again. And you will lie in peace thinking, This is the way it is; this is the way it will always be.

And remember the whirly whirling at the Lammas Fair, swinging the laughing lassies round the circle, throwing their skirts high, tossing their hair.

And remember the church bells pealing, the solemn bells of Scotland; and the chimes you heard in England, making a sweet jangle on a Sabbath morning.

Remember the wish-a-wash-wish of our own shells overhead, flying so softly to the killing.

Remember the murmur of the breeze upon the heather, the great emptiness, the cloud shadows on the hill.

"Dinna' talk to me of winds and hills," he muttered angrily; and for a little he went on alone.

He fell and lay there panting, and he got up. And he fell, this time into a drift which closed about him, coldly warmly comforting.

Then he had company again. Come out, Tam! said the voice, quiet and insistent. Come out now!

But he was drowsy, slipping down and down, heedless of the voice. Sleep was a greater friend.

It's me, Tam, said the voice. It's me. You must come. Remember and come!

I remember, he said, and he climbed out of the snowdrift.

They went on together. Back to the left! You're wandering. It was one voice and it was many. He knew it and he did not know it. It was there behind his shoulder, beside him always.

Who are you? he said. Are you the woman I killed?

Her and him, other folk and other things.

But have you no hate?

Why would I hate when I can help you?

He looked over his shoulder then, expecting to see her, remembering her dark blue eyes and quiet strength.

But he did not see her face. He saw the blackness and the whiteness of the night.

It was soon afterward that the road became level. Then he was alone again on the open ground, and the blizzard was pounding him. He heard the noise of waves breaking. How would he hear that noise on the hill? But it was distinct, a different sound altogether from the whining bluster of the wind . . .

"Well, I made a start with it," Ash said, a start with what he had been working to for all these weeks. He heated the pot, put in one spoonful for him, and one for it, and one for luck, and that was tea, the genuine article, not those dreadful tea bags. Lorna was due back tomorrow evening, Thursday, and he still had the untyped chapter before this one — when the receiving line had heard Diamond coming, but he never reached them.

Ash put that in the envelope, which he licked, the same old horror of anyone but Lorna seeing it, and he wrote her name. That alone seemed cavalier, so he added: *Hope you had a good trip, N.* His famous steady hand was not quite itself.

There was some rain on Saturday night, or he rather thought so; but apart from that, and a light shower or two, it had been good August weather since that thunderstorm two weeks ago, or it might be three.

There was a difference this evening, sultry, humid, but no clouds in the sky except one gray mackerel-bone from south to north. "I wonder," he said, going in to prop his envelope against the pewter vase in the hall. Surprising that they left doors unlocked when they went away. But water running somewhere, and that should be investigated. He found Jake filling a bathtub at the other end of the house. It was almost to the brim and he shut it off.

"What's up, Jake?"

"Just precautions. That hurricane — you hear on the radio?"

"No, Jake. I don't listen much."

"Agatha, darned stupid names they give 'em. Well, Agatha's off New York and stationary, hasn't made her mind up. If it heads for land, it'll blow itself out down there. If it stays at sea, follows the coast-like, we could get the tail end, knock out power lines, blow trees down, mebbe, nothing much. Still, once or twice in my time we've had a fair dusting. Now for them shutters."

They went out, and round the house, Jake checking the screw clamps that held the window shutters open. He tightened a few of them with a wrench. "Well, that's it," he said. Praise the Lord and pass the ammo."

"There are no shutters on the cabin, but I'd better fill the bath."

"And anything loose, Nigel, you could stow it. Come to think, Mrs. Ash, she might be drivin' through rough weather tomorrow. Won't stop her, though, I'll bet. When Mrs. Ash travels, she sure travels."

"I'll be going down, then, Jake. Goodnight."

"Goodnight, Mr. Ash, Nigel, I mean. That name of yours, never known a Nigel, it kind of screws my tongue up."

"Why not practice on Di-Gel? That's on the wrong syllable, but it shouldn't screw your tongue up."

Jake chuckled. "Now you're soundin' more like yourself." He had made no comment yesterday about Ash's appearance or dim mood.

How often had he come back to this cabin, his refuge again and still his prison? He got himself his first drink. He had written no word with drink in him, except sherry at lunchtime, and that did not count. But this drink livened his mind to plan tomorrow.

"I can't back out now," he said, and went to turn on the cold tap in the bath, then out to see what the weather might be up to. There was a rim of muddy cloud in the southwest, and overhead the mackerel had widened, even to dim the sun. It was a tranquil evening of foreboding.

But it was an evening of good luck to him, for above the low hills across the river was the crescent of the moon, not a crescent, the merest curving sliver. "This time I first saw you true," he said. "I didn't deserve it, God knows, I didn't, but I saw you true."

Nigel Ash put his hand into his right trouser pocket where the money was, and he bowed seven times to the infant moon, turning his money, making his secret wish.

What a child I am, he thought, to be discomfited at a first sight of the moon through glass. The few city dwellers who ever notice it must almost surely look through glass. Short-sighted people cannot see it except through glass.

The magpie, the ladder, the salt, the moon, such credulity in the human child. He went in. Bloody idiot, he had let the bath run over.

15

WHEN HE AWOKE AT SEVEN, the sky was heavy with a brownish tinge, and no stir of wind. He listened to the radio weather. Agatha was still at sea, moving fast and parallel to the coast, expected to reach the southwest tip of Nova Scotia in mid-afternoon, gusts of up to ninety miles an hour. If it held to that course, the eye of the storm would pass a hundred miles or so away, near enough for what Jake called a fair dusting.

The rain began as he came in from his walk. It started full force and ended as abruptly, a plout was the good Scottish word for that. The warm rain started and stopped a dozen times before settling to drum continuously on the cabin roof, and wind gathered in the twilit morning, not much of a wind, a fitful bluster above the cabin in the lee.

He considered it now and then, forgot about it, was aware of it beyond him. At the end of the morning Ash read what he had written:

The loch was close beside the road. He could see only a few yards of the angry water; the blank wall of the blizzard closed beyond. And the shed at the water's edge, that must be a boathouse. What else could it be in such a place?

Now that he was alone again and unprotected, he knew that he was very sick. The door of the shed was locked. It was a flimsy door, easy to break if he could find some heavy thing. But he still had the policeman's torch, and him wandering all these miles without the use of it. He dragged it from the satchel.

He found what he wanted on the other side, round there where the gale whistled through gaps in the wallboards. It was a four-foot balk of timber. He dragged it to the door. Then, gasping for breath, he raised it in his arms.

131

The door gave way with a crash. He picked himself up from the floor. The boat lay tilted on its side at one end of the shed. At the other end was a stove. What use was a stove to him, with no strength to hunt for fuel? But he looked round wearily; a rough table, a bench, a frying pan on the wall, a jug, a few old newspapers and bits of boarding. That was all.

Diamond found his matches. They were still dry. Then he put paper and wood into the stove, put them in anyhow, jumbled up. By a miracle the fire caught first time. He went out to the water's edge to fill the jug, doing the whole thing like an automatic machine.

It was warmer already in the boathouse, and the fire lights were dancing on the walls. The frying pan would be for the trout; many a one freshly taken from the loch would have sizzled there. Oh, the lucky folk at their fishing.

He pushed in the wooden boards, heedless of the way they jutted over the floor. The fire was blazing strongly and the chimney pipe was red. The comfort stole upon him, rising over the chill of the fever, drowning him in its warm tide. The water in the jug was hot. He drank that down, every drop, and it soothed his thirst. Then he stuffed the last of the wood into the stove, and climbed on to the long table to rest.

Ash drank sherry, and went on to a slice of pizza, salad, a banana — frugal lunch, his stomach not yet eager, but his mind sharp enough. He remembered some doozer storms under the names of their habitats, hurricanes in the West Indies, a typhoon in East Pakistan, a cyclone at Darwin. He had turned back from them, and skirted them, and once he had flown right through a hurricane that made a capricious switch and pounce on Cuba. He was carrying arms for Fidel Castro, and no hospitable alternative anywhere. Fidel is my pal, he thought. I must go and see Fidel again sometime.

This storm was getting worse, but it was a tired storm, having traveled far, and now losing strength over cold waters. It would amount to no more than a dirty blow.

Half an hour was all the time that he took away from Tam Diamond, sleeping in the boathouse. "I must not hurry it," Ash said. There was an irony that the storm grew here, while his imagined storm died there. He was absent from this turbulent place. He began to write again.

It was heat that was battering on the door of his dreams, a flashing heat. And he was awake in the burning hut.

Already the flames were up the wall, licking around the timbers of the roof. And there was the crackling roaring of fire. The bastards to do this to me now, he thought, crawling to find the door.

No one was waiting for him. The loch and the hills were empty in the light of dawn. He crawled on a little way through the snow and turned to watch the burning boathouse. It was up in a fine blaze, with the roof bare of snow, and a creaking of big timbers, sparks glowing pale. The black smoke went straight up.

It was a clear morning, a wonderful change from the wildness of the night. Even in his exhaustion and fever, even with the coughing that tore at his lungs, he saw the miracle of the new day. His eyes went over the dark loch, over the rolling purity of the snow, up to the green and gold and scarlet in the eastern sky, and across to the west where the snow was touched with pink.

He trudged on slowly, thinking, Here's me sending out another invitation; here's me calling to the boys in blue. They can't help but see the smoke.

But he did not mind. He wasn't caring any more. The whole of that business was away behind. There was only the rare beauty of the morning for him to see.

He crossed the bridge over the river, half aware of the water rushing darkly between snow. But he looked over to the loch. And there he saw the swans.

Something hit the south side of the cabin, a monster bash, like the battering ram that Tam had used. "Tam, I can call him now," he said. He put the cap on his pen, jerked back from where he had been floating, floating in the afternoon. But he had done enough on this wild day, stumbling with Tam Diamond on his road to peace.

There was a bulge in the gyproc of the bedroom wall, and water was pouring in. The wind was in the south, which could mean that the hurricane was passing. A full gale. Force Ten about, it felt like, driving the rain almost flat past the big window, driving the rain through the breach in the cabin wall.

He had no oilskins to resist that deluge, so he took off all his clothes, found a pair of sneakers and went out naked. The missile had been a bough from the nearby apple tree, knocking a splintered hole through squared cedar logs, four inches thick, quite a healthy punch.

He groped his way back along the more sheltered eastern side, and in again, and he found just the thing to patch with — a plywood bookshelf. He started half a dozen nails in that and took it out. The board had a flailing will of its own in the wind, but he managed it, and drove the nails home, a good stopgap job, he was pleased with himself.

The storm held him against the cabin wall, held him safely so long as no more projectiles should chance along. It was not cold. It was quite agreeably balmily wet, one could hardly be wetter.

Three days into the moon, the tides should be dropping off, but high water this afternoon was by far the highest since he had come here. It boiled with its mass of flotsam at the lips of the rocks below the cabin, great balks of wharf timber, treetrunks jostling, the dinghy wallowing on the running line, gunwales awash, and beyond that the spume-hidden estuary. With only a ten mile fetch below the south wind it could not be a big sea, but it was wicked.

Chilled now, Ash went back from handhold to handhold, and inside to dry himself, put on the kettle. "I always did like storms until I feared them," he said. "And this ain't much of a storm to fear."

The electric kettle was singing up nicely. The lights flickered, went off, came on again. "Please," he said. It was his lucky moon. The power held to boiling point, and then went dead.

Gloomy, penumbrous, but a good strong cup of tea. *When Mrs. Ash travels, she sure travels.* If Lorna took the longer way through Maine, she would be well north of the trouble until she turned down for the coast. But if she came by the direct airline

134

route from Bangor to Calais, she would be driving through woods, and some big woods at that. He was uneasy, his imagination quickened in these days of trouble.

The wind veered swiftly to the west. "Goodbye to you," he said to Hurricane Agatha. But he meant a goodbye in futures, for the gale was as rambunctious as ever, and now this cabin and this shore lay open to it.

Water lashed the big window, and a tree crashed down inland. There were no trees to windward of the cabin. Wondering which it had been, he put his head out of the door to be bucketed by icy saltwater spray. Foolish virgin, he could see nothing and retreated.

The tide ebbed, and the spray diminished, and in a while the wind was losing bite. The house to shore telephone might be linked to NB Power, or it might be some sort of adjunct to NB Tel or it might have its own battery system. *Press call button, then lift receiver*, were the instructions. He did that, no answer, but the buried line crackled faintly.

Ash was getting himself a drink when it buzzed for him. "Lorna!"

But it was Jake at the house, heard his ring, and No, Mrs. Ash, she wasn't home yet, about four she had told him, and here it was after six, but she was a real good driver, and hell, it could be trees across the highway, and the power was out everywhere but they said it mightn't be too long, and no damage much up here, not to speak of, but more'n five inches of rain, and his vegetable garden it was a goddam pond, and how were things down your way?

Ash reported cabin damage and his temporary repair, a big tree down but he hadn't seen it yet.

"You keep writin' through all that?"

"Yes, until we got clobbered."

"You sure must have some powers of concentration."

"Jake, I'd like to know when Lorna gets back. Could you ask her to call me?"

"Sure thing. Don't worry yourself, though, she'll be okay.

135

Now don't you worry. S'long, then, Ni-gel." A mistake to mention Di-Gel. Kindly Jake, solicitous at a man's worry about another man's woman. He had his two drinks and ate cold supper.

The rain stopped and the gusts were abating. Out there, he stayed near enough to hear the telephone. As he had expected, the big spruce was the victim. It had not been uprooted, but jaggedly broken off a few feet from the ground. The hurricane had finished the lightning's job.

Blue sky was showing in the west, and the sun came through as it dipped to touch low hills, to broaden, to narrow, a last rim of sun, and it was gone.

He went into the cabin, thinking that Scotland, where he had also been today, was a country of great winds at any season, and this Eastern Canada a country of lesser winds almost every year at every season.

The power came on, and soon after that the telephone buzzed.

"Hullo," he said.

"It's me, Nigel."

"It's you," he said. "I've been worried about you."

"Jake told me you were. The airline seemed like a bad bet, so I went the long way round, and it was easy until the last forty miles south, sheets of rain, I had to stop altogether for simply ages. But I had Congo to keep me company. How are you, Nigel?"

"All right now you're home," he said.

A pause. "I've got your chapter," she said quite briskly. "I can do that in the morning. Will you have another for me tomorrow?"

"In the afternoon, I hope."

He heard her yawn. "Gosh, I'm sleepy," she said. "Goodnight."

Later, as he went to sleep, the world was quiet. The creatures of the night would be feeding, would be hunting, would be fleeing in the quiet.

*

136

They were quite close to him in a small bay, floating on the placid water, two swans, almost as white was the snow itself.

They watched him, the wild birds in their dignity. Their necks were straight, not curved like the swans he remembered, and they were more remote, so still and so strong. And they told him this: We are the wildest of wild things, Tam Diamond. See us and know us. We are alone but we are not afraid. Let us show you the way.

Then they turned and the great wings opened wide and beat the air, and they cut swift furrows on the surface of the loch, ploughing deep and then more lightly, legs pattering on the water, a loud wind rushing in the wings; until the last drops fell back into the loch and it was calm again, and they were wheeling over the far shore.

He watched them, knowing that they were telling him a truth, a thing which he had never found in the unhappy voyage of his life. He did not understand it yet, but it was on the threshhold of his mind.

The birds swung down the loch, turning again before the smoking hut, coming back to him. They passed close over his head; and then they turned and flew to the west, climbing until their whiteness too was touched by the glow of morning. He watched them until they were small, until he could no longer see them. But they called from afar off, and the mingled music of their trumpeting came back to him.

Tam went on, his mind full of the beauty he had seen, of the message which still he did not understand.

And not understanding it, he was tired again and stumbled and fell deep into the snow.

But soon the voice was calling to him: We must go farther, Tam, still farther on the road.

Tam slipped once or twice, but he got to his feet in the end and walked again.

Who are you? asked Tam. He was not easy in his mind.

The voice asked him: Did you see the swans? Did you see the bluebells and the young larch in summer? Did you hear the wind and thunder? Did you smell the warm growth of spring? Did you feel the softness of Ella's lips? Do you remember the last time the Officer spoke?

All those things, Tam muttered. But not you. I don't know you. Unless . . . unless . . .

And the truth rose up and came to him with a flashing speed and a beauty.

Then it's not just for human folk, Tam said.

137

Not just for human folk, the voice said loudly, for everything, for all the parts together.

Tam saw it then, all the things he had not understood, all the separate things which were a part of one another; all the hatred and love, the ugliness and beauty, the storm and the silence.

I found it in the end, he said; even if I didn't deserve to, even if I was a killer. But I found it. I'm sorry for what I done.

Are you happy now? asked the voice from close behind him.

Tam had not noticed that he wandered from the smooth road, that he was blundering across the moor. He stumbled and fell and rose again, but always the voice was there to help him. He was happy. At last he was truly happy.

"Ay," he said aloud, raising his eyes to watch the day. "I'm happy the now."

Tam Diamond never saw the deep place where he fell. He hardy felt the new pain.

Nigel had not stopped at half-past twelve according to the rules. So nearly done, he did not dare to break the flow, and he wrote on for another hour. Finished, thank God, and something gone out of him, it might be virtue, something gone. Now there remained only the meeting of the end with the beginning. But first he must read it through. Tomorrow he would read it through.

A belated lunch, a holiday this afternoon, rest his tired mind with physical work. He borrowed a chain saw from Jake and carried it down, and a can of mixed gas, the woods road being too soft and sodden for even the jeep.

He started on the windfall spruce. Life was always beginning something and doing something and ending something, the one running into the other and on. But then his thoughts were only about the satisfying, tricky, arduous job in hand.

Having grown as a pasture spruce, the tree was knotty, and having been struck by lightning, was split erratically along its whole length. On both counts the lumber was useless for board or plank. But it would make a cord or two of pulpwood.

He cut off the stump and counted the rings, about seventy, a pioneer of this young forest. Then he limbed up one side, and sawed the bigger boughs into four-foot pulp, and that was all that he could do until the trunk was winched downside up.

He had a bath, dressed himself respectably and made the tea. His hand was shaky again, but this time from the chain saw, noisy, potent, jittering beast. Lorna telephoned to say that she had finished typing, and did he have another? She was rather abrupt, not meaning it, he knew, but she did not like telephones, and nor did he.

He read it through again, printing indecipherable words in the early part, reminded, dammit.

Lorna came to meet him at the lily pond. The limber way she walked, the quiet way she looked, all new to him each time again. God, what a woman. He kissed her cheek, and she kissed his cheek, and they stood apart. "I missed you so much," he said.

"Same here," she said.

So it had been spoken, and remained half-spoken, and they spoke no more on the way to the house where Congo greeted him with revived enthusiasm and where, as had happened before and before, Lorna sat to read his chapter, and he went to get their drinks.

He put her glass down, and then, not wanting to watch her read what he had written, he took his glass through the screen door to the terrace. Some maple branches, heavy with leaf, were scattered on the lawn, and a couple of cedars leaned on the hill, but the storm had left few wounds. The earth is strong, he thought, and she called him in.

"It's the first three pages," she said, not looking up. "The rest are quite all right."

"I know," he said. "I should have copied those out again." He looked over her shoulder and solved the illegible words that she had underlined. He had a fearful — in both meanings fearful — a fearful urge to kiss her delectable brown neck, but he went and sat in the other chair. "I'd better tell you. I went on the booze last weekend."

"Did you?" she said without surprise or emphasis. She hesitated and said: "When?"

"On Saturday night," he said. "I suddenly simply couldn't stand it."

"I know," Lorna said, looking at him now. "I know."

"Bobby and the Kellys found me on Sunday and went into action after consulting some doctor sage, I forget his name."

"Doctor Pugsley. He's a lovely old man."

"Well, his recommended therapy was fairly brutal, and it worked."

"Those pages are shaky, not boozy though, surely?"

"No," he said. "The tremulous aftermath."

"I had a feeling something was wrong, and I telephoned on Monday, but no answer, and Bobby said he thought you were having difficulties with the chapter and had taken the afternoon off to visit the aquarium, too casual, he's no better a dissembler than his mother is. All he said to me in the car was that he thought you were under a terrific strain with the book, and he hoped you would be all right."

"They were so damned good to me," Nigel said.

"They're fond of you," she said, smiling at him, for him. "I can't imagine why."

He laughed, alone with her, the stresses and strains not over or resolved, but in abeyance, that was her comfort.

"Your eyelid has stopped dancing. I think the jag must have cured the twitch." She had a droll way of saying things. She stood up now.

"Could be," he said. "Where are you going?"

"I have to change. The Skafes asked me to quiet dinner with them. Are you going to start on the final bit tomorrow?"

"No," he said. "I'm going to read the whole thing through first. It will take me most of the day."

"I think I can finish this by lunchtime. Then I can bring it for you to read too. Poor Tam," she said quietly, and he saw that her eyes were wet, and she looked at him, not concealing that.

"Would you like me . . . ?"

"Yes," he said. "I would like you. What?"

140

"Would you like me to come and cook supper for us tomorrow evening?"

"Are you sure?" he said.

"Yes, I'm sure."

"Goodbye, my love, until tomorrow."

"Goodbye," she said.

16

HE READ MORE THAN HALF THE BOOK THAT MORNING. Diamond in the present, Diamond remembering the past, some bad times and some good — his father drunk in the tenement — one happiest of days when a stranger country girl taught him how to fish, and afterward she leaned across his new bike and she gave him a kiss on the cheek. It was the softest sweetest thing he ever knew, that warm touch, so gentle, so quickly gone. *Goodbye, Tam* — she said. *Don't forget today — I'll not forget*, he said. *Goodbye, Ella.* Then he got on his bike and rode back to the city. He remembered ugly things, a fight in a Dundee pub, and other worse violence; and the Commando raid when Tam carried his wounded officer under fire, and the officer died in the cabin of the boat, the only man who could ever manage him. That was sad, but not sad with ugliness. These were the background to this nightmare present of which nothing was good but the young widowed woman's kindness.

He did not know about its quality. He knew that he, Nigel Ash, was in Tam Diamond's heart. But that afternoon he must switch in part to the enemy.

He had lunch, and went to bail out the dinghy. It was low water, so only a short burdensome haul in. Fortunately it had been at the far end of the running line, and had no apparent damage. It tipped on its keel, but was still too heavy to turn over until he had bailed a dozen buckets. Got it now. He let the boat fall back to wait for the tide. So many things a landlubber forgot, and one was that he should have taken off the outboard before the storm. So he did that now, and carried it up to the brimming drum of rainwater behind the cabin, set the motor therein, wiped off the salted exterior, and behold, it started off first pull, his lucky moon. He let it run a few minutes to clean the innards, a noisy metallic cauldron bubble in the barrel.

She had come and gone unheard, leaving the envelope, and on it: *See you at sixish.* So back to read. He finished at teatime. Now one must exercise oneself along the shore and to below the Kellys' house, but no sign of the brothers to have a word with. It was more like a Scottish than a Canadian day, sunshine and cloud, a few brief showers.

Then there was the table to set for dinner in party fashion. Most of the cabin furniture, except sofa and armchairs, was French Canadian, of carved white pine. He did rather wonder why their modern generation had lost that admirable plain artistic skill. The tray with drinks. The half bottle of Meursault in the refrigerator. Nothing remained but to have a bath, to put on decent trousers, a striped shirt, a tie with the mango pattern she had given him, good-smelling Car on his grizzled locks, a jacket of Glenash tweed, and there we are, we can do no more, and our heart goes pit-a-pat like any jolly decent schoolboy's.

The woods road was dry enough again, so he expected that Lorna would bring supper by jeep. It will be our first meal alone together at my brother's cabin, and we know what may be going to happen, and who suggested it? "You damned hypocrite," he said aloud. "You wooed her to it."

Here came the jeep. "Hullo," he said, giving her a hypocrite's brotherly kiss, and carrying the dinner basket. Inside he said, without hypocrisy: "I do love your jumble of good taste. That's the best taste of all." He meant the same thing about her clothes, this evening a Picasso kind of blouse, a blue cardigan over it, a red skirt of terra-cotta color, nylons, country shoes. But he did not say that. He looked at the fair hair, brushed glossy, a wave only at shoulder height.

Lorna took the things out of her basket. "It's nothing fancy," she said. She put a covered casserole dish in the oven, and turned that on. "Do you want to know what?"

143

"Not me," he said. "Unlike that fellow George Petrie. He and Mother Becker discussed the menus in detail, it seemed."

"That's just a sort of joke they have."

"An odd chap, I only met him twice. That evening on the boat when he brought Bobby and Co. here, I disliked him, brassy and ever so amusing. But next morning he came alone to photograph a heron — had a drink with me, quite different, thoughtful, appealing in a formidable way."

"George is shy, I think." And she added casually, "A brilliant cop, they say."

"That would not surprise me."

"What time would you like to eat?"

"In an hour or so, would that be good?"

"That would be just lovely," she said in a New Brunswick voice. "So I'll put the vegetables on later."

"Sit in or out?"

"You know me, Nigel."

Perhaps he did know Lorna now as well as any man may know a woman he has not known, and then he would not know her. One never knows what is worth knowing.

"Ebbing," she said. "Two hours about. I like the ebb tide too."

"I begin to like it. Go away, come back. It's the life of this place."

"It's the life of all life," she said. "Oh, look, Nigel, the sandpipers."

"The evening I got the first idea for the book, six spotted sandpipers ran from the tide. Soon now they'll be chasing it across the mud. Five weeks or something ago, that was."

"An age ago, that was," she said. No strain between them this evening, to be friends and to be lovers.

"Lorna, do you believe in God?"

"You asked me that before. I believe in Jesus, and I believe that God is in everything. The dogma claptrap leaves me cold. Not much of an answer, Nigel."

"Good enough for me," he said. "Do you go to church?"

144

"Quite often," she said. "Unless the clergyman is one of those hell-fire thunderous S.O.Bs."

"You make me laugh too," he said. But he did not dare to ask her what he wanted to ask. The moon was quite high toward the west, a fair fat crescent. "I was lucky this time," he said. "I saw the sliver of the new moon from here on Wednesday."

"I wasn't," she said. "I saw it through a picture window with the smart set at North Hatley."

"I'll get us top-ups," he said, but she went with him to put on infant carrots, new potatoes.

"It's beginning to be quite chilly," she said. "I don't like high surly summer. But I love these evenings at the end of August. Would you have some item of gentleman's apparel that I could borrow?"

He got his windbreaker. "Will this do? It probably smells a bit."

"It smells good a bit," she said. "Swamps me a bit too."

There was almost no wind, an occasional touch from east to north, a tranquil evening, full sun, sun paling behind cloud, the sun's rays slanting by cloud. Now the sandpipers did chase the tide. "H'sst!" She had seen them first.

They were nearer than usual, walking sedately in this direction, the white-faced mother leading, her child as tall now, if slighter. They came to drink at the freshwater brook, no more than a rivulet, that drained the hillside into the far corner of this cove. They drank side by side, but in turn, one pair of ears and eyes always facing downwind. Then they turned and walked away and fed a little on the rich aftergrass, the clover, the alfalfa. But not for long. They disappeared into cedars as unhurriedly as they had come.

Lorna and Nigel turned to smile at one another, and she said: "They seem to have adopted us."

"For the moment," he said. "Until the rut begins, 'until the bucks are running' is the Canadian expression which I like much better. But I've found four or five different places where

145

they sleep up the hill, a flattened circle in long grass, sometimes in cover, never far from cover. And it's always one mark. They sleep touching one another."

"There's a small poem by Yeats, you probably know it:

> One had a lovely face,
> And two or three had charm,
> But charm and face were in vain
> Because the mountain grass
> Cannot but keep the form
> Where the mountain hare has lain.

"Could you say again? I like it but I don't quite get it."

Lorna said it a second time.

"Of me in vain," he said. "But never of you in vain."

"I don't know how anyone could have changed as much as you have."

"Don't you?" he said. Their nearer hands met, the fingers slipping in to link with one another. "I sure do feel the electric," he said.

"So happy," she said.

"My lucky moon." But he felt a tingle in his neck. If one bows to one's lucky moon, one should not tempt one's luck. ". . . Sorry?"

"You're away up Glenash again. I said: Will it take you long to finish now?"

"Two days or three," he said.

"Starting tomorrow?"

"Yes," he said. "Unless . . ."

That was another thing about her, unlike most women, no *unless what?*

"I went to my father's funeral. Otherwise, I haven't been to church for twenty years. I meant: unless I could go with you tomorrow." And he added: "If he's not one of those hellfire thunderous S.O.B.s you mentioned."

"No. He's a good comforting kind of Presbyterian boomer. It would be lovely, Nigel." Lorna disengaged her hand and

146

stood. "But isn't there the hazard of your alter ego, *that bloody man*, you call him?"

"You know Neil Arnott," he said. "You could whisk me to safety."

"I do not know Neil Arnott," she said with acerbity. "I know Nigel Ash."

"I keep hoping to evade the rough edge of your tongue," he said, following her in, and she turned, laughing, and kissed him lightly, quickly on the lips.

"Seeing as how it's happy evening, lucky evening, shall we have one more, say a martini?"

"English people always switch your drinks." But Lorna blushed, it was so charming. "*English*, what sin have I committed now? Say a martini, but not on those rocks, frosty cold with lemon peel."

He put the glasses in the freezer to chill a minute, and then he poured the necessary into the martini jug, filled up with ice cubes, gave it a stir with a long spoon, cut two thin pieces of lemon peel, and the buzzer sounded.

"Hullo."

"Jake speakin'. Mr. Ash, he just called from London, England, tried the big house first, no answer, so he gets on to me, and asks is all okay, and I says sure, and Mrs. Ash was out to a dinner some place in town, I seen her leavin', and he says to tell Mrs. Ash he'll be calling same time tomorrow, and the meetings was going fine, just finished for the night — some worker, that guy, Labor Day weekend, think of it — and he asks about the storm, it was on their news, and I says nothing much up here, but a bit of a hole in the cabin wall, and he says was Mr. Ash okay, and I says Mr. Ash was okay enough to go out bare-arsed naked in the hurricane and he fixed it good, and Mr. Ash laughed and he says: *that sounds just like him*, near as next door, his voice was, right across the ocean. Well, I guess that's all. Night, Nigel."

Jake was a telephone-shouter, so one had to hold the thing away. "I heard every word of that," Lorna said. "*Some place in town, I seen her leavin'*. Oh, dear."

147

He made the drinks. "Frosty cold, you said."

Lorna was crying, tears on her cheeks, but her voice was sobless: "Cover up by Jake. Why do they want us to be together?"

"You like all the same things, Bobby said to me. And Jake made a similar comment. Here," he said. "It's clean." He gave her his handkerchief.

"The softest I ever felt," Lorna said. "What is it?"

"Irish linen, Silkilon, they're called. One of my luxuries. Father always had them."

"I wouldn't say you have many luxuries, just a few eclectic ones. Anyway, it's mine now." Lorna laughed, tears over, and put his handkerchief in her purse. "Super martini," she said. "Calling you Nigel, that's a great compliment from Jake. Actually, you seem to be well-regarded in these parts, that is, by the privileged few who are granted audience."

People used to admire him for derring-do and all that balls, and people could be amused by him, but always, he thought, they were left with reservations. Perhaps having a true dedicated job at last had changed him a bit, not much. "If that's so," he said. "It's you. I don't have to say it, do I?"

Lorna shook her head. "That's the loveliest thing, you don't have to say it."

"There's some watery martini left." He filled the glasses.

"Let's have fun. Bobby says you sing marvelous Scottish songs, could you do one for me?"

"Broad Scotch, you mean?"

So he sang:

> Och, I'l never forget the day
> We was ordered on review,
> The King came doon tae see us
> And the Queen was wi' him too . . .
> The Queen puts up her royal specs
> And she looks at me and she says:
>   'Oh, he's a braw braw hieland lad
> Is Private Jock McCraw,

148

There's no anither sodger like him in the forty-twa,
Reared among the heather you can tell he's Scottish built
By the wig, wig, wiggly wiggly waggle o' his kilt'.

"There," he said.

"Thank you so much for my handkerchief," Lorna said, employing it. Then she went to get dinner. The first thing was cold, in a ramekin dish, a pâté of hers, with caviar on top and aspic. "That's not just bad," he said. "Caviar, indeed."

"T'is but whitefish caviar to the wing commander."

And she went to the oven for the casserole dish. "This is with Jake's compliments," she said. "He had a brace of young partridges — ruffed grouse, that would be — stached away in his freezer. Anyway, when I said I was cooking your supper, he said: What about it, Mrs. Ash, they're real delicious, you can unthaw 'em quick?"

"So you told Jake you were coming?"

"Yes," she said. "The jeep is absent. It isn't licensed. Where else would I be coming in it? Anyway, supper is no guilty secret."

Nevertheless Jake had elected to cover up to Dan about it. Good old Jake. You know, he thought, people may seem to like me now, but character doesn't change at forty-eight. It slipped across his mind, and he opened the Meursault.

". . . The sauce is fantastic, and real mushrooms too."

"They're early this year. I found a few on the golf course."

"Lorna!" He said, having tasted the wine, and filled her glass and his.

"Nigel!"

So they drank to one another. "I'm feelin' kinda cheery," he said.

"I'm feelin' just miserable," she said. It was such fun, indeed such fun together.

"Coffee?" he said, after the cold caramel custard, again in small dishes. "And there's brandy or creme de menthe."

"Coffee," she said. "But I've had enough drink for the

moment." She stocked his modest cellar for him, and she bought his groceries for him, took his things to the laundry, never questioning that he paid her by cash, initially in Canadian fifties, and in smaller bills as those were broken down.

He made coffee the extravagant way, heated the earthenware pot, put in the coffee, added boiling water, stirred it, left it to settle. Small cups, Demerara sugar, cream. He took the tray through. She was looking across the river, silhouetted against the fading day. She had a beautiful body that might soon be his to share. He did not know. He knew that she also wanted him, but there was honor in Lorna, and steel in Lorna to deny herself if she so chose.

He put down the tray, and did what he had for so long wanted to do. He kissed her neck once and stood away.

"That was most agreeable," she said.

It was dark enough for lights now, so he put on one standard lamp and closed the curtains, and they had their coffee, sitting in two armchairs beside the fire.

"You never talk much about yourself," he said.

"Nor do you much," she said.

"But I want to know about you."

Lorna shook her head. "Please not. Don't you understand?"

"I suppose so," he said. "Sorry, my love."

"But lone wolf Nigel — or do you have a good woman somewhere?"

"Nowhere else," he said. "I had a bitch of a wife once, but that's a closed subject."

"Tell me one thing, just one thing, and I'll never be inquisitive again."

"You're the least inquisitive person I know."

"When you arrived at the door of the Westmount house, held up by the taxi driver who said: *This gentleman sure is sick, Ma'am,* and you passed out cold, what happened before that?"

"I flew into Idlewild the previous day, feeling perfectly all right. I was Nigel Ash, proper tweedy British gent, first-class, on my way to spend a fortnight with cousins near Poughkeepsie. You see, Lorna darling, having been searched God knows how many times in Germany, I'm quite nifty with unalerted customs people.

"The technique is to hang back, never hurry, and when your turn comes, be polite, not too polite, a little anxious because you do have something to declare and you don't know whether it is dutiable. In this case the carrot was the carved Madonna from Oberammergau — on the mantelpiece, my one and only present to the cabin."

"It's exquisite," she said.

"Well, I was taking it to my cousins, and of course the poor chap fell for that, a sacred object to a good Irish Catholic, he pretty well blessed me, and through I swanned to the waiting limousine."

"I can see you," Lorna said, with love. What else? "I can just absolutely see you."

"The fact was that strapped to my chest, with a thin coat of insulation against body heat, were two small canvases, about eight-by-twelve, a Corot of the Italian period, and a Jan Brueghel, you know, one of the sons, both authenticated by every known expert, both recently stolen from the Barnsley collection in London, very hot items worth, I suppose, about a hundred thousand smackers. If this hijacking goes on, one of these days they're going to start body-searches. But I walked through Heathrow unmolested."

"Please stick to the point."

"The point was Park Avenue, where I duly delivered the goods. My courier price was five thousand dollars, and I badly needed it, broke as usual. It was a duplex apartment, upstairs kitchen, dining room, bedrooms, as I later found out — downstairs an entrance hall, a long drawing room full of priceless stuff, some of it perhaps a bit baroque for your fancy; then another room where some types were playing roulette — no women in evidence — and yet another small sitting room to which I was ushered by the burly butler, and greeted by Mr. Pacelli, he did look rather papal. *Mr. Ash*, he said. *What a pleasure to meet you. And this is Mr. Silverstone. Now do please indulge my expectation.*

"So I took off my jacket and tie, opened my shirt and freed the sticky tapes that held the thin parcel to me, handed it over. I had not even seen the contents. I had been told what they were, and where I was to take them, and what I was to get for them safely handed over. As a matter of fact, I hadn't done that sort of thing for years, just one evening a telephone call at the cottage in Scotland from my same old contact.

"Silverstone, presumably the art expert, opened the parcel up and started examining them, and Pacelli said: *Now that you are here, Mr. Ash, would you care to see my private collection, ultra-private, one might say?* He was a debonair sort of chap. He pressed some button, and the end wall slid open to reveal his ultra-private collection.

"They were fabulous, no other word for it, and of catholic variety, a dozen paintings in an otherwise bare room — a Vermeer, a Goya, a small Turner, Cezanne, Manet. *It is a small hobby of mine, he said,* after I had taken my time. It did occur to my nasty mind that he was being a trifle confiding of his masterpieces. He closed the wall behind us, and Silverstone said: *About the Brueghel there can be no question, Mr. Pacelli. But the Corot — I do not think so. Indeed, I suspect that it is a master forgery.*

"Lorna, I'm getting bored with this. I only want to be with you."

She came and sat below his chair, her head back against his thigh. "I know," she said. "Just summarize, then."

"To summarize, they paid me twenty-five hundred, gypped me of the rest, and I didn't bat an eye. I was one alone in a houseful of them. So I joined the roulette game, lost a thousand of that very sportingly with good humour, but one of the others was properly plastered, and he was escorted to bed, and I soon excused myself — it was three in the morning my time by then, and actually I was beginning to feel odd, a headache, dizzy, very odd. I knew the drunk had won a lot of money, and he was out cold, so I relieved him of five thousand, snuck along with my suitcase and the small overnight job to the emergency exit stairs, down two flights, got the elevator, took a cab at Fifty-third to La Guardia, caught a night coach flight to Boston, and in the morning Delta to Montreal.

"By that time I was feeling ghastly. They don't normally bother with passports, but they examined mine that morning, and I came in as Neil Arnott just in case, asked the Murray Hill limousine man to drive around until bank opening time and take me there and afterward to your address in Westmount. It seemed the most sensible thing to do, because by then I knew I was really ill, cold as hell one minute, burning the next."

"He was a decent fellow, as the Murray Hill people usually are, and I said: *Just this one stop and then Westmount. Here's fifty dollars.*

"I managed it at the bank, changed two thousand into Canadian, and put the Arnott passport and the rest of the money into my safety deposit box. The last thing I remember is being at your front door. What happened then?"

"I called Dan at the office, and the ambulance arrived in ten minutes." Her head stirred against him, and she said: "I thought that my stranger brother-in-law, whom I had always disliked so much, was dying. Your breathing was awful, and you were flat-out unconscious. How did you ever manage all that, feeling like that?"

"I made myself," he said. "I think it was the hardest thing I ever had to do, but it only really hit me totally after I left the bank." He put his hand on her forehead; then he stroked her hair. "My swan song," he said. "Farewell to crime."

"Really?" she said.

"Yes, really. Shall I put more on the fire?"

"I will," she said. And when she had done that, she stood looking down at him, not smiling, but not sadly.

"What do you want?" he said.

"I want you this time. And then one more time when the book is done. And then goodbye."

"Mightn't it be bad for you?" he said.

"No," she said. "It would be love for me. But mightn't it be bad for you?"

"Yes," he said. "But better than not. 'Lay your sleeping head, my love, Human on my faithless arm.' Not faithless," he said. "Extraordinary thing."

They laughed at one another. And now they kissed with passion at the log cabin by the shore, standing together, loving together, finding together, and there were two rifle shots.

17

"QUIETLY," HE SAID AT THE DOOR. The moon was down, but stars gave a little light. The Plough, the Dipper, he saw them up there as he climbed smooth ground to the two garden chairs, to his vantage point of days and evenings.

The deer were side by side. Both were alive, and both were propped on their forelegs, hindquarters down, backs broken, either bad shooting or expert immobilizing shooting. Both stared blindly into the searchlight beam. A man with a rifle walked toward them, also in that beam. He walked right up to them, first to the mother deer. He cuffed her on the head, playfully, even affectionately, as one cuffs one's own big dog. "You got yours, Whitey," he said, his voice distinct on a quiet night. And he went to the fawn, and did the same thing, and said: "So did you, Sonny Boy."

"Jesus, Randy, what are you playin' at?" The voice came from behind the light.

"I ain't fuckin' playin'." He hit the young deer one vicious blow on the head with the rifle butt, and it collapsed. "Whistle the truck down quick." It was a piercing human whistle. The man called Randy, what was his other name? It was Dibble. Randy Dibble used the butt of his rifle on the doe, but she did not collapse. "I'll bleed this fucker," he said, laying down his rifle. He took her by one ear, and slashed his knife across the muzzle, one way, the other way, like stropping a razor, and she bled. Then Dibble plunged the knife into her throat. The white-faced doe gave her last and only cough as the blood gushed out.

Ash had seen that done many times. He himself had done it

155

in his stalking days, a quick way to end the life of a wounded beast. But never in his life had he seen such things done as the other things that this man had done.

He heard he sound of a truck farther up and over. "Come on!" he said to Lorna, and he took her hand to guide her until light in the cabin door showed the way.

He went to the bedroom and to the cupboard where Dan's Belgian rifle-gun was in its small case. He put that on the bed and opened it. He had looked at it before, but he had not touched it. It was in four parts — barrels, fore-end, action, butt. The short barrels fitted to the action and pistol grip — so that it could be used as a somewhat cumbersome handgun. And to the pistol grip clipped a butt. He took perhaps thirty seconds to assemble it, only a few moments more to pick up half a dozen three inch shells of .410 caliber, number six shot, and a handful of magnum point two-twos, and he put them in his jacket pockets.

She was waiting in the living room. Her face was pale, and she said nothing at all. He picked up the big flashlight, similar to that recéntly used on the field. "In the jeep," he said. "I'll drive."

He waited until he heard the noise of a truck grow loud as it came on to the field beyond the cove. "They won't hear us now," he said, starting up. He drove without lights until the barrier of woods would hide them, and then he climbed fast. "You're sure there's no other way out except your back road?"

"Quite sure," she said.

"Wait inside, darling," he said at the house. "Wait until I get back."

"I'm coming with you."

"No," he said. "You are not."

"What are you going to do?"

"I'm going to deal with that cruel bugger," he said.

He went down the back road to the metal gate, and stopped the engine. No sound of a truck coming. He got out and took

156

the flashlight with him. They had done just what Jake had said that anyone could do. They had cut a way round the right side of the gate, fairly wide because of one spruce that was too big to fell. Axes being noisy, they had used only bucksaws, three men, probably two with saws and one to take the strain to keep the saws from binding. It was all small cedar, no more than six inches at the butt, sawn off close to the ground. It might have taken them half an hour to clear a track that any middle-sized car, let alone a jeep or a truck, could negotiate. Ash turned the jeep and backed it in, rammed its backside into smaller saplings, barring their road, but out of sight of the truck until it made a final swing.

There was a long bit of nylon string — a lucky fluke, that. He tied one end of it to the headlight button, threaded it round a backbody stanchion, stood forward on the right side of the jeep, pulled the string, indirect pull, the lights came on. He switched them off again, put the flashlight on the ground against emergency, and loaded his weapon, a rifle shell above, a shotgun shell below. At close range it was a lethal weapon, not at all the kind of thing that you would expect Dan to own, but Dan was a gun-buff, among a lot of other bloody stupid and sensible things.

A double-barreled ejector of an unusual kind — forward trigger, rifle — rear trigger, shotgun; no use in gangland because you had to reload after each shot. It was a take-down combination for a man to carry in his pack, shoot a rabbit, shoot a partridge — excellent for that. But slow for this job.

Still no sound. Ash had time for a little practice, working out a quick reload. Between the third and fourth fingers of his right hand was a four-ten shell. That left his trigger finger free. Between the first and second fingers of his left hand a magnum twenty-two. Thus, both hands were operative. Whichever barrel you fired, you opened, spent shell ejected, reload with left hand, or reload with right hand.

You got yours, Whitey. He saw the pale-faced doe of these

many evenings. He saw the White Stag of his story. Once long ago he had seen the White Stag on the hill, a great beast, known across fifty miles of the Scottish Highlands.

The truck was coming. The engine was rough, missing on a cylinder, but it came quite fast. He saw the sidelights through the trees, and the headlamps came on now as it swung to the diversion, turning this way, the jeep still not lit up, and then the left front of it was. He pulled the cord and he had the cab illuminated in enfilade. It was a half-ton pickup truck, and someone in the back jumped and ran for it.

Randy Dibble was at the wheel, another man beyond him. "Stop the engine," Ash said, "and get out this way, hands on top of your heads."

For answer, Randy Dibble rammed the jeep, and for answer to that, Ash shot him neatly in the left hand on the steering wheel, opened, spent case ejected, reloaded with his left fingers and thumb, he was quick, but then he had always been quick. He took another twenty-two shell from his jacket pocket. The engine stopped. "Come out," he said.

Dibble came out with his right hand on his cap. The other, much younger, sallow, terrified, came with both hands up.

"Stand still, Dibble," he said. He stepped forward a little, so that they could see him now. "You," he said to the other one. "Get out of here. Go on, run." He spoke quietly. He heard his own quiet voice, and the youth ran, stumbled, picked himself up, and ran along the gravel road of Daniel Ash's country place.

There was movement in the back of the truck, which was in darkness. Ash picked up the flashlight and switched it on and held it out. "Here," he said. "Point this into the back."

Dibble did as he was told. Blood bubbled from the young deer's mouth, and the forelegs twitched weakly. Ash shot it in the head, reloaded, looking at the two dead beasts. "You got yours, Whitey," he said. "And so did you, Sonny Boy."

"Jeezus, Mister. I didn't never mean . . ."

"You meant everything, you wicked sod." Ash waited,

158

watching Randy Dibble, a few days bearded, his left hand bloody, his right hand holding the flashlight, still switched on.

Ash stood before one headlamp. The other shone on Dibble. His eyes were hot, hateful, desperate. They flickered one way to darkness, the other way to darkness, and to the gun, held in one hand at the point of balance, held casually, a man might think, without killing intent a man might think.

"You can drop it now," Ash said.

As the flashlight clattered on a rock, the eyes betrayed the moment of the movement. Dibble broke for darkness. From a slow man he would have escaped. From Ash he had no chance — gun in both hands, gun up, rear trigger, shotgun barrel, middle of the back at a few paces, perhaps one second gone.

"You got yours, Mr. Dibble," said Nigel Ash. He had done what he had done, and the slasher of the white-faced deer was dead.

He opened up, and the spent case ejected. He took out the live twenty-two with his fingers, closed the gun, picked up the broken flashlight, took the ignition key from the truck and threw it away, got into the jeep, started, backed a yard or so, and drove to the house.

Lorna stood there on the lighted porch, and Jake was with her. "What happened, Mr. Ash?"

He recounted it briefly and completely. ". . . Then he made a run for it, and I shot him in the back."

"In the back," Jake said. "Holy Jesus! Did they try anything?"

"Nothing," he said. "I decided to kill him when he ran, and so I did."

"I told Jake what we saw him do," Lorna said. She was perfectly calm.

"But in the back," Jake muttered. "Self-defense wouldn't hold for in the back."

"I don't care a damn about self-defence," he said. His head had been cold and clear about what he would do, and he had done it. "What's the time, Jake?"

159

"Near a quarter of twelve."

That gave about six hours of darkness. "Will they report it?"

"Two dead deer in the back of the truck — hell no, they won't report it."

"I must think," he said. He walked away from them into the dark to think. He would not give himself up. That was settled already. He must therefore vanish. Across the river? No, that was out. "Jake," he said, coming back. "Is the jeep gassed up?"

"Filled it this mornin'."

"Good," he said.

"I'll do anything," Jake said. "Just you say."

"I think the best thing," he said, speaking slowly, his plan was forming. "I think the best thing is that you should be at home asleep, having heard no shots."

"I wouldn't of," Jake said. "Bedroom faces south, sleep like a hog and so does the wife. Hell, once I shot a coon below the window and she never stirred. I was up late because I told Mrs. Ash I would walk Congo, was why I heard."

"Okay, then. You come in the morning at eight as usual, make your rounds as usual. Report to the police. What you find in the morning is all you know. Okay?"

"Okay," Jake said. "Anything else?"

"That's all. Goodnight, Jake, and thanks."

"You sure are a man," Jake said. He meant a man-killer too. "Best of luck, Nigel. I'll go then." He hesitated, shook hands in a countryman's awkward way, and went.

"Hullo, Congo," he said in the house.

"That awful brute," Lorna said. "So horrible." She kissed him. "I would have done just the same." But she qualified that: "Would have tried to."

"May I take the jeep?"

"Oh course," she said.

"Have you got any camping kit?"

"Bobby has oodles. Just tell me."

"A pack, light sleeping bag, compass, groundsheet, plastic

160

rain stuff, a billy, a mug, matches watertight, basic food, bully beef, tea and so on. Can you lay it out? I must go to the cabin. A pair of hunting boots too, if they would fit me."

"Dan's or Bobby's, yes, I think so. We have all that."

"I won't be long," he said. At the cabin he changed into a khaki shirt, cotton neckcloth, sweater, whipcord trousers, old jacket, razor and soap, shells and bullets, cigarettes, one hefty drink. "Goodbye to you," he said to the whisky bottle. And he looked at his typed manuscript in its folder, the end not yet met with the beginning. *"Au revoir,"* he said to it. "Be seein' ya," he said less dramatically, light off, and to the jeep.

She had everything laid out on the dining room table, mahogany, Chippendale probably. They filled the pack carefully, methodically while his mind raced on. He put the hatchet and the hunting knife on his belt, the compass in a pocket. The rest he selected as she packed. "I think that's all. No, two more things. Do you have a map of New Brunswick?"

"Only a road map."

"Better than nothing. Any small plastic garbage bags?"

"Lots," she said, and fetched the map and two bags. They were a chaste shade of green. He took them and the map and the pack to the jeep and came in again.

"Listen carefully, darling," he said. "You were down having supper with me. They're sure to find that out, two lots of fingerprints all over the place. But you came up and were in bed by ten. Then some shots woke you. You thought there were three. You went back to sleep."

"But that isn't true," she said. "If they catch you, do you think I'm going to say nothing?"

"They won't catch me," he said. "The point is that you must be kept out of this altogether, and so must Jake. Drill it into him again first thing in the morning."

"Where are you going, Nigel?"

"I'm not telling you that, and you don't know anywhere I might be likely to go."

"Right," she said.

"Are you going to stay here much longer?"

"I planned until late September. Jake and I always do the perennials together."

"The point is," he said, "that I disappear now. Nigel Ash disappears. But I have to get to the bank in Montreal for that other passport. I must go myself, do you see?"

"Yes," she said. "What can I do?"

"If I telephone you from a call-box in a few days' time, say, at about four P.M. or so, and you're sure it's safe and they haven't bugged you, can you bring me my smaller case with a suit, pajamas, shirts, a pair of shoes, and so on, not much? It will have to be a quick drop-off. You'll be going somewhere else, say to Fredericton."

"That's easy if they don't tap our telephone. But if they suspect I know anything, or if they think you might call . . . The same could apply to Jake. If only there was someone else. What about the Kelly boys? They're here another week. I could warn them. Or could I even tell them what really happened? They're dead reliable, and very fond of you."

"That pair of cool cats, yes, you could tell them. Better let me have all three numbers." Lorna wrote them down for him.

"The typescript — shouldn't I bring it up?"

"No," he said. "Say you've been typing for me if they ask you. But leave it there."

"And that guncase — did you hide it?"

"No point. On the bed. Now I must go."

"Are you coming back?"

"Yes," he said. "Somehow or other when the shouting dies down, I'm coming back. That's where I began it. That's where I'll end it, and then I'll go."

"And if I stay here, will you love me once?"

"I will," he said. "And always."

"Your lucky moon," she said. "My unlucky moon. We haven't been so lucky, my love."

"No," he said.

"Poor you," she said. "Poor Tam."

162

"There is a sort of irony," he said. He could not see her very well.

He got into the jeep, wiped his eyes with the back of his hand, drove up the paved front drive, and headed north. He kept well below sixty in case there might be a patrol car. But on the main highway he met only two cars, and they were not police, and on the dirt roads he met no one at all.

It was still an hour before dawn when he reached Anvil Lake. The wind had gone south, and the sky had clouded over. He put the jeep in low ratio four-wheel drive, and he climbed fairly easily up the smooth rock toward the anvil, some bad bumps, but no bottom scraping.

Then the hill was too steep even for the jeep, and he must not leave tire marks by spinning his wheels. Engine off, in low gear, parking brake on, he went round to open the tailgate and take out the old floormat, which he needed.

But on the mat, in his invariable favorite place, lay the black labrador. "Oh, damn you, Congo." He had put his pack in the jeep, gone back to say goodbye, left the front door open, and Congo had jumped aboard, quite simple. He would lie all day or all night in his favorite place on earth.

Ash took out the pack, and summoned Congo and told him to sit, and to stay, which he was trained to do. Lorna had trained him. He saw Lorna's face now, and she was smiling at him, crying. "Every bloody thing I've ever done," he said.

He took out the mat and went up front for the winch hook and hauled the cable after him. It was a hard clamber, and then less steep. Above him, silhouetted against the paling sky in the east was the solitary wire birch. He had sat there once, planning on with Tam Diamond's story, the hunters and the hunted.

Now he wrapped the mat round the tree, hooked the cable back into itself, went down again to the jeep and listened. Nothing. A stir of wind, nothing else. He got the winch in gear, started the engine and began hauling himself up. It was slow, easy, inevitable.

When the slope eased, he unhooked the cable and wound it

right in. Then he ran on under wheeled power past the tree to the beginning of the anvil's gentle gradient, stopped again. Now what else? He opened the hood or bonnet, put both plastic bags over the oil-filling cap, and tied them tightly with that useful nylon cord. He also employed it to anchor the steering wheel two ways, insure straight running. There were a couple of yards still to spare, put it in his pocket, a leash for Congo. Now was there anything else that might float? Only the floormat. He laid it on the engine and shut the bonnet.

Then he put the jeep in neutral, let off the parking brake, and jumped out smartly. There was no need for that hurry. The jeep began sedately, picked up speed, and was going a fair clip when it dipped and disappeared over the anvil.

He listened to the mammoth splash, and then he went back for Congo and his pack. It was a framed pack, well balanced, not very heavy. "Walk, Congo," he said. The dog was an incidental complication, but would be company, might even be a valuable companion sentry.

Ash had driven thirty miles and dawn was breaking. He should make another five before Jake discovered a truck with the carcases of two deer, a man's body nearby. He and his black friend would be two needles in the haystack of New Brunswick. He saw one snag only — that some one of the very few who knew might let slip that his only landward excursion since he came to the cabin by the shore had been to a place called Anvil Lake.

Ash kept to firm ground beside the shallowing cliff. Then he skirted the pebble beach and headed north up the logging road. It was much grown over since he had come the other way from a plane crash eleven years ago, but it was still passable to a man on foot.

Rain had begun, and it soon fell heavily. That would be a help in obliterating any treadmarks he might have left. He unstrapped the groundsheet from the pack. It made a good cape in the rain.

He saw no reason to reproach himself for the murder that his cold anger had caused him to commit. He would do the same

164

thing again. *Your lucky moon. My unlucky moon. We haven't been so lucky, my love.*

"Dear Lorna," he said, and the labrador looked up. "What have I done to her?" Nigel Ash walked on.

18

THE ALARM WOKE HER AT SIX. She had taken a sleeping pill, loathsome feeling, not worn off. Why so early? But then it came back, a jigsaw of pieces not fitting together, gradually fitting together much too well, and she remembered what she had to do.

Lorna washed her face, a little better, put on old slacks, a sweater, loafers, went downstairs for instant coffee, a little better. She called Congo, but he was not in his basket in the back porch, not in the house. She whistled outside, no Congo. He never wandered unless there was a bitch in heat. That was a possibility, remote. She guessed it at once. Congo had jumped into his favorite place to go along for the ride.

It was raining, so she put on a slicker with a hood, and took another to keep the suitcase dry. She must get Nigel's clothes before they could check the contents of the cabin. There were two cases, one a big Revelation, and one much smaller, what he called an overnight job. Three suits in the cupboard — a tropical, too thin; a medium countryfied herringbone; the dark gray narrow pinstripe he had been wearing when he collapsed at the Westmount house. They looked like London-made suits, but they had no tailor's tags on the inside pockets. If one has two names, one has no name tags.

The herringbone said Englishman. The pinstripe said anyone well dressed. She put it in. Two shirts, underpants, socks, the super handkerchiefs, a camelhair cardigan, black shoes with rubber soles — he always wore rubber soles: *I like to gumshoe.* — two silk ties, and one of them she had given him, his green hair stuff in a traveling bottle, a comb, an ivory hairbrush with

166

N.M.A. on it. Complete? Just the Burberry to add, no hat. He had been wearing his tweed cap, and that would do in rain. He never wore a suit when he was here, she thought. I would like to see him in a suit, with that casual air of his, *d'une elegance.* She had a disloyal thought about Dan being poured into his clothes.

One last thing: There was a half bottle of Remy Martin, almost empty; she poured it away, rinsed the bottle, filled up with Scotch whisky, and stowed it in a soft place between shirts and suit.

Leave everything as is, he said. But what about the dishes? She had been to supper. Surely she would have washed up afterward. Might dirty dishes not suggest that they had been disturbed? She did that, put the remains of her partridge fricassee in a small bowl in the refrigerator, and the casserole dish to soak.

The case was quite light, an easy woman's load. She avoided the muddy bits going up. One had to remember that one had driven home last night before the rain. It's the lies that bother me, she thought. I never could tell a decent lie, probably why I never tell them. But now there were lies to tell decently. Lorna took the case to the storage attic off Dan's study, and put it among empty ones.

She managed toast and marmalade, and then she watched for Jake Tovey. He came at the same time on Sundays, eight o'clock, but only to feed the hens and do minor chores, like watering. Was there a chance that Congo had spent the night with them? No such chance. After Jake had left, Nigel walked into the house and said *Hullo, Congo,* always the same lackadaisical voice to a dog, to a person; and she remembered noticing the calmness of that voice, quite unchanged after killing a man.

Jake was walking across, and she went to meet him. "Congo's gone," she said. "He must have hopped aboard just before Nigel left."

"Oh, hell," Jake said. "Well, I guess that don't matter, not too much."

"It does matter, though, Jake. If Congo sleeps in the house,

167

and he is gone, that means Nigel came to the house. So Congo doesn't sleep in the house. He sleeps in the back of the jeep. He would too, if I would let him. And you didn't take him out last night. I did, and put him in the jeep. I've moved his basket to the living room, daytime basket."

"Good thinkin', Mrs. Ash. Yes, that's okay. What isn't is about the jeep being gone. They know darned well we have it because just last month I was takin' it in to be serviced, and the young Mountie stopped me for not being licensed. No need to license a farm vehicle if you use it on your own property and you don't ply for hire-like. They never get that into their thick heads. But I showed him he was wrong, so he won't forget we got a farm jeep, and where the hell is it? Excuse the bad language, Mrs. Ash." Jake laughed, but shortly.

"Nigel was determined that we know nothing except what we're supposed to know. The first thing you know at all is when you find the truck. I had supper with him, came up early, was woken by some shots, went to sleep again. And neither of us has any idea where he has gone."

"I don't neither," Jake said. "He never left the place except the once to go fishing with Bobby."

"That's just what I mean," she said. "You know nothing about a fishing trip."

"Anything else, Mrs. Ash?"

"No," she said. "Nothing for the moment."

"Are you okay, Mrs. Ash? You look kinda washed-up, and I wouldn't wonder." What a kindly man Jake was. Nigel said that about him: *Such a kindly chap*.

"I'm all right," she said. "I've just got to learn to tell a few decent lies, and not too many of them."

"I'll do the hens, and I'll do the greenhouse. That's another half hour. Then I'll find the truck, and from then on its for real, to you, to the cops."

"Right, Jake," she said. She knew nothing yet. The best thing to do was to get ready for church. They would have gone to church together this morning. After sinning, I suppose, she thought.

Jake arrived in a hurry to break the news. ". . . And don't you go no place near there, Mrs. Ash." Then he called the police, gave the details, gave the license number of the truck, said: "Okay, I'll be here," and hung up. He had sounded suitably outraged, and totally convincing.

The police car came soon, and in it the young one, Constable Simpson. He had caught her speeding in the town limits lately, and she had turned the charm on, got away with it. *Nice Lab you've got there, Mrs. Ash. What's his name? — Congo,* she said. *Thanks, officer, I promise to drive slowly.*

Jake went with him. They were up there for an hour or more, until nearly church time. "Do you need me at the moment, Officer? If not, I think I'll go to church. I'm pretty well shattered be this news."

"I'm not surprised, Mrs. Ash." He was a nice looking boy. "Oh, sure you go to church." He was shy of her. "You'll be around later, won't you?"

My mature appeal, she thought. It still works on males of every age.

She sat alone in their pew, stood, sat again, leaned forward to pray, heard his sermon booming on. She did try to pray a bit. She could pray for Nigel, and she could pray to be a respectable liar. But mostly she could rehearse. And she could sing the closing hymn:

> . . . Goodness and mercy all my life
> Shall surely follow me.
> And in God's house for evermore
> My dwelling place shall be.

Goodness and mercy, she prayed. But as Lorna prayed for goodness and mercy, she saw that sadistic savage on the field. *Goodness and mercy all my life,* she prayed. She was the last to shake hands with the minister, and she left that dwelling place.

The rain had stopped by lunchtime. Vehicles moved down and up the back road, a part of which was visible from the house. Lorna heard them through the screen door, but she did not watch them. It was not until two o'clock that a car came from there, and stopped. She answered the doorbell.

They were a thin narrow-faced man, and a beefy younger man. Plainclothes police, she knew already as the thin one produced a green card in a cellophane case and said: "Sergeant Borton, R.C.M.P., and this is Corporal Leblanc. Mrs. Ash?"

"Yes," she said. "Do come in. This is the most awful business. I haven't seen — I mean Jake wouldn't let me see. Please sit down." A good flustered start.

"Just a formality, Mrs. Ash, but we need to check up on a few things."

"All I really know it that I was woken up sometime in the night by shots, I told Jake that."

He held his hand up. "I am not concerned with what you told anyone, Mrs. Ash." It was no formality with this cold man. "My concern is what you did and saw and heard. Begin with the evening. Now calmly, please."

She told it quite well, she thought, about going down in the jeep for supper with her brother-in-law at the cabin, and up early because she was tired and had been sleeping badly, so she took a pill and was asleep by half-past ten. He permitted himself a slight frown at that, no doubt about rich women taking sleeping pills, probably to keep her off balance. Just a mild pill, she said, and then the shots, she thought there were three, and she went to sleep again. "That's all I know," she said.

"Did you put the jeep away when you came home?"

"Yes," she said, "in the shed near the house, the jeep barn, we call it. Congo, our labrador was in the house, and I took him for his run, and he hopped into the back of the jeep where he sleeps, and I gave him biscuits and shut the door."

"And the dog never sleeps in that?" Sergeant Borton pointed to the basket.

"In the daytime. I tried once or twice at night, so much less

170

trouble for us than his beloved jeep. But he always howled. The jeep is Congo's idea of heaven."

The corporal, who had been taking notes, smiled faintly, not so the sergeant. "And did you hear the jeep being taken in the night?"

"No," she said. "Even if I hadn't had a pill, I don't think I would have. We have these Rusco double windows, and our bedrooms are on the river side of the house, so unless it's a very hot night, we hardly ever open the other ones across the hall, and the Ruscos make that side almost soundproof. I bet if we shut the front door now and one of you drives away, we won't even hear it."

The corporal, who seemed fairly human, nodded. The sergeant said, "That will not be necessary, Mrs. Ash." He was a gray bloodless man, and she feared him, and she feared the next thing that was coming. It had taken a surprisingly long time to come.

"Your brother-in-law, Mrs. Ash. Have you been in touch with him since last night?"

"No," she said. "Nigel is writing a novel, and he works at it all day long, so I never disturb him."

"Not even when there has been a murder, Mrs. Ash?"

"I didn't think of it," she said. "After Jake told me, I went to church to try to pull myself together, but that didn't seem to help." She crossed and uncrossed her hands. I'm not such a bad actress after all, she thought. "I don't know," she said. "I don't know. I could call him on the house-to-shore phone if you like. It's by the kitchen."

"Please do," he said, and nodded to the corporal, who went with her. She heard a voice at the front door: "Sergeant! Something else just came up from the Dibble lot." Lorna buzzed a few times, then back to the living room. Sergeant Borton returned.

"No answer," she said. "I think he sometimes goes for a walk about now."

"Mr. Ash is an Englishman?"

"A Scotsman," she said. "He does talk like an Englishman."

"And nobody else is living on your property?"

"No," she said. "The Toveys, myself, Nigel at the cabin, that's all at the moment."

"No one named Diamond has been here?"

"Diamond!" she said. "But that's extraordinary — that's the man in the book he's writing."

"How far is it to the shore? Can we drive there?"

"About half a mile," she said. "You can't drive in an ordinary car, we keep the road that way on purpose. But I could take you in our Wagoneer. It has a good clearance and four-wheel drive."

"Thank you, Mrs. Ash." He was a disagreeable suspicious man. But his job was to suspect. On the way down he said nothing.

He knocked at the cabin door, and went in. The large corporal stood aside for her. *A beefy bugger,* Nigel would call him.

Borton stood in the middle of the room, turned completely round once, and went straight to the bedroom and the bed, upon which was the open leather guncase, well made, expensive. There was a small pamphlet in the case. The sergeant glanced at it. "Corporal," he said. "Walk up. Have them start looking for empty twenty-two magnum shells, three inch four-ten too."

"Right, Sergeant." Were detective teams usually so formal with one another?

Borton went out also, presumably to say something else, and came back, and to the manuscript in its folder. "Mrs. Ash," he said. "How do you know that the man in his book is called Diamond?"

"Because I'm typing it for him," she said tartly.

"And did you know that Nigel Ash had had an encounter a few weeks back with the deceased, Randy Dibble, had told him his name was Diamond, and then had knocked Dibble down?"

"No," she said. "I know nothing about that, never heard of it."

172

"So Mr. Tovey said. They agreed not to tell you."

"If you know that, why ask me?"

"Because it is my business to check statements." He was looking at the first page of the typescript, but he turned again. He watched for her answers all the time. The eyes were a mustardy color, not brown, not gray. "Did you see the carcasses of the deer?"

"No," she said. "Jake told me it was all too horrible, and not to go there."

"Have you ever seen a white-faced doe and a fawn on your property, on that field where they were shot last night?"

Nigel had told no one else, so he had not told her. "No," she said.

"You're sure, Mrs. Ash?"

"Quite sure," she said angrily. "I told you."

"And your brother-in-law never spoke of them?"

"No," she said. She saw them come decorously down to drink last evening. "Why keep on asking me?"

"Because on the first page of this book are the words: *The White Stag was resting.* And on the second page: *They called him by that name, but he was not white. He was a gray beast and only his face was nearly white.* The gray and the white of the dead doe are precisely the same, Mrs. Ash."

"We never spoke about the story. He wrote it, and I typed it for him."

"Was the book finished?"

"No," she said. "But nearly, I think. In the order of things I think it must be."

"And you say you never discussed the book?"

"No. I suppose we would have when it was finished. But I think Nigel was afraid of losing the story if he talked about it."

Detective-Sergeant Borton nodded to that, at last one acceptance. "And the theme of the book?"

"Tam Diamond kills a woman — it's manslaughter, really, not murder — and he runs away across the Scottish Highlands."

"And the character of Diamond?"

And, and, and, his remorseless ands. "He was a good-hearted man with a temper he couldn't ever control."

"*Was*, Mrs. Ash. Is Diamond dead?"

"I don't know," she said. "I mean I'm not sure."

"And would you say that your brother-in-law has an uncontrollable temper?"

"I don't know," she said again. "I never saw him lose it. I never even knew about him hitting that man Dibble." Another nod, a second acceptance. Better say more: "I suppose one could sometimes feel a sort of explosve thing in Nigel, just feel it, not know it, because he's a quiet casual man." Perfectly true. "You see, Sergeant Borton, although I had met my brother-in-law a few times before, I've only got to know him at all really in these past five weeks. He came here to convalesce after being ill, and then he started on the book. Since then he's been living for his novel, and for nothing else. I've never seen anyone so, what is the word?"

"Consumed, perhaps," said Sergeant Borton, being quite reasonable, watching her. "I'll just have a quick look around, Mrs. Ash, and then if you would be good enough to drive me up."

The quick look around was a lightning systematic examination of every drawer and cupboard, the snibbing of every window. Why had Nigel gone? With her evidence and his, and evidence grilled from Dibble companions, surely no jury would convict him of murder. She was beginning to think straight while this unpleasant policeman conned the cabin. The first reason was for her sake, a personable man and woman alone together in a log cabin at a quarter-past eleven at night. The second reason was his other passport. To get away now, he had to be Neil Arnott. But the third reason might be the strong one: like Diamond, he could not bear the thought of prison; unlike Diamond, he had known that for three years of his life, and of those three years, four months were in solitary confinement, she had extracted that from him. And he had said something like: *I've lived in the country almost all my life, but I don't think I really cared much about the natural world until I lost my freedom for a while.*

"Right, Mrs. Ash." He held the small guncase by the handle, and with his other hand picked up Nigel's manuscript.

"But you can't take that."

"I must take that. There seem to be parallels to be examined. It will be returned. And presumably there is a carbon copy, Mrs. Ash?"

"Yes," she said. "I keep it for him at the house in case of fire or anything."

"And there is a key to this cottage?"

"It's usually in the top middle kitchen drawer, and we have a spare one up at the house." Simon Pure, that's me, she thought.

"I shall have the door sealed until an inventory has been made," he said, getting the key, letting the catch off the Yale lock and standing aside for her.

"But why on earth do you seem to link this thing to Nigel?"

"Because of this," he said, swinging the case a little. "Dibble was shot in the wrist with a small caliber rifle, and in the back by a shotgun at pointblank range, and your brother-in-law has disappeared.

"But why would a guilty person leave evidence against himself?"

"That I do not know, Mrs. Ash," he said, once more fixing her with his curiously blank eyes.

They got into the car, and she drove uphill, and he said, turning to watch her again. "Did Mr. Ash make many excursions while he was here?"

"He went on a boat trip once, I think."

"I mean inland, upcountry, Mrs. Ash?"

"Not that I know of," she said. "He didn't leave the place. He simply lived and slaved for that book."

"And your relations with your brother-in-law, Mrs. Ash. Were they friendly?"

She had been waiting for it. "Yes," she said. "We did become quite good friends in a casual way. We went for bird

175

walks occasionally. But mostly we only met to swap chapters, the one typed for the one to be typed.''

"And so your relations were not intimate?''

She stopped the car. "What do you mean?''

"Just that, Mrs. Ash, intimate in the usually accepted meaning of the word?''

"How dare you make such a horrible suggestion! We were plain ordinary friends, I told you.''

"I made no suggestion, Mrs. Ash. I asked a question. It is my duty to ask questions.''

"Your dirty duty,'' she said, and drove on, turning the Gospel round . . . *Looketh on a man to lust after him hath committed adultery with him already in her heart.* "Perfectly innocent,'' she said about their comparative innocence hitherto.

"Thank you, Mrs. Ash.'' He got out. "I must ask you to stay here in the meanwhile. We may have further questions.''

"Stay housebound?'' she demanded.

"Oh, no,'' he said equably. He was the most loathsome cold fish she had ever encountered. "I mean stay at Gallery, Mrs. Ash. Thank you, then.'' He walked away. Her mature appeal certainly had no impact upon Sergeant Borton.

Having made sure that the house was empty — she would hear the front door or the back door open — Lorna did two things quickly. First, she telephoned her sister's house in Quebec and got Bobby. "Listen, Bobby. Don't speak, listen, and not a word to another soul.'' She told him about the deer, about the man being killed, and that Nigel had gone, and that he and Bobby had never been on a fishing trip together.

"Right, Mum,'' he said. "Oh, gosh!''

And you don't know anywhere that I might have gone, Nigel said last night. That pointed straight to Anvil Lake. Then she telephoned the Kellys' house, got Nelson, and arranged to meet them later in the woods.

". . . That's what really happened,'' she said. "I still can't quite believe that any human could be so cruel.''

176

"They do worse than that to one another, Mrs. Ash."

"I suppose so, Keith. But what human beasts do to one another — oh, never mind. Did you know that Nigel got the kernel of his story, the first spark to it, from seeing the white doe at the shore?"

"No," Keith said. "We didn't know that. We didn't know about any white doe."

"It was a secret," she said, And they smiled at her, these brothers, so different and so strong.

"What can we do?" Nelson said.

". . . So if you could just take the phone call, and pass the message on to me."

"If they can tap your phone," Nelson said, "they can just as easily bug your car. It doesn't make sense for you to go."

"It makes much better sense for us to go," Keith said.

"But that implicates you. Nigel would never dream of implicating you beyond passing on a phone call, and nobody would know about that."

"He didn't want to implicate you either, Mrs. Ash. That's obvious."

"Do you have the case ready?"

"Yes, Nelson. I packed it and brought it to the house first thing this morning."

"Right, then. We'll pick it up after dark tonight, say about nine. Would the terrace door be best, if we're sure the coast is clear?"

"Yes," she said, looking at the one, the other. "You're cool," she said. "That's what Nigel called you: *A pair of cool cats.*"

She went home, and had the drink she badly needed for Dutch courage and decent lies if Dan's call came through. *What tangled webs we weave when first we practice to deceive.* She had said something like that to Nigel once, annoyed by him.

It is absurd, she thought, that I never have deceived, I never had to. But last night I would have deceived my good and faithful husband without much of a qualm, and I would again. And

177

now I have to tell him a pack of extra lies, and that repulsive sergeant probably has me tapped already.

She got a second drink, and the call did come, not from London but Sunningdale where Dan was spending the night after thirty-six holes of golf.

"It must have been lovely for you to have a day off," she said. "But listen, Dan, a very bad thing has happened here . . ." And she gave him the official version.

"Oh, God!" said Dan, who never invoked the Deity. "I suppose he caught them at it, and lost his famous temper."

"I didn't know about his temper," Lorna said.

"You weren't his brother. But in the back! That's murder."

"I suppose it is."

"Jake said he thought you'd gone to town for dinner. He saw you leaving."

"I did go to town, or nearly. I went to the golf course to pick a few mushrooms for the casserole I was taking down."

"Well, thank God you left early and weren't involved."

"Yes, I know," she said. And you don't know, she thought to her husband, that I had a nightie with me in my capacious purse.

"Where would he have headed for?"

"I haven't a clue," she said. Quickly change the subject. "When are you coming home, darling?"

"Wednesday afternoon. I'll call you from the office. Are you all right alone there, Lorna? Why not come up?"

"I'm all right. I think I'll stay, Dan." She did not say that she had been instructed to stay. "It's been a bit of a shock, all this."

"Poor darling," he said, a good kind man, he always was. "That brother of mine, I knew it was too good to last." He paused and said: "We'd better send flowers to the funeral."

"Send flowers to the funeral of a man who jacked a doe and a half-grown fawn?"

"There are worse crimes," Dan said. "I think it would be the right thing for us to do. Goodnight, then, darling."

178

"Goodnight, Dan."

He isn't suspicious of me, she thought. It isn't in dear Dan to suspect me. But send flowers to that monster's funeral? I will not.

19

Ash walked for some hours but not far on that first morning. The spruce budworm had chewed the life out of this stretch of forest, and there were many windfalls, deadfalls across the logging road, to be skirted, or climbed over with a burdensome pack.

"Let's have a bite," he said when the rain had stopped. He opened a can of bully beef, shared half of it with Congo, and kept the rest for evening. A slice of bread and cheese between them, a handful of blueberries for him, a drink of water for them both. "A little sleep is overdue," he said, and Congo lay down near him.

How pleasant in the woods in the warm afternoon. Peaceful, he thought. I feel curiously at peace, and he drifted into dreamless sleep.

It was Congo's small whine, a scarcely audible undertone, that awoke him, and then the spruce grouse clucked on a nearby branch, a handsome black-chested bird, and it knew no fear. "You do ask for it," he said, throwing the hatchet, and the grouse moved a foot or two along its perch, and clucked. He rescued the hatchet and scored the second time. "Fetch it, Congo."

The blunt head of the hatchet had broken a wing. He wrung its neck, and said: "Sorry, fool hen, but business is business." He put it in his poacher's pocket. "On we go." And they walked again, the dog a pace behind him. Congo had been well trained by Lorna. Kindness training, he was not subservient like a keeper's dog at home.

The road swung with the contours of the land, but headed

on north in average direction. He crossed two small streams, from rock to rock, dry-shod, and passed a lake. At the far end of it, a mile or so away, a chain saw buzzed. It was high-pitched, one of the new small saws, he thought, somebody cutting wood for a campfire at Labor Day weekend. He could see no one through his binoculars. The noise fell behind and faded to nothing. It was the only sign of man that day.

The fir and the spruce were green again here, and there was paper birch. He began looking for a camping place as the sun dropped to low hills in the west.

Another lake, a hollow not far from it where he could make his fire. Perfect, he thought. We're in luck again. But that about luck did rather jerk him from the comfort of the wilderness.

Ash decided to keep the bully beef for breakfast, so he skinned the bird and spitted it to cook and boiled a few potatoes in the billy-can. Lorna had persuaded him to take them. *Isn't it best to have nearly as normal a diet as possible? You told me that yourself once.* He could not imagine any other woman he had ever known who could have coped as she had done last night. He could not imagine any other woman.

"Here, Congo," he said, putting his share on a piece of birch bark. Spruce grouse could taste like essence of turpentine, but this fat young bird had been feasting on blueberries, and was delicious. A mug of tea, powdered milk and sugar from the screw-topped bottles, a cigarette, the last of today's twenty, and he had three packets left, Monday, Tuesday, Wednesday.

He was stiff after all that burdened walking, but what could you expect in middle age? He tied the groundsheet to low branches overhead to keep the dew off, spread the waterproof top and pants, unrolled the sleeping bag, and he was still half a night's sleep behindhand. He took Congo for a short stroll in the gloaming, the evening star bright already, a breath of wind from the west, it felt like fine weather.

And so to bed, the loaded gun on his right, Congo on the

other side. We weren't chased today, he thought. I'll know soon enough if we're being chased. *We*, including the innocent hound. He went to sleep.

Congo's low growl woke him in the night, and he touched the dog, and the dog was quiet. Some large animal moved nearby, a lumbering moose on its way to the lake. Far off he heard HOO-HOO-HOO, the sonorous hoot of the Great Horned Owl. HOO-HOO-HOO-HOO, *I'll come for you.* But nobody was coming, and Ash slept again.

It was full early daylight when he woke. He had been right about good weather, a heavy dew, not quite a frost. How delicate the cobwebs were. "Let's have a swim, Congo." But while the dog paddled about, enjoying himself, Ash shaved at the water's edge. Long ago in prison he had learned to shave without a mirror — it was easy, even in those pre-Wilkinson days. He had a thing about shaving every day. On the run in Germany, he always shaved if water was available, which all too often it was not. But here thirst never bothered you for long, another point in Canada's favor.

He took off his clothes, and waded down the sandy beach, up to his thighs, and he sat in it, being a dipper rather than a swimmer. The water was warmer than the air, quite perfect, and he heard a plane coming from the south. "Heel, Congo, quick!" He scooped up his clothes, and sought shelter for his nakedness. "Bloody fool." It was carelessness, out of practice, leaving clothes in the open to be seen.

The single-engined plane, low-winged, red and white, a Micmac, flew directly overhead at a couple of thousand feet, and the sound dwindled to the north. He was going somewhere, not looking for somebody.

It was Labor Day, Monday the first of September, and one must expect people in the woods. But the people advertised themselves with a fusillade of shots, giving time to take cover behind rocks. They were a boy and a girl, quite a pretty buxom girl, and the boy had a semi-automatic twenty-two, which he loaded down the magazine slide, and pooped off another ten

182

shots at nothing much, at this tree trunk, at that, a ricochet uncomfortably close. Ash did not like it.

"I'm feelin' horny."

"What, again?"

There was an urgency of zippered clothing, and they went at it, vocally with grunts. The boy was a slow good performer. "Oh, oh! It's killing me."

He finished killing her, and there was silence, and Ash was pinned; it was honest animal, and rather catching. But soon they got dressed and went away.

He started looking for it in the afternoon, a conical rock where he had come onto the logging road. A distance to the left, beside the plane, there had been a big hemlock. He remembered it because he had avoided it, gliding down to pliant balsam fir.

If this was the same road, and it was, the rock must still be there. The shadows were already long when he came on it. Now turn due west. One did want to find the wreckage of one's plane. First find one's hemlock. It was dead, a skeleton of a tree, what woodsmen called (and feared) a dead shakoe, perhaps torched up in his forest fire. The plane was a slanting tangle of aluminium, hidden in second growth.

Ash wondered whether anyone else had ever found it, probably not. Nobody, except perhaps a prospector, would have any reason to visit a cemetery of burned-out woods, or the useless poplar and wire birch that first grew again.

Having found the wreckage of eleven years ago, he lost interest in it, and became interested in finding a reasonable camp. That meant turning south, away from his fire. He knew that there was a brook that way, having crossed it on the road. He came to the brook. Much more important, Congo looked busy. *Ha-loost, then,*" he said, and the dog went to work.

They were a family of young ruffed grouse, commonly called birch partridge, the other species, not tame like the spruce grouse, but new to it. It would be dark soon. Even if that boy and girl were in earshot, which was unlikely, they would be making for home after the long hard day of it. Congo flushed the birds up trees where they sat. He shot one sitting with the .22, and one flying with the four-ten, competent work.

He listened while Congo fetched them to him. Someone might have heard, but nobody called. It was a babbling brook, a cheater of ears, so he moved away until he could not hear it, and made camp for the second night.

So far so good, he thought as he lay with the dog and the gun beside him, watching his moon, which was nearly a half moon now. There were no mosquitoes to pester on the first night of September. He had killed fresh food twice, and his stomach was holding out, vitally important when on the run. He had seen small trout in the brook, and that might be breakfast. So far it was more like a camping holiday than an escape.

One walked by day with vigilance, and with the sharper senses of a dog for added warning. One did not blunder across Germany by night, being chased half the night, having one drink from a muddy puddle, and then lying up the whole waterless day. One did not stagger, fevered and exhausted, through a blizzard in the wild March weather.

So far it was cushy. All well, unless — there were two unlesses — first, unless he made a bad or unlucky mistake. Second, unless and until they found his trail from Anvil Lake, he was fairly safe. Cushy, he thought, closing his eyes to shut away that moon. Just a mite too cushy. Then he had quite a different thought, dogging him from time to time. *We were happy until you came*, Lorna said. He grunted, and the dog stirred, and soon he went to sleep.

The third day began very well. Worms were none too plentiful, but he turned over rocks and found a few, cut himself a pole, baited one of Bobby's hooks, and caught four unsophisticated trout for breakfast.

He came to the end of the logging road, which debouched on to the main highway at a settlement. Congo had whined his quiet warning half a mile back. Congo knew the score by now — people were to be hidden from.

184

Ash sidetracked west through hellish thick woods, turned north again, and bided his time. There was some traffic, but you could hear it coming. "Heel, Congo." They crossed the highway, safe again.

But he had to make two long detours that day. The first was to the west round a blueberry barren. There were bear tracks in the woods and purple bear droppings everywhere, but no bears. Blueberry time was not quite over yet, and one had to be careful not to eat too many. At the edge of the forest the goldenrod had faded, and the last and best of all the flowers was coming out, the wild blue aster. Already some maples were turning for the fall, not the sugar maple, the red, an occasional crimson splash among greens.

He headed north by compass again. The second detour was for a lumber operation, and a big one, the throaty harshness of many chain saws, the clank and roar of skidders. This time he went east through forest slaughtered a year ago, and was into budworm country.

They were using DDT in the summer that he had sprayed. There were no birds and no insects in the woods, and salmon parr floated on the rivers. They had finished most things off except the budworms which grew resistant and flourished exceedingly. Recently they had switched from deadly DDT to things called organo-phosphates, supposedly less persistent and less toxic to the animal world, and still the budworm prospered. He had thought in that year, when he was making good money doing a dangerous flying job, that the job was madness, a colossal ill-informed mistake, perpetuating the infestation instead of letting it run its devastating course. He still thought so, and so did everyone with any sense. And on the spraying went.

That third day was a hard one, and he made little progress to the north. "You know, Congo," he said, after bully beef and the last of the loaf for supper. The dog cocked his head to listen to whatever gems of wisdom temporary master might impart. "You know, Congo, you're a wonderful help to me. You're fun to be with, and your senses warn me every time. But how the hell can I jump a freight with you in attendance? And it wouldn't be cricket to man's best friend, it is entirely out that I should leave you in the lurch. You do present complications, Congo." The dog put his head between his paws and watched him in that way he had.

If there had been no Congo, he would have changed his original plan, formed hastily — that Lorna should drop off the suitcase for him at some place prearranged by telephone. If they suspected any involvement on her part, it would be far too risky for her.

If no Congo — he would have reached the main C.P.R. Montreal line, single track, and he would have walked to a siding and have waited for an express freight train. With any luck, there might even be a car transporter, he saw himself climb to the top of the stack, that damned imagination of his, pick the lock, and ride in comfort to, say, Sherbrooke, buy clothes there and rent a car to Montreal, he had his Arnott driving license with him.

"You have no collar and no tag, Congo," he said. It was getting dark, and for the first time he was very tired. "She took it off. No, that's wrong. Jake took it off when he put you to bed. So supposing I tie you by the nylon cord to a tree outside some tidy respectable-looking house, say *Stay, Congo*, and leave a note simply stating the owner's telephone number. Then, if she is tapped or Jake is tapped, they know instantly where I have been. Or I could write down the Kellys' number, I suppose. That might be it."

It was all so damned muddling. They would be watching main roads everywhere, so roads and hitchhikes were out. They would be watching commercial flights from Fredericton, so they were out. Yes, difficult. He slept fitfully on the third night, his back aching on hard ground. The railway is only fifteen miles north, he thought, awake again. I must decide tomorrow.

But in the late afternoon of tomorrow, which was Wednesday, he heard the sound that he had feared all along. It was the inimitable blatter of a helicopter, turbocopter, growing from the south, passing out of sight, fading to the north. But it faded no more. The noise remained constant, as was the way with a helicopter landing. It might be discharging passengers and awaiting them. Ash heard the engine slow, and heard no more.

It could mean that they had picked up his trail at Anvil Lake, had leapfrogged north, picked it up again, leapfrogged again, found it again. Leapfrogged this time, no trail to find. They might have him bracketed.

Ash was up at dawn on Thursday morning, and so was the helicopter. This time it chopped from north to northeast, steadily across on what sounded like an easterly heading, not checking in movement until the sound was cut off abruptly beyond wooded hills this side of the Mallabec River.

He had no appetite, but he managed a partridge leg, and the crust of a loaf for padding, having stripped the other leg for Congo.

"Bloody helicopters never fly for fun," he said. It could be doing various things. It could be making a geological probe for anomalies, some kind of prospecting job. It culd be undertaking a hopeful post mortem to the summer's spraying, or a check on the night migration of the adult moths, that kind of entomological fun and games. And so on. It could be trying to pick up his trail.

If that was the case, and commonsense dictated that one must proceed from such a premise, the obvious thing to do was to head in the direction where dogs might now be drawing a blank. It was paradoxical, ironical, that his plotting and planning of Diamond's flight had been practice for this, just as his own escapes long ago had been.

Compass variation: call it twenty-west, so a magnetic course of roughly sixty-five. That put him near enough to the highest point in those inconsiderable hills. He had not had to use the compass in earnest before, and if he could have fairly frequent glimpses of that hill to keep him right, he would not need it again this morning.

The first bad thing was that the pull of the packstrap had done something to his right shoulder, which ached tiresomely.

The first good thing was that a half-grown rabbit, the snow-shoe hare of winter, hopped across slowly. "Fetch it, Congo."

Congo brought the screaming beast. Unlike tender-hearted Diamond, Ash wrung its neck, expelled the urine, and put it in his poacher's pocket. That was one anxiety relieved, because food was running short.

The second good thing that happened was that he came to improved woods, selectively cut, in pleasing contrast to the usual charnel heaps of butchery. They were the first cared-for woods that he had encountered since leaving Jake's domain. Walking was much easier, but one was more vulnerable.

The third good thing that happened was the placid brook, a few inches deep with a sandy bottom, sometimes a foot deep, no more than that, and it meandered in his general direction. The brook, not marked on the roadmap, must be a tributary of the Mallabec, which he had to cross.

He walked in the water for a slow but unobstructed mile or two, and Congo needed no persuasion to stick to a popular element. The brook curved gradually left from the hill that had been his aiming mark, yet taking him an easy way to where he wanted to go. But the fording of the Mallabec might be by no means easy.

The helicopter flew again, and they took cover under alders at the bank. It seemed to make a steady beeline from north to south, passing invisibly in the east. That helicopter departed, but there might be more than one. He was not sure about far mutterings behind him.

Any mutterings, if they were not only the children of his tired imagination — and tired ears played tricks by day, just as tired eyes played tricks on the walker in the night — any mutterings were soon lost in the rushing of the Mallabec.

Loud water usually, not always, meant shallow water, too. The wind was capricious here at a low point between the hills astride the river. Congo whined once at the scent of something, and the something in Congo's new way of life more often than not meant *Homo sapiens*.

Ash hid at the junction of brook and river. Here, in this upper reach, the Mallabec was some thirty yards wide. He saw nobody, and Congo whined no more.

It was a shallow riffle, with some white water at larger rocks. Below that, the Mallabec dropped over an unbroken ledge to tumble into a black deep pool.

The water was crystal clear, and he could see sunlit stones all the way across. It should be easy enough if one kept one's footing. He cut himself a wading pole of alder — too pliable, but it would have to do — and went upstream a little for leeway. To stumble, fall, be swept into that pool with a pack on one's back would not be funny.

He transferred the precious gun to his left shoulder, took the pole in his right hand, and started out, prodding for depth, planting downstream to secure each step. He could have done with some wire round the rubber soles of Bobby's hunting boots, but he had no wire. To be in Dan's shoes would indeed be very nice, he thought absently or absurdly. But at the moment he preferred Bobby's boots.

Congo, trying to keep at heel, and just out of his depth, was losing ground. "Ha-loost, over there," he said. Given a free rein, the dog jumped, splashed and paddled, and was soon across. Ash made it cautiously through the deepest part, halfway up his thighs, and the bite of the current was strong, his pole thrumming under thrust. But that was past, and the stream eased in shallower water, and he was over.

They rested in cover beyond the river. There was one slice of bully beef left, which he ate, and a hardtack biscuit. He gave a corner of that to Congo. "Good supper coming," he said. "Now we must push on."

It had been slow in the brook, slow crossing the river. The wind was quite strong, veered into the north, he thought, but fickle in the valley. A puff came from the other way across the river, and the hair on Congo's normally sleek back stood on end. The dog growled.

190

"Sit, Congo, stay!" He went back to investigate, dropping to his hands and knees above the river bank.

On the other side stood a police dog, a German shepherd, dark-muzzled, paler in the body. It was motionless but for a questing nose, held high for airborne scent. It wore a harness.

Ash put up his binoculars. Above the dog's shoulders, at the meeting point of the harness, was a round object. One might instantly guess at that — a transmitter. The dog would be trained to follow a known scent on the ground, or the same scent by air, to hunt slowly, the handler homing by volume and direction on the signal. The dog would hunt free, and keep a distance from its quarry.

Ash thought that might be it. Whether it was or not, he had no choice. The dog still stood there. No man was in sight. But probably a man would be within earshot.

He ran back, tied Congo to a tree with the nylon cord, unrolled the sleeping bag, wound it round his left arm, and drew the hunting knife.

This dog would be trained to kill in last resort. It was a powerful animal, and its jaws moved ten times quicker than any movement a man could make. On terra firma he would not have much chance of matching it. In water he might match it.

The dog still stood there, but wind on the back of Ash's neck now carried scent to it, and it waded in and swam.

He waited until it was halfway across, not yet at the deepest place, and he went to meet it. The dog came on, the lips drawing up, the fangs most evident, but Ash heard no snarl above the loud rushing of the Mallabec.

He held it off with his sleeping bag shield, which it tore apart, and he came in under and knifed the dog twice, the first time stopped by the rib cage, the second time through, and the dog thrashed in death.

He hauled it to shallower water by the harness, sheathed his hunting knife, drew the hatchet from his belt, and bashed the transmitter to bits and to silence. Down floated away from his ruined sleeping bag, and blood from the police dog. He looked at the south bank, the right bank of the Mallabec, no one.

Without entirely leaving the water, he turned the torn bag inside out, manipulated the body into it, added four sizable boulders, tied the bag shut with the tapes, and dragged the whole caboodle down to the ledge where the river dipped. The last bit was tricky, but he managed it, and the loaded sleeping bag, dark green, plopped into the pool and sank out of sight. Some down floated up, and then no more. Ash was exhausted.

His left forearm bled from a few punctures, and began to sting. He washed it in the river water, looked back once more, nobody, and went to join Congo. There was a small first-aid kit, even that provided. He put Mercurochrome on his bites, opened a bandage, tore it down, knotted it, wound it on to discourage bleeding, and tied the free ends clumsily with hand and teeth. He was dizzy, his heart slowing down.

Time lost again, but time spent on thwarting pursuit and on averting infection might be held to be rarely wasted. He climbed the valley side, which was steep, and over the brow into hardwood forest, beech, rock maple, the birches, once more vulnerable, not from the air for the canopy was dense, from the ground.

"What would she think of me for that?" he remarked to Congo. But he guessed that Lorna, who felt much as he did in such matters, would heartily approve. Dogs trained to do a man's dirty work were outside the pale of decent dog, damned unfair on them too.

He crossed the hardwood ridge. Then the land dropped again into evergreen forest. The wind blew steadily from the north, where he was heading. By using the old trick of walking through water, he would have expunged a surface trail, but this wind had taken his scent to that dog. Another similar dog could follow upwind. To continue north at present made no sense at all.

Ash began to swing east, and in a while he came diagonally to meet a survey line, a claim line, a boundary line, some kind of a line running due east, compass bearing a hundred and ten.

192

It was a cleared strip, about six feet wide, cut a year or two ago by the look of the stumps.

He stopped to consult the map. He had an ex-pilot's eye for a map, even one as deficient in topography as this. To his right, beyond the ridge, was the Mallabec River, a mile away. To his left, also about a mile away, a secondary road paralleled the river. Ahead, and to the right, Route 301 crossed the river at Mallabec Bridge. Ahead and to the left was a place named Huntingtower, a small dot on the map, two miles north by road from the bridge. Roughly four miles north of the Huntingtower crossroads was the railway line.

His mind recorded the details of the map, such as they were, and he folded it and put it in a pocket. "Come on, Congo," he said to that faithful friend, invaluable ally, number-one-problem dog.

They had been on to him once. They would be on to him again. If he stayed on foot, it was a matter only of time before they cornered him, his one hope the railroad, and tonight. He had decided long ago, long before all this, that prison was not for him again. Dibble's demise did not initiate, it confirmed. His resolve about that had not weakened and never would. He did not feel desperate. He felt remarkably calm at the possibility, the probability of a shoot-out, a withdrawal, a running action against magazine weapons. But Congo?"

The clear strip ran straight to the east, uphill, downhill, it never deviated. He went over a rise, and, climbing unhurriedly toward him, came a bull moose, black-backed, enormously antlered, big as a Clydesdale horse. "Our yield sign, Congo," he said stepping aside. The ungainly, magnificent beast ambled past, paying no attention whatever to them, moose highway, very convenient with a head like that.

Ash left the trail, and climbed to the right, up on to the ridge above the Mallabec valley. He wanted to spy that bridge. The land dropped off ahead, a glimpse through trees of road winding up from river. He took off the pack, a relief to his shoulder, but it still ached badly. "Stay, Congo." He crawled forward to a narrow gap between rocks, safe except from overhead, and no aircraft were sounding. He had a clear view through glasses of the covered bridge, a quiet dark reach of river. Nobody was visible, and gaps in the sides showed that no car was on the bridge. He saw parts of the road, which wound up quite steeply from the river to a side valley or cut. Opposite him, due east, where the valley ridge began again, was a stone quarry, disused, for grass was growing across the entrance.

Things did not seem hot at the moment here. He could cross the road and continue east, or he could turn north again, where he wanted to go. The wind held steady. Go north for a while, keeping back from the road.

He had not gone far when he saw the house. There were a few well-kept houses and neat gardens along the main highways of New Brunswick. But this was a secondary road in the back of more or less beyond, and the house was modern, pleasing, functional, a black shingled roof, painted clapboards, off-white, a faint blush of the pink that looked so well in snow.

The garden was good too, a terrace, a drop wall to the lower lawn, a clump of hydrangeas to one side, a mixed shrub border on the other, annuals against the house, a rock garden too. It had the quality of landscaping that Lorna might have done. It would be an unusually appealing house and garden anywhere.

There was a sign with lettering on it beside the curved driveway, at the head of which stood a station wagon. Ash moved on until he could read the sign through his glasses.

COLBY PARKER

Farm Machinery

Lumber   Feeds

Fertilizers   Insecticides, etc.

OFFICE: *Huntingtower* 216

A modest sign, but new. "It looks like the very place for you, Congo. But how?"

A young woman came out to stand on the terrace, one arm akimbo. She was a dark-haired girl, her nose too long for prettiness. She wore narrow slacks and a high-necked sweater, a certain grace, a difference about her that was in keeping with the place. She stood, perhaps listening, and went in again.

Ash decided what to do. He would retrace his steps a bit, cross the road, take Congo as near to the edge of the garden as he dared, and tie him there. But first the message. He tore off a section from the bottom of the map, far south of here, and wrote on the back: *Please call* 539-3040. A tied dog gives tongue sooner or later, usually sooner, and so would Congo.

But she came out again, carrying a child's push tricycle. She lifted the small boy on to it, tickled him, kissed the top of his head, happy young family, rather good to see. It was one of the things that Ash had missed in a life that was a wasted procession, leading so justly, so inevitably to this, a hard and painful thought, and he crouched in the bushes.

She was weeding her dahlias, legs straight, bending with a girl's suppleness. At twenty-three or whatever she had a figure almost as good, not quite, as Lorna at thirty-eight. He was not desperate about his plight, which could hardly be worse in probable futures. But he had a desperate longing to see Lorna again, be with her again, be with her at last.

The girl straightened, and lifted a hand. "Listen, Dickie!" she called across there, her voice distinct, excited, tuneful. "Daddy's coming!"

It was a while before Ash heard the plane. Then the sound grew rapidly from the east, beyond the house, and it came into view, red and white, low wing, a Micmac, like the one the other day, some other day in the tiring march of days, a coincidence.

The plane circled twice, in one long continuous steep turn while the girl danced up and down on the terrace, waving both arms, and her small boy did the same. It was indeed good and happy and sad to see. The plane flew away north, and she picked up the child, ran to the station wagon, drove out, and turned in that direction.

Ash had changed his mind before she was out of the driveway. "Stay, Congo," he said for the n'th time, and took the gun. He ran to the road, looked right and left, both ways deserted. It was soon after four, the time of day that he had said he would try to call. The living room with the big window was to the left, a telephone on a table. He knew from the number that it was not a party line, and there was no dialing tone.

"Five, three-nine, three-oh-four-oh," he said assuming a suitable accent, which he could do.

It was answered at the second ring. "Hullo. Nelson Kelly speaking."

"Hullo, Nelson. Route three-oh-one, the Mallabec Bridge."

A pause. A rustle of paper. "Yes, got it."

"Climb out of the valley northward. At the top of the hill, half a mile or so, a disused quarry on the right. Coast clear, turn into it."

"Yes, got that."

"And say that our darkie friend is with me. Oh, and I could do with some cigarettes."

"Okay. Keith and I are coming. Too risky for the other party. You know the balloon is up?"

He laughed. "Yes, I do." But then his thought was that he would not see her.

"In two hours about. If no good the first time, we'll go farther on and come back later."

"Okay. Thank you, Nelson." Thanks to this unflappable young man were much in order.

He wiped off the receiver, not for prints, but because it glistened from his sweaty hand. Safely down and across the road, not with much to spare.

A car came fast from the river direction, slowed and stopped. It was a police car, radio crackling. A constable got out and went up to the house.

196

Ash moved closer to Congo, who whined. "S'ssht!" And the dog was quiet.

"Come in, two-three."

The constable ran down. "Two-three," he said.

"Where are you?"

"At Colby Parker's, just checking, but nobody's home."

"Listen, then! Larry lost transmission from his dog, west of you, south of the river. We're pretty sure the guy's headed north. But the other dog's bin on a lost-kid job over Moncton way, we'll get it tomorrow if still needed. Turn left at the Huntingtowers four corners, watch that two mile straight, dead flat, you can see the whole of it."

The constable acknowledged and drove away.

A respite from dogs until tomorrow. But they were pretty sure the guy was headed north, and north meant the railroad to them as to him. What else?

"Nothing else," Ash said. He shouldered that pack again, and turned back to the south.

21

". . . NOT EVEN A SNAPSHOT, MRS. ASH?"

"Not that I know of. You see, Corporal Leblanc, he was living really like a hermit here. Well, not a hermit, because he saw us quite often, but he never went out."

"You mentioned a boat picnic, the sergeant says."

"Yes, that's quite right. I didn't go on it." Bobby had said, when his film came back *Y'know, Mum, I wanted to get a decent one of Uncle, and look what happens! Keith shoves in front of him. Like a hole in the head I need a picture of Keith Kelly.* "No photographs, Corporal. Or I've never seen one."

Leblanc nodded. He did not quite overflow his jacket and his pants, but bulged muscularly in them. Nice cop, and he fancied her mature appeal, still nicer. "Would you describe your brother-in-law, Mrs. Ash?"

"Let me see — he's about six feet, no, a little less. His hair is what they call iron gray. His features are sort of boney, with a high-bridged nose. He's tanned, and he looks a bit weather-beaten. And his eyes, let's see, they're a rather pale blue. He was very thin after his illness, but spare would be more like it now. That's really all I can think of, Corporal."

"His weight, Mrs. Ash?"

"Gracious, I don't know men's weights."

"Mr. Tovey says about a hundred and seventy-five."

"Jake would know. Just average, I guess, wide in the shoulders and narrowing down. That's all I can think of." Too many alls she could think of, or much fewer than.

"Any visible scars and marks, Mrs. Ash?"

"None I can think of."

198

"Mr. Tovey thinks he's taller than you say, around six-two."

"He might be, Corporal. Heights are difficult." I'm five-foot-eight, she thought. And I fit all right to whatever it is. "Is there anything else I can help about?"

"Would you say that Mr. Ash would stand out in a crowd?"

"In a crowd of country people, I don't think particularly. Quite a lot of the older generation around here have that kind of lean face. But among . . . But in a city crowd perhaps Nigel would look different."

She had stopped herself from saying: *But among overfed city types.* Corporal Leblanc, being overfed himself, would feel a little hurt. One should never hurt the feelings of a well-disposed policeman. The telephone rang beside her chair. "Hullo . . . No, she's busy at the moment. Please call later.

"That was *The Herald Advertiser.* And I suppose there will be others. What do I say to them?"

"That you have been instructed to say nothing pending police investigations. That won't stop them asking questions, but don't answer, Mrs. Ash. *No comment,* is your answer. If you say nothing, the media can think up nothing."

"There isn't anything to think up."

"No," he said, the "No" sounding equivocal, perhaps. Supper with Nigel was the cause of it, the rub, the trouble. He continued: "The sergeant would like you to write out a statement."

"But I've already made statements *ad nauseam.*"

"Notes were taken only of the first part, Mrs. Ash, when I was present. It would be helpful. Just in your own words, I could pick it up tomorrow."

"Oh, well," she said. "Anything to please that sergeant-sleuth of yours."

Leblanc h'mmed, getting up to go. "That might take some doing, Ma'am." He thinned his lips, no love lost there. "Goodnight, Mrs. Ash. Get a good rest now."

The Herald Advertiser came on again. "If you want information, please ask the police."

"Did you see your brother-in-law last evening, Mrs. Ash?"

199

"No comment." But how rude that sounded, guilty too. "I'm so sorry," she said. "Them's my orders. Goodbye."

Then Grace Skafe called to say that her Husky was away — *my* Husky, oh, my God — and would Lorna like to come for lunch on the boat tomorrow, just the two of them, grass widows? An escape to cozy chats with Grace. "I'd love to," she said. "But I have a sort of statement to write out. Would twelve be all right?"

Keith and Nelson came for the suitcase, and after they had left, she went out to the terrace again. HOO-HOO-HOO — HOO-HOO, a deep pleasing voice down in the woods. And Lorna turned to trace the pointers to the Pole Star. I wonder if a Great Horned Owl hoots tonight for Nigel too, she thought.

There's no story until it's done, he said. It was not yet twenty-four hours since these deer were dead. And she supposed that the deer of his unfinished story might be dead at the finish of that story, but she did not know.

The telephone unplugged, the sleeping pill taken, two in two nights when she hardly ever took the wretched things, and her prayers and into bed. Hoot again for me, Owl. But her wish was not answered.

Mabel Tovey came to clean on Mondays, and Jake brought *The Herald Advertiser*, displaying headlines: *Bank President's Brother Sought in Killing*. "No thanks, Jake," she said, knowing that in a part of himself, despite himself, Jake would be titillated about the horror drama. "If anyone comes or if anyone calls, please say I'm out all day. And if the cops want me, I'll be in this evening."

"That sergeant is a mean foxy sonuvagun."

"Loathsome cold fish, I hate him."

"I wouldn't tell him so, if I was you, dear, no, I wouldn't," said comfortable Mabel.

She shut herself in Dan's study and wrote the statement of events as they were known to her, and that meant almost nothing. It tallied exactly with what she had said, and she added

200

minor embellishments to be the little woman anxious to tell all, like the two Milkbone biscuits Congo had at bedtime, and the funny doom feeling she had had for no reason at all when she was going to sleep, a hunch or something. And she signed it.

The Skafes' boat rumbled in shipshape splendor. ". . . I didn't know Simon was away."

"He went to David Dorrien's funeral in Ireland," said Grace at her petit point. "That's the artist, Anna's husband. Such a nice weak man, and the bottle got him. Poor Husky didn't want to go one little bit, but he felt he had to for that Anna's sake. Well, let's have a drink."

Subject closed, after the nearest thing to a carpy comment that Lorna had heard from Grace. She had met Simon's first wife once in Montreal, a splendid I-don't-give-a-damn female creature, as different from this sweet conventional as a woman could be.

But Grace was genuine, a respecter of persons, quite incurious. She neither enlarged upon whatever lurked concerning that Anna, her predecessor, nor beyond saying: "I feel so much for you and Dan about this thing," did she allude to the killing of Randy Dibble.

A fifty-foot cruiser, a crew of two, a couple of grass widows in the sunny stern, tucking into pâté de fois gras, the real thing from Strasbourg, *ça va sans dire*, watching a whale blow beyond the islands, where it was so much cooler, quite nippy today with a rug over one's pampered shoulders. "It is September, dear, after all." And back again, and she prattled on. "I always think it's so nice between the islands." That too-nice word from the good woman.

Dan loved these plush trips on their ocean-going vessel. But it, they, would make Nigel climb the wall. Or he might endure it once to watch the phalaropes. A myriad small birds bobbing on the water, yielding last moment passage to the intruder, settling again in a chop of current.

". . . I always think Labor Day draws a line across the year."

201

"Yes," Lorna said. You always think, and you don't have an original thought in your nice noodle. But she was grateful, and said so nicely, and escaped home.

"Any word, Jake?"

"Nothin', Mrs. Ash. The corporal was here, but I said you was out in the boat, and he'll be back tomorrow. He as good as said they haven't a clue where Nigel's gone."

On Tuesday, Leblanc came, and he read the statement. "Funny things, hunches," he said, not being a policeman for the moment. "I remember having a kind of uneasy feeling when I went to bed that night, no reason for it. And the next thing they called at two ack-emma to say my Aunt Yvonne was in a head-on collision, killed outright. My Aunt Yvonne raised me, Mrs. Ash."

"Oh, I'm sorry," she said.

But he reverted to being a cop. Did her brother-in-law have camping equipment at the cottage?

"Not that I know of," she said. Do her very very honest best. "But we have some here."

"None missing, Mrs. Ash?"

"There couldn't be. But come to the cellar and let's have a look."

The cupboard was still loaded with camping stuff, not quite so crammed full as it had been. Dan showered things on Bobby: the latest pup tent, gas cooker, lantern, compass, the latest anything.

"It's all here," she said.

"And plenty," Corporal Leblanc said thoughtfully, not in his Aunt Yvonne mood. "That lot would outfit three men."

"My husband used to be a mad keen camper, and he always hopes our son will get the bug. But he never has yet, not even in his Cub days."

"They do or they don't, Mrs. Ash. Make it too easy, and they don't."

How right the wise corporal was. Upstairs again, he said: "We checked the cottage. Here's your key back, Mrs. Ash."

People came and went. The telephone rang. Was it tapped? Did they really suspect her of being an accomplice, of being, what was it called, an accessory after the fact? As if that mattered. *They won't catch me*, he said. *I will not be taken*, he meant.

Jake returned from his dinner to say it had been on the news there was a lead to the Saint John docks, a man answering the description. "Could be, Mrs. Ash. With a bit of luck, he could easy have run it through, no traffic to speak of at that time of night."

"I suppose so," she said. "Jake, I think I'll go down to the cabin. You could give me a buzz if anything happens."

The Saint John docks, a long way east of here, would take the heat off north of here. A Saint John lead might account for the absence of that pestilential sergeant.

Tuesday afternoon at the cabin, alone and undisturbed except by Nigel everywhere, time dragging on. He said once: *Time has no meaning until it's forgotten.*

She walked along the shore, hoping to find a Kelly, and she did. "Nothing so far, Mrs. Ash," Keith said. "And if we do get a call, we may have to move pretty quickly."

"Please try to tell me somehow, just that you've had word."

"Nelson thought he might phone you as from Rob's Grocery about an order. He worked there two summers, he knows the jargon." Keith looked at her, and looked away. "I don't think it's likely Nigel will call. He can't thumb a ride or take a flight. He can't pinch a car and get far with it. We think a freight train is what he'll try for."

"But, Keith, don't you see, a man and a dog can't jump a freight. And he'll never leave Congo in the lurch. That's what Nigel is like."

"Yes," Keith said. "I guess that is what Nigel's like. But he might tie Congo outside the right sort of house, leave a telephone number, ask them to call it."

"And that number will be yours," she said. "If it's ours, and we're tapped, they can close in on him right away. I am so sorry to have dragged you into this."

Keith laughed. "Not to worry, Mrs. Ash, as Nigel himself would say. Besides, Nelson and I are bored with virtue."

"I know the feeling," she said. "Thank you, Keith. So a call from Rob's Grocery means you've heard." She went back to the cabin, thinking that the ultimate compliment such reticent young people could pay was to call an elder by Christian name. I'm still Mrs. Ash, she thought, locking the door. I haven't graduated to the eminence.

Dan was flying back on Wednesday, and would call from the office. He did, soon after three.

"Oh, hullo, Dan, safely home. Did you have a good flight?"

"The usual," he said. "Are you all right, dear?"

"Fine," she said. "It's been a bit of a hoo-ha."

"Any news down there — developments, I mean?"

"Not a thing," she said.

"When I'd been through the Customs, a fellow came up, plain-clothes R.C.M.P. and he wondered if he could ride into town with me. So I said sure, and he said he had been asked to ask one thing — did I know whether any of the country round Gallery was familiar to my brother. So I said I didn't think so really, but I believed he once had a plane crash north of there, and he had walked out to a place called Anvil Lake, where our son went fishing with him last month. Did you tell them that, Lorna?"

"No," she said. "I forgot about that."

"But Bobby went on about it."

"If you had heard Bobby going on about as many things as I have this summer, you would have forgotten them too. Do you know you've only been down three weekends? What kind of life is that for me?"

"I know," he said. "It's been very bad. I'm sorry, dear. Things keep piling up. Couldn't you close the house and come?"

"No, I couldn't. There's all the garden to put away. And besides, you know how I love September here."

"Even after what's happened?"

204

"What's happened has happened."

"Lorna, you don't sound like yourself at all. I have a mountainous backlog on my plate, but I think I'd better . . . Yes. I'd better . . ."

She broke into that: "It has been a bit of a shock, Dan, but I'm perfectly okay. Really, I am. Don't you dream of coming."

"I'll come any time, anywhere. You're all that matters, you know that, don't you?"

"Dear Dan," she said, and meant, and she soon escaped him, damn him.

It was not until noon on Thursday that Sergeant Borton came, alone. "You will be interested to learn, Mrs. Ash, that your jeep is at the bottom of Anvil Lake, or so we deduce from tire tracks, scratches on rock, cable marks on a tree, a small oil slick on the surface below the anvil that gives the lake its name."

"At the bottom of Anvil Lake? Good gracious! Anvil Lake — my husband reminded me that our son Bobby went fishing there with his uncle." It sounded like that old game, Happy Families. "I had quite forgotten."

"Your forgetfulness cost us three days, Mrs. Ash."

"I suppose it did," she said. "I'm sorry. You've no idea what a rat race the summer season at Gallery is, particularly with a teenage son on the razzle-tazzle. So much happening, I forget things from one day to the next."

"It would have been more sensible and more economical of jeeps if he had got you to drive him there."

"What on earth do you mean? Are you being sarcastic, Sergeant Borton?"

"No, Mrs. Ash, I am stating the obvious."

"You are stating the ridiculous. I know nothing about it. I was asleep."

"I have a few suggestions to make, Mrs. Ash." His curiously blank eyes left her face only while his left forefinger tapped his right small finger. "I suggest, first, that you were at the cottage with your brother-in-law when the deer were killed." Next finger. "I suggest, second, that you drove up with him. How else would he have got here quickly enough to intercept them? As to your presence or not at the murder of Randy Dibble, I make no suggestion." Next finger. "I suggest, third, that you out-fitted Nigel Ash with food, and with camping equipment from the abundant stocks that Corporal Leblanc has seen. It is not possible to trek through the New Brunswick woods without at least minimal equipment. He had none at the cottage, you say. Someone supplied it." Forefinger to forefinger. "And I suggest, lastly, Mrs. Ash, that one convenient lapse of memory serves only to confirm what I suspected already — that you were lying in order to shield your brother-in-law, just as he, for reasons best known to himself, was at pains to shield you. Now, Mrs. Ash, there is still time for the truth, which rests, I would surmise, more easily with you than falsehood."

"That is slander," she said. "You bloodless surmising gargoyle, I'll sue you for that."

His expression did not change one whit. "I am giving you a chance," he said. "If you don't take it, you will in all probability be prosecuted for an offence much more serious than slander."

"I have told you the truth," she said, "and nothing but the truth."

"Very well, Mrs. Ash, on your own head be it." He opened his briefcase, took the typed manuscript and laid it on the table. "I found this interesting. It serves to explain what one might call a *crime passionelle* by a man of obsessive mind. Much more clearly than that, it tells us what kind of a man we have to deal with." He closed his briefcase, so neat, so economical, so prim in movement. "I suppose I would be wasting my time, Mrs. Ash, if I asked you where your brother-in-law is trying to go."

"You would," she said. "I haven't the slightest clue. Why don't you add that to my pack of lies?"

"Very well, Mrs. Ash."

"I suppose I would be wasting my time, Sergeant Borton, if

I suggested that you apply for a transfer to the N.K.V.D., where you belong, and perhaps you do."

The blank cold eyes came alive to glare at her, and his mouth was working. "Rich bitch," he said.

The car drove away. Could it be that she had made the champion guess of all time? Ridiculous, impossible. And what was impossible?

They began on the terrace perennial border in the afternoon. Jake dug and she divided, and they spoke only of the job in hand. They were not seeking him now; they were hunting him down in the mild September weather, just as his man Diamond had been hunted down in wild March weather. "The wind's veerin' east," Jake said. "We'll have a change tonight."

She heard the telephone through the screen door, and she ran to it.

"Rob's Grocery, Mrs. Ash. Just to say we're holdin' your order for the Black Diamond you was wantin', and that's due in on the transfer truck. So we can deliver in the morning. Hope I didn't disturb you, Mrs. Ash."

"No, no," she said. "Many thanks."

Black Diamond cheese. Black Congo dog.

She thought of telling Jake, and didn't. "I guess that's all we have time for," she said.

"I'll put these in the shade, and water 'em." The wheelbarrow squeaked. Why would he never oil the thing?

It had been bad enough the first few days, the police, the media — she disliked the word as much as she disliked the media — solicitous people calling, chance meetings in Gallery when they would say how sorry to hear about it, awkward brief encounters. But now they left her alone, and she was a prisoner in this house, not knowing, not able to help him, intolerable. *It tells us what kind of man we have to deal with.*

"I think the rich bitch will get a bit tight tonight," she said. *Quite amusing*, Nigel would say to that. Just as he would be quite amused about her mad parting shot at Sergeant Borton. Just as Dan would be appalled.

207

But it rang again. "Hullo."

"Hullo, Lorna. It's Simon Skafe. I wonder — would I be intruding if I dropped over for a while?"

"No, Simon. Do please come. Would six be all right?"

A man to talk with, a sure and certain man. She got on well enough with women too, but men were something else again. A bath, a woolen dress, Jake was right about a change of weather coming. She made herself presentable for Simon, a still attractive older man, let's face it, sort of Uncle Simon, who arrived at six and gave her a kiss.

"Grace told me about Anna's husband. It must have been hard for you."

"Not quite a picnic," he said. "Anna is very cut-up, but as wonderful in trouble as she always was. John is staying on to keep her company. Sally and Brian came back with me." John their son, Sally their daughter and her husband. "Ah, well," said Simon Skafe.

The story was that the passionate Anna could not endure being an absentee tycoon's wife, nor the social trappings thereof — hence David Dorrien, hence doting Grace. But the whispered postscript to that story was that it had never ended between Anna and Simon. "Ah, well," he said again, helping himself to the drink she offered him.

Deflated would be the wrong word about Simon, but he looked older, a little stooped. He filled up with water, no ice, and drank half of it. "That's much much better," said the abstemious man. "Just what the doctor ordered. He did, actually."

Easy and disarming, but not dissembling. Straight to the point, as was his way. "Dan telephoned, Lorna. He's worried about you."

"He needn't be, Simon. I'm quite all right."

"Having been away, I'm not well clued-up, but this place seethes with rumor, and the latest one is that your jeep is at the bottom of Anvil Lake."

"So that miserable sergeant told me."

208

He glanced quickly at her, and turned to stand at the window. "There's no question that Nigel killed the man?"

"I don't think there can be, no."

"In cold blood in the back?"

"There were the deer. That wouldn't be quite cold blood."

"But rather more hot blood than jacking deer would seem to warrant."

"Who are you to judge?"

He turned to look at her again. "I'm not judging, Lorna. I am quoting what the world is saying."

"I suppose the world is," she said.

"Your water lilies are still in bloom, I think I see. Shall we stroll down there?"

"Oh, well," said. "Okay. We'd better put on coats."

The weathercock on the flagpole pointed east, but down here the wind eddied, gathering. "Jake said a change was coming."

"Lorna, I detect sore trouble. Would it be a help to tell me?"

"You haven't seen the police?"

"Have a heart, my dear girl."

"I guess I do need a shoulder to lean on." So she told Simon Skafe, a hard man, it was said, an understanding man, it was also said. She told him about the link to the book, about the killing of the deer — "oh, no," he said — about everything then and after, omitting mention of Jake and the Kellys. ". . . I never had to lie before. It makes such a ghastly escalating muddle."

"I used to, but I gave it up, just for your escalating reason."

They went as far as the water lilies. "Very handsome," he said, hardly noticing them, not his kind of thing. "It's a classic case," he said. "One wonders what one would have done oneself. And the answer is that one would not."

"I know," she said. "I come to see that. But Nigel isn't us."

"Who is Nigel? I have something to tell you, Lorna. It wasn't in their news, of course, nothing that happens in Canada ever is. But Grace called while I was over there, so, flying back yesterday I asked Brian — you know Brian Fiske, our son-in-law?"

209

"Yes," she said. "Go on."

"I asked him what he knew about a pilot in the North called Nigel Ash. You see, Brian flew a great deal there in DEW line days, and he still runs our air operation among numerous other things. Well, he had never heard of a Nigel Ash, and would I describe him? And when I had, he said: *The only guy who would answer to that was Neil Arnott, a crackerjack pilot. I knew him quite well, in so far as anyone knew Arnott well.*"

"Did he say any more about this — Neil Arnott, was it?"

"Yes, Neil Arnott. Not much more. Brian said he was a likable chap if he happened to like you. But he had a caustic tongue and an explosive temper, and people were afraid of him. Disillusioned, might be it, nothing worth believing in. A chip on the shoulder, might be it."

"Disillusioned, yes. A chip on the shoulder couldn't be less true of Nigel. Brian's Neil Arnott was somebody else."

"The only time I met Nigel Ash, he certainly gave me no chip-on-the-shoulder impression. But that was here, Lorna, with you."

"Yes, I remember."

"Yen-watching, a deplorable pastime of the elderly."

"Could you hang on a moment? I've been meaning to shut the filter off." She went round the pond, and did that, and came back. "Not a particularly appealing expression," she said. "And not a bit like you."

"Sorry, Lorna. But lately I have been reminded that not even the old are spared that particular sore trouble."

"Yes, Simon," she said. "Yes, it's true. It just happened to us. And now he's gone, and I have nothing to remember."

"Ah, but you have," he said. And they walked up to the house where he downed the rest of his whisky and water.

"Could you do something for me, for us, I mean?"

"Tell me, Lorna."

"Could you make sure that Brian doesn't link Nigel Ash to Neil Arnott. It might be desperately important to him."

"I'll see to that. Not that Brian will. He asked me why I brought up the name of Nigel Ash, and when I told him, he clammed up instantly. To be precise, he said he was quite wrong, because Arnott was a stocky chap, he now remembered. It was a case of the pilots' league, members in good standing, I would suspect. Well, home for me, and thank you, Lorna."

"And thank you for not moralizing."

"I am hardly one to be moralizing. Do you know that . . . ?" But he shook his head slowly. "Better left unsaid."

THE NAME BOTHERED HIM. There was a Huntingtower in Scotland. There was a Buchan novel. But Huntingtower, N. B.? Some tantalus of memory, he could not place it. The more he tried, the more elusive. If there was a Huntingtower, N.B. to be remembered, let it come.

Ash changed his mind again. He had changed it to telephone. He changed it now to reverse direction, have a look at Colby Parker. It was a self-satisfied theory of his that people who could not change their minds were usually petrified vacillators. He lurked in thick cover by the roadside, a hand on Congo's shoulder. A brief tremble as the dog sensed something, and then Ash heard the car. My eyes are better than his, he thought. And with binoculars they are very good indeed. But Congo's nose and ears — how long will I last without him?

The station wagon turned up to stop at the house. Tall girls tended to have husbands to look up to, but this one's husband was inches shorter, a foot broader in the beam, a veritable square man. He took a zipper bag and a rolled cylinder of papers from the back seat. "Why the flight maps, Colby?"

"There's a guy in Ottawa I must see, and that means tomorrow afternoon. You ever hear of a goddam civil servant work Saturdays?"

"No," she said. "Nor Sundays, Labor Days, you-name-it days. Away last night. Away tomorrow night. Lately, it just never stops."

"There's no other way," he said, reminiscent of brother Dan. But there was an earthy punch to this young man, not reminiscent of brother Dan. "Sorry about it, Karen honey. Why not come along?"

But she shook her head, leaning against him. "A real pretty home you made us," he said. "The garden looks better all the time."

"I love it more all the time," she said. "Did you wow the farmer boys up Garvey way?"

"I guess it's paying off," he said. "First, I give a few of 'em your friendly neighborhood dealer buzz. Then I put her down somewhere central and handy. Then I ride around on the bike, getting orders and good farm snacks. Yeah, I guess it is paying off, a new slant to selling."

"Everything you do pays off," she said. "Take the lumber operations. Take the particle board."

"Take you," he said.

"Go on, then," she said, looking down at him. It was a good clinch to watch, but soon he moved his mutton fist from her bottom to her knees, and swung her up over one shoulder. "Me ride, Daddy."

He put his son on the other shoulder, and went for a jog with the giggling pair of them, not a jog, a dance, light-footed as an Eskimo. "That's the phone, Colby." He put her down, and the boy astride his neck. He jumped from the drop wall, jumped up it again, jumped over a flowerbed, gracefully too, like a ballet dancer of rare configuration. "See, Dicky! We can do a lot better without fat Mum."

"Fat Mum!" she said at the door, looking at him with the same woman's look as Lorna's look that last night at the cabin. "It's the Mounties for you," she said, and sat on the doorstep, their son on her knee until Colby Parker came out again.

"Have they caught him yet?"

"Not yet," he said. "But they know he's right around here somewhere. They will."

"I hope they don't."

"Hell, Karen, you can't go around shootin' jackers."

"Yes, I could," she said. "'What was that about?"

"They wanted to know, is the plane secure. He's a pilot, this Ash guy. So I told them it's as secure as in the bank vault, key out, plane locked, hangar door double-locked."

"And the keys are all together," she said.

"It would take a bluebird to find those keys." Colby Parker put an arm round his wife, a slender, full-breasted girl, not pretty, rather beautiful. "I just got to touch you," he said, "and I get these funny feelings."

"Me too," she said. "Come and play with your toys, Dickie. Dad and Mum gonna have a little snooze until suppertime."

They went in. The wind had gone farther to the east, and Ash was cold in his hiding place across the road. He stood now, a rendezvous to meet, to keep, and he walked toward the Mallabec River.

He remembered about Huntingtower. *Jim Hodges bought it at Huntingtower. His engine quit on take-off. With these short-arsed strips, what chance do you have? Too bad about old Jim.*

Too bad about old Nigel Ash. It would take a bluebird to find those keys, which were all together. And if that charming insect-eating bird — so much rarer these days for reasons that were obvious — if it found the keys, the bluebird would be no better off. "I couldn't do it," he said, the wind louder overhead. "I simply could not do it."

But you can. You've been afraid before, and you have faced it, and you've done it.

"Not this," he said. "Not palpitating terrified."

After nine thousand hours, what nonsense! An aircraft you know well, a Micmac, handed to you on a platter. Were you palpitating terrified before?

"No," he said. "I never was. Not until I got what was coming to me."

And are you afraid of other things, of men for instance?

"No," he said. "I'm not."

214

They're closing in on you. You know they are. And you know they'll be waiting for you at the railroad. So there is no alternative. You must grasp your lucky moon.

"For Christ's sake shut up about my lucky moon," he said, afraid.

Tam Diamond was never afraid.

"I'm not Tam Diamond, damn your eyes."

You made him, didn't you?

He had reached the ridge above the river, opposite the quarry. Two hours, Nelson had said, an hour still to go. He sat, rubbing his sore shoulder, eased of the burden of the pack, which Congo sniffed, and then whined at him. It was not a warning whine, but a word of supplication. Like everybody else, Congo had faults, and one was greed. But greed was hardly a fair word for honest hunger. Congo's last proper meal, not even a square one, had been nearly twenty-four hours ago.

"Okay," he said, picking up the pack. He had no hunger himself. He had a bellyache among other aches, but a good officer never forgets the bellies of his men.

A fire was a risk. All risks seemed minor but the risk he dare not try to take. The wind was strong, though, scudding birch-bark smoke flatly away to dissipate. He took the rabbit from the big pocket inside his jacket, skinned and gutted it, and by then the deadwood hardly smoked at all.

The fire burned with a reddish glow, cooking Congo's supper. And in the red glow he saw the red desert at Alice Springs, losing height to it, the thermals terrific in the afternoon, and he took another swig, feeling hazy and happy, bucketed about, let's smarten them up a bit — but the power line, black, thick, sagging, swooped at him between the huts.

Ash wiped sweat off with his sleeve, and stripped the half-cooked meat for Congo. The sight of it nauseated him, so he withdrew to be sick. In a varied experience, being sick and having the trots together had happened to him only once before, and that was with malaria.

But he came back, feeling better, feeling well enough to smoke his last cigarette, seeing that power line in the dying fire. "I can't," he said. "I simply cannot do it."

And a man from somewhere in memory said to him *You must believe. Be silent and sit still.*

He was silent and sat still, and it did not help. As always, action helped a little. He found water and dowsed the fire. "Come on, Congo. Time to go."

The object of all this was to get dog home to mistress safely, so perhaps one last precaution: He made a leash of the nylon cord and walked into wind. *An east wind ain't bad,* said Jake, the pundit. *Southeast to south is bad.* But the sky was overcast, and clouds were low, and it was blowing up.

He leashed Congo to the pack, and moved forward to the same place as before to spy the covered bridge. They would come that way, but what they would come in, he did not know.

Life was waiting, as he had so often thought, waiting for the better, or the worse, or simply waiting. In this immediate time, it was waiting to do a swap, one black dog for one small suitcase. And beyond that, what? Beyond that, either or. Either try to face the element which he used to love, as Saint-Exupéry had loved it in a godly if too fanciful way, the element of freedom. Either try to face that once again, or be extinguished in a sordid little gunfight. If he must die now soon, he would be ready. It would be sad for him, having found what he had never found in — what had it been for Diamond? — in the unhappy voyage of his life.

"Perfect nonsense," he said. "My life has been a fruitless cock-up, not unhappy. No contentment, true. But contentment also is a cow."

He laughed, amusing fellow. Bluejays were crying up for wind and weather. A green car passed from the Huntingtower direction, wound downhill, in and out of sight, and stopped at open ground before the bridge. Two men got out, a thin man and an outsized man, a beefy bugger, one would call him. They were quite dressy in tweed jackets. He watched them through

216

his glasses, cops, awaiting something, someone. Cops must also wait.

The second vehicle on Route 301, also headed south, was a laden pulp truck with its own grab-loader. It came almost to a stop. Colby Parker, Huntingtower, N. B., on the cab door, ubiquitous Colby Parker, pulling New Brunswick up by its worn elastic bootstraps. A modicum of intelligence and good judgment, a spur of ambition, a barrel of energy — they were what it took. Ambition is what I lacked, Ash thought.

The driver engaged his lowest gear, and started slowly and noisily, a tricky descent with a heavy load. So loud was the noise of the truck downwind that the helicopter gave him almost no warning as it came upwind, too little warning to do more than bury his tired light head in his arms.

It hovered, descended to the open place, and the smaller man, ducking his head and clutching a briefcase, climbed aboard. The turbocopter rose and made an angled beeline for Huntingtower. The beefy bugger got in and drove off south. The pulp truck arrived to line itself up, to squeeze by a smidgen through the covered bridge.

By good luck rather than good management Nigel Ash had escaped unseen. Good luck and lucky — if he thought those words again, he would emit a banshee scream.

He looked at his watch, six twenty-three, they should be coming soon. His immediate first problem was that cover was sparse opposite the quarry, so he should be there as briefly as possible. Therefore it made best sense to stay here, exposed as he was to a small segment of that element — segment, element, how stupid works did link. He would wait until he saw a likely car, and then move quickly.

The black Volkswagen swung down to the bridge and emerged this side, a battered beetle, its front bumper askew. It had the right sort of look, a Kelly ambience, one might guess, and one might guess wrong. At any rate, it was not the kind of car in which a self-respecting policeman would go about his business.

He ran back to Congo and the pack, so much lighter now, so much more burdensome, and he slithered with dog and encumbrance down the steep slope to crouch in brown brush-killed vegetation at the roadside. 2,4,5,T was the stuff they used here, as in Vietnam.

The car announced itself with a Volkswagen's faithful rasp and stopped short of the quarry entrance, Keith Kelly driving, engine off, Nelson out on the other side. He made a circuit of the machine, ostensibly a tire inspection, stood still, head cocked. Then he jerked his thumb once, a nonchalant economical gesture toward the quarry, into which he walked, turned a full circle, and pointed to the left.

Ash followed the car. It was a small quarry, the sides broken and untidy except where Nelson had instructed his brother to park against a vertical wall, giving some cover from the west.

Congo was pleased to see his neighbors. "Things are hotching a bit," Keith said. "Good boy, Congo, in you hop."

But the dog did not obey. He stiffened and gave his brief bothered whine. Now the pulsating beat of the helicopter. It gathered swiftly, passed low and close and out of sight, flying south. "Which way do you head from here?"

"On north, it'll have to be. A plainclothes corporal stopped us a couple of miles back. He showed his card, had a good look at our tent and fishing gear in back, and waved us on. They know Congo's missing, so I guess we turn right at Huntingtower four corners and make a wide sweep before we head for home. Eh, Nelson?"

"Right. But this place isn't too healthy. Can we take you on?"

"Did the corporal have a car?"

"Green. No markings."

"That's it, two of them, one got into the chopper." But gripes in his belly, he doubled up, couldn't help it.

"You look tuckered up," Nelson said.

"My stomach is in slight revolt," he said. "Okay otherwise."

"We brought some of Doctor Pugsley's special stuff, it's in the case."

218

"How in God's name did you think of that?"

"Mrs. Ash said you wrote it in the book — about a man's stomach being the first thing to go."

"Well, I hope old Pugsley's treatment does the trick like last time."

"Still the same old Nigel Ash," Keith said, with some affection.

The wind boomed about this place, and Nelson went to the road to watch and listen. "Nothing. Can we take you on?" he said again.

"There's a house on the right a mile up the road, a chap called Colby Parker. After the bend beyond that, could you drop me?"

"Sure. Colby Parker — isn't he the flying guy?"

"That's him," Ash said. "I called you from the house when his wife went to meet the plane."

"Let's go," Nelson said. "I don't like this place. Can't see. Can't hear." He went to the road again. "Okay Keith. Come out."

A crush behind of Nelson, Congo, the pack, their gear. Ash sat in front with the gun. It was bad enough to make them bring the suitcase, fetch the dog. But to incriminate them by riding with them, a craven craving company.

"Where does he keep his plane?" Keith asked.

"At the spraying strip west of Huntingtower. I've never been there, but we knew about it for forced landings."

"Yes, I see. Your case is under the hood. Cigarettes, old Pugsley's potion, and we squeezed in a few sandwiches and bananas. Presumably we take the pack with us?"

"I don't know," he said. It was so obvious what he should try to do, and could not do, but what else to do?

Keith glanced quickly at him and back at the road. "You don't look in any shape to carry both," he said.

"I'm not," Ash said.

"Why not stay with us?" Nelson said behind. "If we keep to the back roads, we might get away with it, even cross into Quebec or Maine."

"Not a hope," he said. "Here's the house." The station

219

wagon was there, no lights, no sign of activity. Parker might still be having a little snooze with his smashing wife. "Not a hope," Ash said, "because I killed a police dog, and they know it's missing. But how did they cotton on about the jeep?"

After a pause, Nelson said: "I guess they just came on wheelmarks or something."

Keith slowed and stopped, and Ash got out. "My only chance is the one I can't take," he said.

"That plane?"

"Yes," he said. "I pranged one half-sozzled in Australia three years ago, and I lost my nerve, never flew again, plain terrified."

"You can will yourself to anything," Keith said, taking out the suitcase. "Do you know the type of plane?"

"Yes, well," he said. "It's the type I pranged. That only makes it worse."

"Yes, I see," Keith said.

"I don't see," said Nelson, square-jawed, implacable. "And the person I'm thinking of is Mrs. Ash. Don't you know what she's been through about all this, having to lie and lie and lie for you?"

"Yes," he said. "I was wrong. I was trying to keep her out of it, though."

"We know that," Nelson said.

"How is Lorna?"

"She's just great." Nelson scowled at him. "Do you want us to tell Lorna you've chickened out?"

"That's a dirty crack," he said.

"I know. I'm provoking you. Wouldn't she do the same?"

"I suppose she would," he said. "Goodbye, then, Congo." He leaned in to pat him. "Congo warned me of the police dog. He warned me of people a dozen times. You might tell Lorna that, and ask her to buy him a super steak, I will reimburse the lady."

"Any other messages?" Keith said.

"Oh well, love and that sort of thing."

They both smiled about that sort of thing, his sort of trouble, which they seemed so well to understand.

"Good luck, Sir," Nelson said.

"Good luck, Sir," Keith said.

I call you Sir, you measure up, you old poltroon. "Thank you," he said. "You're a pair of cool cats, as I have remarked before."

They did not ask him again about the pack. They drove away with it. He shouldered his weapon, picked up his suitcase, and entered the forest. *Lean, wind, lean,* he thought, wishing that he had quoted Keith's words to him. The wind did lean loudly on the treetops, and that helicopter came beating up again. Much more wind would ground the bloody chopper, but so would darkness.

It was early twilight. He walked through young Colby Parker's timber limits, presumably his timber limits. "I know what I should have done," he said. "I should have pointed my little gun at Colby Parker, stuck him up to fly me." But he was inclined to think that the muscleman would take a bit of sticking up.

He went north, crossed the road east of Huntingtower, turned west, crossed the other road into dense woods, moving parallel to the two-mile straight, which one patrol car was, or had been, watching. He reached the strip as darkness fell, not provoked into courage, but more afraid.

BLUNDERING THROUGH THICK WOODS was bad enough by day. In the fading light it had been hideous, but now at last open ground ahead, a narrow avenue in the forest. He lay down to rest, the suitcase a hard pillow for his head. He had eaten little that day, and he had lost what he had eaten, and the chills grew in him.

"I should eat," Nigel said, an abhorrent thought. He opened the suitcase and used the pocket flashlight to find old Pugsley's potion, *two tablespoons four times a day, shake well*, were the instructions. A sup and a sup approximated two generous spoonfuls. The taste was awful, but he felt or imagined an immediate soothing in his guts.

A car turned in to cross the strip, its headlight on a low building, Parker's hangar, set back from the north side of the runway. A man in uniform walked forward to the building door, looked at it and walked back. The car turned away to rejoin the road, lighting first the windsock, streaming horizontally, then the far end of the strip.

Ash tucked the binoculars back inside his jacket. Even supposing he could force himself, will himself as those damned Kellys put it, will himself to have a try, how could he possibly if they kept checking the aircraft hangar?

The wind was stronger, and very cold. He took his Burberry from the top of the case which he shut again. It helped a little, even in this dry-mouthed fearful pit, to consider from outside, as it were, his tatterdemalion self, wearing an old cloth cap, a smart raincoat, sodden hunting boots and filthy trousers, a suitcase in one hand, a gun on the other shoulder, bumbling along a graveled airstrip.

222

The night was starless, but not dark, a waxing moon above the clouds. He kept to the edge of the strip, long grass on his right in which he might hide. He had no Congo now to warn him if somebody lay in wait. He could stop often to listen with inadequate ears, to watch with tired eyes, and they were playing tricks, just as they had done to him long ago, just as they had done to Tam Diamond on the steep side of the glen — the cluster of reeds that was a man, the tree that was a steeple, the white flashings of exhaustion. Old Pugsley's quick easement had worn off, and if there was also an antibiotic to quell the little monsters rampant in his stomach, it would take hours to work.

He hid among gas drums, rusted relics of pre-Parker vintage. The access road was opposite him, running a hundred yards south to meet the east-west highway which paralleled the strip. He kneeled in a crouched position. Some would be quick to call it a fetal crouch, but it helped his bellyache. He saw the lights of a car passing to the east; he did not hear it through the wind.

It would take a bluebird to find those keys. Perhaps a cryptic comment; surely not a random comment. The bluebird was no jackdaw, seeking shiny objects to expropriate. But it had its housing predilections, known to any bird-watching man or woman. Ash left his suitcase, and took the gun with him round the building. There were oblong windows near the eaves, for light, presumably, but below them nothing broke the even laminated clapboards. The hidden moon showed that clearly — side wall, back wall, side wall, no holes in them, and nothing fixed to them. The sliding doors were of metal, locked together at a handle, double locked by a padlock and a hasp below. There was also a gas pump, and that was padlocked.

Ash went back to the empty barrels. He stumbled against one, making a loud clank, and his heart jumped up. "I've tried," he muttered in the wind. "What is the point?"

There is every point. You call your life a fruitless cock-up. Weaken now, and you make it precisely that.

"But people have phobias — tunnels, heights, even open spaces — and there is nothing they can do about them."

Flying means heights. Is that your phobia?

"Of course not," he said angrily. "It's power lines." He saw the black thing sag at him.

You fell off a horse. Climb on it again.

"Oh, Christ," he said. "Can't you leave me alone?" But he was very much alone.

A car turned in from the highway. What was all this bravado about never being captured, never enduring prison again? It would be so easy to do what he had instructed Randy Dibble to do — put his hands on top of his head and walk to meet the headlights. But he cowered there, useless among a lot of useless barrels, too much of a weakling to give himself up, too much of a weakling to try to mount the horse that he had ridden superbly.

The man did not get out this time. He drove close to the hangar doors, circled on the concrete apron, and drove away. Nigel Ash had a different thought — he shrank from everything, and more than all the rest, he shrank from killing a man again.

Somehow or other that thought put a little backbone into him. The wind had steadied now. The gusts and lulls were periodic, but they held to a strength, a tempo cycle. He went on another bluebird expedition. The hangar was no good. Two lone trees between it and the woods were just a possibility. The first was a sugar maple, hidden from the highway by the building. He circled it with the flashlight, seeking above eye level, at eye level, below eye level, nothing.

The other was smaller, with an eccentric contradictory splay of boughs that could mean only old apple tree. It stood alone, exposed to a watcher from most directions, and he could not use the flashlight. He circled the rough trunk, stooping, and found nothing. The first crotch, or division of limbs, was at about five feet from the ground, a favorite bluebird height, but they did go higher.

He laid down the rifle-gun which, in its former capacity had wounded a man, finished off a deer, potted ruffed grouse, in its latter capacity had killed a man on the run and a ruffed grouse on the wing.

224

Tired though he was and rather sick, he managed to climb into that crotch. He steadied himself with one hand, searched with the other, nothing. Oh, to hell with it, he risked the light, and there, at intertwining apple elbows — they curved around one another quite voluptuously — was a bluebird's nesting box. He lifted the hinged lid and found the ring of keys hanging from a nail.

To Colby Parker it would be one vault up and one leap down. To him it was an exhausting laborious business, but he had the keys, reluctantly sought and found.

He took cover among rusty barrels. One had the means of entry; one must have a look. But the sliding doors faced squarely to the access road. Binoculars again, no car was parked there. He had five keys — two for the doors, two for the plane, one for the gas pump, that would be it. First thing: get in there, check the wing tanks, get out again.

Ash took the suitcase with him. The padlock key was easy. On the third try he found the right doorhandle key. They rolled apart smoothly and quietly on dolly wheels. The starboard wing tank was almost full, the port half-full, sufficient gas.

He unlocked the pilot's door, put the suitcase in, took the gun with him, and locked the hangar doors as the lights of a car came along the highway from the west. But the lights went off. Back among the barrels, he saw nothing — and then a shadow in movement loomed across the runway.

One minute or so earlier, and he would have been caught. Not very fair, Ash thought about the sneak approach. The headlamps lit locked doors, and once more the policeman got out to inspect them.

"Come in, Two-Three."

He ran back. "Two-Three."

"Where are you?"

"At Colby's hangar. All secure."

"Okay, then, go get some rest. We'll give you a shout around five. The railroad . . ."

But the car door closed, and Ash heard no more. Soon it drove off, turning left and away as before. The west end of the runway showed clearly and briefly, but he could not see whether there was a recessed apron where a plane would be out of sight from here. He walked along to find out, three hundred yards, a thousand feet or so, a short walk. Yes, there was a rough space tucked into the south side. He headed back into wind, weak, muddle-headed, stomach empty, but it did not ache. From that conversation, one could expect things to be quieter until five A.M.

It had been easy until they had picked up his trail. There had been alternatives until then — a freight train, simply a matter of patience and a bit of luck. *Luck.* — Or spend the whole of September in the woods, the best month of the year, what could be easier in New Brunswick or in Maine? And there were others, vanished all of them. The only alternative now to the horror that was offered to him was to wait in the cold night, clobber the cop at his next lock inspection, and make a run for it in the patrol car. But his revulsion from cold-blooded clobbering was just as bad as that damned haphazard black thing sagging across the eye of his mind. He had almost forgotten it in these three years.

Nigel Ash listened in the wind, heard nothing, saw nothing. He unlocked the doors, slid them wide, eased the Micmac out nose-first with the towbar, put that away, closed and locked the hangar doors and got in.

The propeller milled once, twice, and the engine coughed and took. He taxied fast to the end of the strip, turned left, went in as far as he could, turned again, cut the engine and got out. He was well off the runway, hidden from the hangar.

Unless someone checked along here, or unless Colby Parker himself had second thoughts about the bank-vault security of his Micmac, Ash was safe for the present. But at this hour, nearly midnight, surely young Colby Parker would be sleeping with his delectable young wife.

The hours dillied and dallied away, and it was time for a

226

second dose of old Pugsley's potion, which seemed to be working, Jehovah Pugsley. He had that, and then he managed one ham sandwich and a banana, and he felt a good deal better. In those days one did not have antibiotics to fight the battle of the belly. In these days as in those days one also got excruciating cramps from calf to thigh, one's whole leg knotted up. He climbed out to the cold, rubbed it, hopped about, and the cramp went away as suddenly as it had come.

The next item was to change clothes in the passenger's seat where there was more room. Oh, God bless her, between jacket and shirt was a half bottle of brandy, but it was whiskey, he took a small sip. Funny thing, booze, he had been on the go for five days and nights, and had hardly thought of it, more important things to think of. But now it could be of vast importance. *Any messages? — Oh well, love and that sort of thing.*

It was contortionist dressing, but he managed it, with occasional assistance from the roof light. His dog bites hurt when he touched that arm, but they did not throb. Now Lorna's tie with the mango pattern, his cardigan, the jacket, finally the Burberry, much needed against cold. He packed his other clothes away, dry sweater round sodden boots, and the hatchet, not the knife and not the gun. Then, the light still on, he turned to consider Colby Parker's ingenious contraption which replaced seats in the workhorse's broad backside. It was a small trail bike in a cradle, held down by guy wires. The cradle was on a telescopic rail affair. One opened the door on the passenger's side — a sliding door, not standard in a Micmac, or in Micmacs of his vintage. One extended the rail and dropped it to the ground. There was a hand winch on the cabin wall. One eased the bike out until the front wheel was on the incline, then one winched it down slowly on its cradle, or one winched it up and in.

A gimmick in the derogatory sense, one might first think. But for a farm salesman cum timber merchant covering a wide territory, it made sense. In fact, it offset the prime disadvantage

227

of airborne business, country style. He had panache, this Colby Parker on the up and up, too sure of himself, but that was no bad thing. I was sublimely sure of myself when I was young, Ash thought. And look at me.

It was much darker now that the moon had set. The wind buffeted the plane, playing a heaving game with the wings in turn, and the aircraft creaked. At dusk he had drunk about a quart of water to replace what his body had lost through sickness and diarrhea, but he was thirsty again, and nothing to be done about it. One could not go water-divining in citified clothing in black night, and neat whiskey was not the best thirst quencher.

He dozed and woke and slid into troubled sleep. *You bloody bludger. Get sobered up and come and see me. — Yes, Allan? — You're the best pilot who ever flew for me. I'll give you one chance. Climb into that thing out there and fly it. — I can't, Allan, I cannot.* He woke up from the dream that had happened, old Allan of Strathallan Air, what the Australians called a fair dinkum bloke. He dozed again, and she said to him: *We were happy until you came. You made me unhappy, Nigel darling, and I am going to hate you. Yes, I will.*

Unhappy dreams, and it was half-past two. *Who is Tam Diamond now? Wha's yon? Yon's Nigel Ash, Tam Diamond's Daddy.*

"Oh, please," he said in the restless cabin, wide awake, and it came to him:

> . . . The Garden called Gethsemane,
> It held a pretty lass.
> But all the time she talked to me
> I prayed my cup might pass.

> . . . It didn't pass — it didn't pass —
> It didn't pass from me.
> I drank it when we met the gas
> Beyond Gethsemane.

It was ten to four. He unscrewed the top, took two long swigs, and put the bottle in his right jacket pocket for future reference. He leaned over to slide the starboard window open to the wind. He heard only the wind as the whisky took warm hold.

Master switch on — trim for take-off — mixture full rich — carburetor cold — two notches of flap — gas on full tank — fuel pump on — throttle an eighth. It was all in his bones. He listened once more, shut that window, harnessed up.

I never was cornered before, he thought in his palsied corner, from which he had to blast without running up, without checking mag drop, carburetor heat drop, precautions that he had never failed to take, not even in those last boozy days before the powerline swooped at him.

The engine fired, oil pressure rising steadily, brakes off, swing to the runway, lights on, throttle, and she rose to full revs without a falter. Against this strong wind, she needed less than half the runway to fly herself off, lights out, but let the airspeed build now, a climbing turn to port, to the north. It was a fair chance that he would not be heard that way.

The plane bucketed about in turbulence, in cloud, climbing on, turning on until he reached two seventy magnetic, steady at that for the first leg over the wilderness of Maine, north of Bangor, south of Houlton, off the beaten radar track was his idea.

It was not so bad to be flying again. I did climb onto my horse, he thought. Out of desperation, aided by the whiskey bottle, I climbed on. No more whiskey. He broke into the clear just after six thousand feet and leveled off. It was miraculous, but fear had left him. There were no powerlines in limbo at six thousand.

It was calm up here. It was serenity, a part of him, the Pole Star riding on with him, the red beacon light on Mount Washington falling back from him, he and Mount Washington alone above the clouds at six thousand, four hundred feet.

The White Mountains were. well south of his intended course, but he had a sure and certain fix, it could be nothing else. Now his heading was due west, two hundred and ninety-five magnetic, five extra for drift, to meet Lake Champlain, sixty miles of lake square on, one could hardly miss it if the weather lifted.

There were breaks in the cloud cover, occasional pinpoint lights to see and lose at once. The radio was useless to him because he had forgotten frequencies.

They might have heard him take off from Huntingtower, but with a strong east wind the odds could be even, or slightly in his favor. Once he had reached altitude, no chance that anyone could have heard him, more than a mile aloft in a loud night of wind.

In his flying days he had never bothered to analyze it, to seek the reasons why he loved the air, and loved it best alone with it. Not joy, but serenity, that calm word again. He had felt serene on the first warm afternoon, falling asleep with Congo by his side. A peculiar serenity after killing a man. He would have felt serenity if it had been given to them to love one another as lovers were made to do. But that had not been given to them. And his battle with poor Diamond had been a battle renewed, not over yet. Another battle yesterday, last night, this night, won with the spurious aid of whisky.

Now he was serenely happy, joined again with his element of freedom, their world together. He had feared, and he knew that he would fear again, but not now, it was a blessing. *Are you happy?* the voice asked Tam. *Ay,* he said. *I'm happy the now.*

And so Nigel was, not fleeing, but flying yonder to begin his journey back.

He glimpsed a city's lights ahead, it would be Burlington. This weather system was passing to the east, cloud thinning rapidly. He turned north for Canada. Day was an hour away, but night had begun to pale.

His timeless time was over. Now dawn and the place must meet. And there were mundane things to do. Another dose of stomach medicine, a sandwich to chew slowly in his parched mouth, a banana, which went down more easily. He flew on beside the uniformity of water, Lake Champlain. A factory chimney, spewing its filth away in secret while men still slept, gave him the change of wind.

Daylight was coming fast as the lake fell back and he flew north-west for Montreal. It was flat country, with the steep isolated hills peculiar to that region. He circled at altitude, not unmindful of commercial flight paths into Dorval Airport. Then he throttled right back, five thousand feet to play with in slow quiet gliding turns, a town not far away, a brownish field, new stubble, a shed against a strip of woods, no farmhouse near, no telephone lines, powerlines, definitely not. But what was that pole? His heart raced up, not a pole, you fool, a dead old spar.

Three notches of flap, and he sank like an inclined elevator, down, a complaint of undercarriage, bounce and down. How easy it had been to meet his element again. He taxied for the shed, which turned out to be an open barn, straw bales to the roof. He parked Colby Parker's Micmac in decent obscurity between barn and trees.

A quarter of an hour later he was riding Colby Parker's trail bike into a town which announced itself as St Claude, and along the deserted rue Principale in search of a call-box, which he found, and consulted Yellow Pages. It was a fair-sized place, with a population of five or ten thousand by the spread of it, sure to be a twenty-four hour service, and there was: *Dandurand Taxi, rue Principale.*

He wheeled the motorcycle into a junkyard just off the main street, La Belle Province, hardly the tidy province. He untied the nylon cord which secured his suitcase to the luggage carrier, pocketed the bit of nylon, it had become a good luck kind of thing, and walked to Dandurand at 432 rue Principale. Once more in luck. Half an hour from touchdown Monsieur Dandurand himself was driving Nigel Ash to Montreal, and to the Motel Bonne Chance on Decarie, where Neil Arnott took a room.

231

24

"Neuf heures et demie, Monsieur."

He felt quite ghastly, dragged by the telephone from two hours sleep, from dreams that were a cheerful hodgepodge of what had and had not happened in these last weeks or days or nights. Cheerful dreams, extraordinary.

He made himself a cup of instant coffee with Coffeemate for cream by courtesy of the management. It was that kind of a sanitized for your protection, mattress vibrator for your tired back or libido (but it cost an honest quarter), triple-size-bedded up to date motel, and clean, for which one could be truly thankful.

He shaved and had a much-needed bath and, getting dressed, warned himself against euphoria. "Now, steady down," he said. In the worst case, they had heard him take off, and there would have been an alert in all directions hours ago. In the best case, Colby Parker, who had an Ottawa appointment in the afternoon, might not go to the airstrip until eleven o'clock or even twelve, Atlantic time, ten or eleven this time.

In the worst case, the farmer would have gone for straw. In the best case, he had no present need for straw, lately taken from that stubble field. And then there was Monsieur Dandurand, a taciturn Frenchman, handsomely tipped.

In any case, worst or best or in between, the first priority — not of ultimate importance but of immediate action — was to go to the Laurentian Bank. The second priority was to get out of Montreal, Quebec and Canada as soon as possible.

He had heard it said that bananas were the only food upon which man can subsist entirely or exclusively. He ate the last one, bland padding for his still grumbling stomach, and had another dose of medicine. He locked the suitcase, pocketed the essential ring of keys, went out to the fine morning and the busy street, and took a taxi.

The mysterious cockahoop feeling — not so mysterious, recent events considered — persisted even in the city. Ever since those crowded prison days, a press of humanity dismayed him. But not this morning. He regarded his hurried harried fellow-men with something like affection, scruffy outfit that they were, and nowhere more plainly so than on St Catherine Street, his cab paid off, a block to walk to that branch of the Laurentian Bank, one of his young brother's larger outlets.

He signed Arnott in and to the safety deposit box, employed his key after hers, and withdrew to the cubicle, where he removed passport, three thousand dollars in American money, and one check form. If he cashed five hundred, that would still leave four hundred and sixty odd, plus accumulated interest in the savings account. Sometime, if a leisured sometime should present itself, he must get Dan's minions to bring the bankbook up to date. But not now. Now lock up, cash the check, and get moving. *No rest for the wicked.* He wondered how those wise old shopworn aphorisms found their way into human tongues, so absolutely true. *All's well that ends well,* same thing again, and it would be so.

The teller at savings was an eager-beaver youth with a custom-made customer welcome, not quite Ash's type, but he said good morning politely, made out the check, identified himself by passport without being asked, and said: "May I please have it in two hundreds, four fifties, three twenties, three tens and ten ones?"

The teller flipped the bills, pushed them and the passport through, serving with a smile again, and said: "Have a nice day now, Mr. Arnott."

"Thank you," he said, and turned to go. At the Current Accounts wicket along was a man. He was a man of about Nigel Ash's build, with similarly longish hair, wearing a similar dark suit, with even a similar make of boney countenance. He was the brilliant bird photographer, Inspector George Petrie, R.C.M.P. He frowned a little, two fingers touching the top of his left ear, perhaps deliberating. Then he put that hand down to hold the check book.

Ash left the bank. Heard, not heard? Recognized, not recognized? It was the lot of the restless wicked ever to be guessing odds. He guessed the odds in this case to be ten to one on. It had happened to him only a few times in his life, but he knew it very well, the irrational authentic tap of fate.

He also remembered how and when and where Neil Arnott and George Petrie had met in a winter, not a summer, and it was the pointed top lobe of Petrie's ear that told him.

None of which altered his immediate course of action. He made a purchase at Eaton's toy department, rented a Chevelle with a New York License to drop off in New York City, picked up his suitcase at the Motel Bonne Chance, and took the shortest way to the border, Route 9, Champlain in New York State. His customs bait was an outsized teddy bear on the seat beside him. "I have this to declare, Officer," he said.

"Is it a gift, sir?"

"Yes," he said. "For my little niece in Boston's birthday. It cost fifteen dollars and ninety-two cents. I have the sales slip."

He was a decent courteous man, tickled about Teddy, and he waved him on, saying: "Have a nice day now."

It worked like a charm, it always did, and the rifle-gun was in his suitcase. One did rather cling to things. One clung to one's friends. One clung to one's sanity while losing it.

Nigel Ash crossed into Vermont. He stopped for a quick bite at a diner — bacon and one egg, vanilla ice cream, a cup of coffee with a slug in it to perk him up. There was still some whiskey left, abstemious fellow. But he soon paid for the whiskey's encouragement with a mountainous need for sleep amid the mountains of Vermont.

So he stopped again at a drugstore. He had first bought them

234

at Innsbruck when similarly afflicted, but that was after skiing all day and beating it up all night for weeks. The inscription on the bottle said: *Wenn Mann bis zum Totenpunkt gekommen ist.* When one reaches the very point of death, then one takes a whatever-it-was-called, ever afterward a *Totenpunkt* to him. "Do you have Totenpunkts?" he asked the baffled girl. "Sorry, I mean No Doz, you know, caffeine pills?"

She did and he chewed up three and drove again by the lesser roads and the smaller hills of that charming state until he reached a suitably retiring place called Bellamy, with a semi-motel, The Sleepy Haven, into which he booked, and from which he walked down the street.

He could not walk quite straight, being at the very *Totenpunkt*, but he managed it to a liquor store and to one each of Dry Sack and Highland Cream, and to a call-box and a telephone call. Unlike his memory for some things, his memory for numbers was quite good.

"Hullo."

"Mrs. Colby Parker?"

"This is she."

"Tom Roberts of Canadian Press calling from Toronto, sorry to disturb you, Mrs. Parker, we would like to follow up about the report of your husband's plane."

"I'm afraid I can't help. Quiet, Dickie, Mummy's on the phone. Sorry, Mr. Roberts, that's our little boy. The plane simply vanished in the night, and we don't know any more. My husband just called me from the office. You might get him there, but no, I guess not, the line's sure to be busy. Quiet, Dickie!"

"A darned shame, Mrs. Parker. I'll call again later, if I may. Goodbye, then."

Such an appealing girl, he had expected better of her than *This is she*, she must have been reading Emily Post or the *Ladies' Home Journal.* The heat, he thought, walking back. Well the heat was certainly off New Brunswick. The heat was

235

dissipated to anywhere within a four or five hundred mile radius, and far beyond that by commercial flight. But what about that bugger, Petrie?

No matter, nothing mattered now but sleep. Oh God, what bliss the silk pajamas in between Sleepy Haven's sheets. It was a lovely view as he went to sleep. It was a view of her nice brown shoulders, nice brown arms, a hand on each dinghy thwart. It was his guess, from sly inadequate observation, that Lorna was nice brown all over . . . He laughed, and she heard that above the motor purr, quite a decent purr, it was. *Joke?* she said, turning, pleased.

It was happening to us then, he thought, asleep.

"Sixteen solid hours," he said at eight on Saturday morning. He lay a while longer, totally slept out, the feeling not too bad, his stomach rumbling but now for food, his dog bites ticklesome, his right shoulder only one of the minor aches that were a middle-aged man's portion after a marathon like that. "I've made a balls of everything," he said, getting up. "But just lately I haven't done too badly, self-respect, I mean." He was not pleased with himself like yesterday. George Petrie had put a quick stop to that.

Voices next door reminded him that The Sleepy Haven was anything but soundproof, and that he must watch it about talking to himself, a habit caused by being alone so much, or by incipient madness, or a bit of both. When he was in solitary in the cooler, he used to mumble all day long.

Eating breakfast at the coffee shop across the street, he made plans for this particular day. They were simple plans, involving mental activity but not, unless anything went wrong, involving physical movement. At the drugstore he bought a pad of cheap quarto paper, and back to the motel where his room had been made up, as requested, and his neighbors had departed.

Agreeably quiet now on his side, facing away from the street, The Sleepy Haven was a perfect place for it, an armchair to sit in, a reasonably distant prospect of a cattle herd, Black Angus, chunky beasts grazing on the hill, no human bustle and no near distractions.

He would make a beginning with the end of Tam Diamond's story, so nearly done. The notes were in his head. They had been building in his head through every troubled day and night.

It always took an hour or more to begin for him. A wait, a gathering, not yet, interminable wait, a gathering to come alive.

But this morning it never came. This morning time did not slide away forgotten, it never came, he did not write a word. "I've lost it," he said. "I can write just as well here as there, why not? So I've lost it, down the bloody drain. *It's the last straw,* another tired pearl of wisdom. I give up."

He had a maxim for when all seemed lost, and it was do something, do anything, but do it. He went to the office to ask the motherly old bag if he could have the room for one more night, yes, he was very comfortable thank you, a great chance to catch up on the week's paperwork, crossed the street for two hamburgers, a chocolate ice-cream sundae and a Coke to take out, back like a yo-yo or a monkey on a string to his temporary haven for sherry out of the tooth glass, and for adequate nourishment. "I must have lost a stone this week," he said. "Too bad when I was just getting pretty again. Well, I lost it and I gained it. In the end I got my flying back, funny way of getting it, but got it."

"You know," he said, becoming or become the introspective club bore, "I didn't think things were worth believing in, and so I didn't bother. But this was a thing I did believe in. *Never say die,* you bloody old fool. Now try again."

He could not see or feel that place. He could not see or be those people. He was here and only here, staring out of a window at fat black cattlebeasts now chewing the cud on a field below a wood, peaceful rustic scene. There was nothing for it but a walk.

In flight — not in airborne flight, in fleeing — one was more alert to danger in the world around than to beauty in the world around. But a day of respite had been given to him. He had hoped to put the day to some use and he had failed. No matter, he was free, and nobody was chasing him, and the world was good on a balmy afternoon, the fall on its way, but only hinting.

His mood of tranquility did not last long, pinched between the nightmare that had been, and what might be. He was going there to finish it. He was going there to find her there. And after that he did not know. How could he know when Interpol might by now have added Neil Arnott and Canadian passport to Nigel Ash and British passport?

George Petrie's concern was not with common murderers. According to Keith Kelly at a casual enquiry on that boat picnic, he had some top secret security job with a public relations front or cover, but nobody had a clue what the job actually was. *That cool cat George, a PR man — how dumb can Ottawa be?* said Keith. It was then that he had thought of the *cool cat* appellation for the Kelly boys themselves, a pair of cynical idealists, they made you think a bit.

Nigel closed his eyes, trying to see Lorna — sad or happy, irate or thoughtful, any mood would do — but he could not see her. He opened his eyes to see across this valley touched by autumn, to remember sharply his other encounter with George Petrie at Camford Point on the DEW line in the Arctic.

He had no sooner cut the engine than the blow arrived. It was as near a thing as that. Sometimes the winds came stealthily. Sometimes they came full strength out of calm. He had seen it as he dropped off height for the landing, an indeterminate rim of cotton wool below the blue evening sky, above the white sea ice. This blow rolled down on Camford Point as fast as a southbound express.

Five minutes earlier, the wind — five minutes later, the plane — and he would have been dead. But he was alive, and in black anger. He would give those soft sods in Met something to remember him by, but first he had to warn Murdoch about the shipment which they were unloading in a blizzard.

238

It was only a stone's throw up to the store hut. He was not halfway there before his eyelids were frozen shut, and he turned and stumbled backwards into the killer wind, backward, forward again to find the door, and he went in.

The wind roared about the hut. Through the porch and the second door, his face thawing out, and there were voices from the cubicle at the other end where Murdoch slept. He had to see Murdoch alone, and he would have left and come back later, were it not for the subject being discussed.

"Mr. Murdoch," said a voice, a quiet cool voice in the hut in the wind. "There are twelve cases of Carnation stacked beside your bunk. Three of them have a small blue daub of paint on the tops and ends. Please open one."

"Get lost." Murdoch was a Scotsman. *Gut lawst*, he said it. He was a bad and dangerous man, and strictly honest in the booze racket.

"I have identified myself. Do what I say or you are under arrest."

"You just try it, arrestin' me."

"A lethal weapon won't help, you know. Put that knife down."

The cop evidently unarmed, Murdoch with a knife, and Murdoch's record of violence and killing stretched a long way back.

Neil Arnott picked up the wooden hand mallet, useful tool for pounding things like lumpy sugar, and he went round the half-partition, seeing the young man in profile, and the young man turned perhaps half a second before Arnott conked him. He collapsed.

"You stupid bugger, drawing a knife on him."

"I'd've more'n drawn it on 'im." Murdoch was not a stupid bugger, but a plain wicked honest killer five times over, a man with a kink, a teetotaller too, and Murdoch's name was no more Murdoch than Arnott's name was Arnott.

He knelt to feel the pulse, which was steady but very slow.

"He'll be out for half an hour anyway. There are six cases in this load. I'll be right back, and we'll decide what to do. Get rid of the lot, I guess."

His anger, which had been in abeyance for that minute or whatever it was, came back full force. He struggled through a blinding blast of snow to the module where the Met people and the radio operators lived in comfort, playing at being Northern men for their fourteen months away from television, playing gin rummy now.

"Oh, hi!" a couple said, and the others did not look up.

"Don't you hi me, you useless twots. Look at your temperatures — forty-eight below at six this morning, thirty-seven below at noon, fourteen below at five. Look at the barometer readings — twenty-nine point nine at six, down to twenty nine point one. Any half-wit would know a blow was coming, and you let me take off from Yellowknife without one word of warning then or later. You sit here on your fat bottoms in perfect safety letting other people kill themselves, and what do you care, God damn and blast you to bloody hell."

He threw their card table across the room, and they goggled at him, terrified of him. He had vented that wrath and that contempt and he felt better for it, stumbling back to decide what to do about this damned policeman.

"Where is he?" he said in the store hut.

"I put him out for to cool," Murdoch said.

"Outside, you mean?"

"Ay," Murdoch said. "He'll no be much trouble if he gets right cooled off."

"Where?"

"I'm no tellin' ye," Murdoch said, his left hand moving to the right sleeve of his windbreaker.

"Aren't you?" he said. His boot was quicker than Murdoch's hand. He kicked him in the crotch, a dirty trick against a dirty knife. He bent over Murdoch, relieved him of the knife and held it to his cheek. "Now where?" Murdoch groaned. "Where?" He jabbed the point in.

240

"Fornent latrine."

Fornent, opposite, beside or near. He threw the knife away in the snow, in the hellish thundering storm, but he found the man between two huts, half drifted over already in that brief time, slung him across his shoulder and took him to the doctor, whose dispensary was at the other end of that same module. "Doc, I found this guy lying in the snow. God knows how he got there."

The face was frozen white, and both bare hands. "That goddam booze again, I don't smell it on him, though. Pulse is just okay. A few more minutes, a goner. Thanks, then, Neil."

Dismissed by the Doc, a competent misanthropic type, he went to deal with the man Murdoch, whose real or proper name was McClintock.

Two days later, when the blow had finished, Neil Arnott flew the patient out to Edmonton. He was on a stretcher, face and hands bandaged, with holes only for his eyes, nose and mouth.

Arnott did not know his name. He knew only that he had worked as a cat-skinner at Camford Point for a week or two. "How do you feel?" he said, as they were going to lift him out.

"So so. Thanks for flying me. We met once, didn't we, somewhere?" The voice blurred with dope.

"I don't think so," Neil Arnott said. "But . . ."

"But my mummified condition . . ." He chuckled, and caught his breath behind his bandages.

"Hellish painful, I know," said Arnott, smiling down at the enemy, whom he had clobbered and also spared. Of no importance. He made for the head office of Arctic Construction, Jeremy Prentice, of some importance.

The shape of a human ear, a Mephistophelian peak, covered in these days of long-haired fashion. How slender a clue to memory it had been. He strolled back to the motel, and unlocked the suitcase that held the gun that had been the cause of all this trouble. But the cause of this trouble was not the gun.

Nigel Ash decided to do one more thing on this day of respite.

It might be a pointless thing to do, he did not know, but done fast enough, it could do no harm, and he would do it.

He had his drinks, rehearsing what he would say, went across for supper, and after that, armed with numerous quarters, he repaired to the Bellamy call-box.

"Hullo."

"Nigel speaking. Listen Lorna, I'm at Idlewild, I mean Kennedy and in a hurry, last call for my flight. I just want to thank you and Dan very much for all your kindness, and say how sorry I am about everything." He slurred his words a little to be a little tight. "I would have tried to get Dan, but he's so elusive. You will tell him, won't you?"

"Yes," she said. "But where . . .?"

"The wide pampas beckon. Oh, and one last thing, I'm afraid I came away with that excellent Parker pen you lent me. How typical, but I'll mail it back sometime. Now I must literally fly. Many thanks again."

He hung up. If her telephone was being monitored by tape recorder, it might seem odd to the most thick-headed law enforcer that a man who had pitched his host's jeep off a cliff should bother to mention a borrowed fountain pen. On the other hand the quirks of the lunatic mind were well known. On yet another hand, he had not borrowed a Parker pen or any pen from her.

He went to pay for his second night at the motel, and he would be leaving early, *Goodbye and thank you,* and *come again, Mr. Arnott.*

And so to bed on his day of respite, a bamboozling day for the puppet strutting, but his mind eased off to let him sleep.

242

25

"Could you fill her right up? And I guess we'd better check the oil."

"Sure." He was a lanky individual with a lugubrious expression. T. LORIMER, TUNE-UPS, not the smartest of rural garages, reminiscent of the junkyard where he had stowed Colby Parker's trail bike, a proper dog's dinner of a dump, cars without wheels, trucks without engines, bodiless chassis and chassisless bodies, upside down and right side up. The discarded artifacts looked quite comfortably at home amid long grass, clumps of burdocks, faded goldenrod and wild blue asters. There were also sheds in variously dilapidated condition. This might just be the place.

By way of contrast to outer chaos, the workshop was tidy, tools neatly stacked, testing equipment, a gleaming black Mercedes of senior vintage on a hoist.

"That's a good-looking car," he said.

"Best engineered automobile in the world, and you know what? My Merc's got a squeak and can I find it? No, sir. So we're out for the Sunday ride like usual, and that squeak is drivin' me half crazy and I says: *Hell, I'm sure it's some place in her backside,* and the wife gets mad and she says: *You care more for your Merc's squeakin' backside than you care for mine.* Two different things, I told her." Mr. Lorimer did not crack a smile. "Well, the oil's okay."

"They say in Europe that one beautiful good car is worth several beautiful bad women."

Mr. Lorimer's lips twitched slightly. "Do they say that?

I must tell the wife." He washed the windshield. "From the flies you picked up, you've bin drivin' a ways."

"Yes," he said. "All day."

"Headin' on down for the big city?"

"Not now," he said. "In a day or two. As a matter of fact I have some rather private business nearby, and I just wondered — could you store it for me?"

"Well, I guess so." He looked puzzled, and then glanced sharply at him. "This car ain't hot, no phony business?"

"No phony business," Nigel said. "You see, the person in question is alone, and a strange car outside the house might draw attention. Well, I mean: she's beautiful and she isn't bad — does that explain it?"

"Explains you're a lucky fella. That one's near empty. Drive her over."

The Chevelle squeezed in with a snowblower and a Ski-Doo. "Better take your keys."

"Let's see — the gas was six forty-nine. What about storage?"

"You said a day or two. Call it ten even for the lot."

"But that isn't enough. In New York City . . ."

"Yeah, I heard of that place. Tell you what, Mister, we'll toss double or quits, twenty or nothing, what do you call?"

"Heads," he said, and paid up twenty. "I hope you fix your beautiful good car."

"Same to you," said Mr. Lorimer, totally deadpan.

He left that engaging man, and walked down the road toward the shore to meet the main highway. But he stopped short of it. There were more summer cottages on this side of the river than on the other, and they were to the left of him. Ahead was the chimney of a disused sardine factory. To his right, downriver, a small bay, the red speedboat at its mooring, a dinghy on a running line.

A mile away, or a little more, was the place that he had come from, the log cabin at the water's edge, the cove and the field, the woods above, the house on the hill. He watched through the binoculars which had belonged to his father, half the size of

244

others of equal power and light capacity, three times as expensive. He watched from hiding. When had he not been hiding? When would he ever not be hiding?

That thought occurred, but to go to do, and to go to meet, they were not hiding. Nothing moved on the Canadian land, and on the Canadian water only the dinghy moved, swinging slowly on its line before a thrust of tide or a touch of wind. In the sky between here and there the gulls were soaring, as they often did, wheeling high and white for no purpose other than evening fun. Below him cars passed intermittently, most of them heading south, none of them stopping.

And then one did. It was some make of open sports car like an MGB, turning off the road and down a lane. A man in rubber boots walked to the water's edge and hauled in the dinghy, waded a little, untied the rope, climbed in, rowed to the dinky speedboat, tied dinghy to mooring, freed speedboat from mooring, handed himself aft in the dinghy, and went aboard, holding the dinghy alongside by a light line to a cleat.

The preliminaries to the ritual evening spin, done adeptly, economically, and now Ash saw with particular care that he did not take a key from a pocket, but felt under the dashboard for a key, put it in, checked throttle handle, turned key, and the big outboard started. He threw away the line to the dinghy, moved out to swing to his starting point, surged on to the step and shot downriver, leaving a flat white spread of wake.

He was a middle-aged man with a dinky sports car and a dinky speedboat having his evening fun like the herring gulls, a soar or a spin, what was the difference? In due course, and on his unvarying circuit, he rounded the red buoy for home, went through his gamut in reverse, slightly farther to row because the tide was flooding, and he drove away.

Nigel waited for dusk. When lights came on at Lorna's house uphill across the river, he moved tentatively, cautiously, crossed the highway, and waited again. There were no lights at the cabin shore, and no near lights at this shore. He got his feet wet, but that was unavoidable. Then, rather clumsily and

245

slowly in the moon-hidden night, he followed the precise routine that had been demonstrated to him.

The big motor purred in a gentlemanly fashion, a deeper but not much louder sound than the dinghy motor at half-throttle. He was beyond midstream when excitement became more exciting than was comfortable. A powerful spotlight came into view round Gallery Island not yet beamed to here. So he ran at full spanking speed for Canada. But the light had turned away. It was probably that infernal R.C.M.P. patrol boat hunting smugglers or any kind of vermin down the bay, and it might be back to hunt the river. He was a sitting duck should that occur. He must therefore risk it. Take the dinghy in tow, and head back to Maine as fast as possible without swamping the thing. It was safer over there beyond their jurisdiction, and at the home of the red speedboat, which they would know.

Boat to mooring, dinghy to running line, all accomplished except the voyage home, a mile and a bit of sitting duck all the way for home. "Not home," he said, unable yet to see the dark cabin, but he saw Lorna's lights until they were hidden by the woods, and then he was near enough to see the cabin. "Not home," he said, "but more home in a way than I ever knew a home."

At half-flood he was able to come alongside the rocks, put out his small suitcase and follow it and haul the dinghy off.

It was eight evenings ago that he had asked Lorna whether he might go to church with her the next morning. He listened to the owl, a trilling sound, not an owl call that he knew, but he supposed that it would be an owl. There were no other sounds except the lip-lap of the tide, a mutter of traffic occasional across the river.

The cabin door was locked, a problem if the unscreened window on the kitchen side was also snibbed. During his term of office he used to put out crumbs, bacon and such delicacies on that window shelf. But it was free, and he climbed in.

It was dark inside, and he used the pocket flashlight, now getting dim after faithful service, pulled down the kitchen blinds and closed the curtains, shut the door to the living room, and put on the oven light, enough to see by.

First task, assemble the gun — barrel, action, fore-end, stock, load in one of each. Second task, have a well-earned drink with two lumps of ice and up to the brim. He was thirsty after that small adventure, thinking that things had gone much better than expected, ever a dangerous thought.

The remains of her partridge fricassee were still in the refrigerator, potato salad, cherry tomatoes. Being ravenous, he gobbled up that delicious snack, bread and butter and Liederkranz cheese, a transparent apple. Neither the potato salad, the cheese, nor the early apples had been there last Saturday night.

It was after half-past ten, and she might be asleep, or Dan might be down for the weekend, but he never stayed for Sunday night. Shilly-shally, better wait until the morning? But in the morning Jake arrived, and some days Mrs. Tovey.

He heard the noise of the patrol boat growing, went into the living room and stood at a curtain chink. The spotlight was on this shore, moving upriver and past and on, no specific point of attention.

When the rumble died, he used his flashlight again. Everything was as he had left it, except that the guncase was not on the bed, and on the living room table, where his manuscript had been, there lay a fountain pen, not a Parker and not his.

That made his mind up the way he wanted it made up, the way he knew that the willful intemperate Nigel Ash had fully intended to make it up. He buzzed on the house to shore.

Nothing happened. Nothing. Nothing. Then a click as the line came alive, but no word spoken.

He whistled the other call of the chickadee, a high note and two low notes. He used that to draw them to him in the woods, and it used to please her too.

"I'm just going to check," Lorna said, and he waited again until she said quietly: "Lights out now, and window shut. Are you okay, Nigel?"

"Yes," he said. "A bit part-worn, but quite okay. Are you?"

"Oh, me," she said. "Madness. It *is* madness, darling."

"I know," he said. "But I said I would, and here I am."

"I asked you, didn't I?"

"What about the police?"

"They haven't been here since Thursday. The plane was found yesterday. Dan told me that when I called him right after your messages from Kennedy, which I passed on faithfully except about the pen. That clued me up, so I left one just to let you know."

"Yes," he said. "I saw it."

"At first Dan flatly refused to tell them you had called. He said: *I can't help them hound my brother down to Argentina.* But I told him he had to, or he would be obstructing justice, and he said he would sleep on it. But he did tell them, because the sergeant on the case called me this morning. A loathsome creature, for the very first time he seemed to believe me."

"Do you think they suspect I might come back?"

"Surely not so soon. But there are two reasons why they might. One is the manuscript. The other is me."

"The other is you. Nothing is anything but you."

"That Sergeant Borton suspected it from the first."

"My fault," he said. "Like everything else."

"Oh, poppycock."

"I spent two nights, one day, in Vermont, trying for the ending. It went dead on me. I couldn't write a word."

"You will, at the cabin. I know you will. You will."

"I'll try." He yawned. "So damned sleepy. Just one more complication: I saw Geroge Petrie in Montreal, and I bet he saw me. He isn't here, by any chance?"

"He came this morning for the Aquarium Trustee meeting tomorrow. But that's been arranged for ages. It's nothing to do with you."

"He might just chance along to renew acquaintance with that bloody man, Neil Arnott."

"Oh," she said.

248

"But how did you know about Petrie?"

"Keith and Nelson told me when they came to say goodbye."

"I'd forgotten old Congo. Is he okay?"

"He rolled up himself in the middle of the night, whatever night it was. Trust the Kellys to slip through."

"Yes," he said. "I'm going to try to make a start tomorrow morning. Shall we meet after lunch?"

"Yes," she said. "And I'll buzz you if anything odd happens in the meanwhile."

"Goodnight, my love."

"Write well, my love."

Write well, she had said that to him at the beginning. *Write well, my love.* To come, to begin, to finish, and to go. To be in danger, and to be serene.

Are you happy now? asked the voice from close beside him.

Tam had not noticed that he had wandered from the smooth road, that he was blundering across the moor to the west. He stumbled and fell and rose again, but always the voice was there to help him. He was happy. At last he was truly happy.

"Ay," he said aloud, raising his eyes to watch the day. "I'm happy the now."

Tam Diamond never saw the deep place where he fell. He hardly felt the new pain.

Those were the last words of that last chapter. He found them in his hand-written manuscript, still in the cupboard. Then he filled the pen, which was a Parker, and his own. Then he stapled ten yellow sheets together, laid the gun on the floor beside him, sat in the armchair, lit a cigarette, looked through the gauze-curtained window. It was a morning of cloud and shower and sun.

All the last journeys had been his own. The journey from Vermont to Scotland had been even more his own because he could not make it.

But now he did go there, to be and to watch those people at the burning boathouse by the loch, which was Loch Ash adapted, the hill loch of his boyhood, the loch where the trout were small and quick, where the whooper swans were at home in March. The place was still his. The people were their own in him: Inspector Thoms, McNaughton the stalker, young Robert Graham who saw all this, and four policemen, anonymous bobbies.

Thoms left two of them to put out the fire, and the stalker led.

"He crawled as far as here," McNaughton said. Beyond that the tracks narrowed. They were clear-cut. No snow had fallen since they were made.

"How long since?" asked Thoms.

"It's hard to say. The sun's begun to soften the edges. An hour, two hours mebbe. It was just after dawn they reported the fire."

He stopped again at the bridge. "Waited here a bit," he said, pointing to the rough circle of marks.

Robert looked over to the loch. There was an extraordinary sharpness and purity about the morning, as if the sky and the hills had been washed clean by the blizzard: the stocky Scots pines beyond the loch, trunks russet red under white branches, the immaculate hills reflected in still water, the sparkle of the warm March sun. And yet it was unreal. It was like a glass of champagne before a football match. It was too fine, too ethereal a setting for the harsh business they had in hand. Robert saw the beauty, but he did not feel it, he who was never happier than on the hill.

"It's a rare morning," said McNaughton abruptly. "It's a Sabbath morning you could enjoy."

Nigel got up for coffee. *You will*, she said. And he was. It moved for him, this relentless thing. He heard a splatter of rain on the roof, and he watched the dark furrow of squall run down the river, and that shower had passed in Canada, and he was in pursuit on a distant hill.

They went on again, a glum little party in single file, Robert leading now. The snow was above his knees, but it was not difficult walking in the broken track.

"He fell here," he said. "And here again." Diamond had fallen many times. The road was almost level, the line of it clearly marked by the banks.

250

He might do it yet, Robert thought. Another two miles and it's downhill. That's what the others are thinking too, that he may have escaped again. And yet in a way I don't want to catch him. I want him to be free after all he must have suffered. Here, steady! That's a queer idea. You can't want killers to escape. But you do have sympathy for a man who falls and gets up and falls again and doesn't give in.

"Look at this!" he said when they came over the next rise. The tracks turned sharply to the right, over the bank at the roadside, and went off across the moor. It was rough undulating ground, a mass of dips and hillocks.

"This looks like it," said the inspector.

"It does so," McNaughton said. "He's in among the peat hags. I'll no say it till we get him, though."

Nigel read the beginning of his ending, and was humbled.

"There was no hope for Tam," he said. "No hope but in the dreams that called him on. No good woman but a dream of woman. And he never did give in."

But the buzz brought the good woman who was not yet his to him. "All quiet on this front," she said.

"All quiet here," he said.

"Did you?"

"Yes, I did."

"I told you so."

"Yes, you told me so."

"Where do we meet? It can't be for long."

"Where the doe and the fawn used to lie — would that do?"

"Oh, well," she said. "It reminds me. But I suppose so, a hidden place. At two?"

"At two," he said. "I'll whistle you up."

26

THERE WAS NO ANSWER TO HIS WHISTLE. *I'll whistle you up.* He had not intended an arrogance, although from the beginning he had whistled, softly whistled Lorna up. Arrogant, he thought. That was always me. But where is my arrogance?

Two apple trees, the fallen-in foundations of a cottage, a shard of barrel hoop still at the well, the tumbled poles of a cedar fence, a cattle skull, an archaic harrow, the tangled grass, the faded goldenrod, the burdocks and the wild blue aster. It was not so different from that marriage of growth and decay at T. LORIMER, TUNE-UPS across in Maine. It might be, it would be, the face of the world in a hundred years or less. That's been my trouble, he thought. The core of my disbelief. Man and his world, my bloody foot.

But Lorna whistled the high note and the low notes of the chickadee, and he answered that, and left Dan's gun, and they met at a place where people had struggled and built, lived loved begotten envied hated died and gone, and where lately the deer had lain together.

"It's you," he said. "It's really you. I tried so often to see your face."

"You're as thin as a rake again," she more or less accused him, her mouth puckering to laughter.

"You look all right to me," he said, a hand on each shoulder in her tatty raincoat, at arm's length from the shadowed face, it was thinner too. "You're bonny," he said. *Bawny*, he said it in the Scottish tongue, and that seemed to please her.

There was no passion. There was comfort. But passion knocked as is the way. "No, darling," Lorna said. "We tempted

252

providence once, and look what happened. You must finish first."

"What is mine end?" he said, going with her to sit on a long granite block of the foundation, all that was left of a settler's home.

"Meaning?"

"Oh, nothing, only old Job speaking."

"Please tell me what happened."

"It's such a dim story. Some other time?"

"Ah, yes," she said. "Some other time. Just a little about the flying, though. Keith and Nelson said next day that your insides had gone wrong, but I knew something else was worrying them about you. And then Simon Skafe telephoned while they were here to say that the plane had disappeared — old robber baron, he liked that one — and you should have seen the Kellys, they rolled around like lunatics."

". . . Terrified," he said when he had summarized that episode in his unfinished journey. "Dutch courage with your whiskey helped. But in the end I got it back."

"That's the very best thing for you," she said.

"A good thing as things go. Hardly the best thing." And they looked at one another.

"I meant that you can write about flying now. You never would have, would you, not if I know Nigel Ash?"

"No," he said. "I suppose I could, if the right idea came along. No airborne pursuits, though, thank you very much. I've had my fill of people being chased."

"Oh, dear," she said. "Just get it done. When do you think it will be done?"

"Tomorrow," he said. "Even by lunchtime possibly, if I go back soon."

"And I could type it in the afternoon. Nigel, your eye has begun to flutter again."

"I know, I know," he said.

"I must go too. Jake is bringing back the jeep. He took a mechanic to dry it out. The scuba diver experts at the station

had a lovely weekend party tying a deflated sausage to it, and
they blew the sausage up with airbottles, whatever they may be,
and the jeep bobbed to the surface from a hundred feet or something. They were as happy as schoolboys, or is it sandboys?
Anyway, we're getting our jeep back."

"I played fast and loose with your jeep, and forgot about it,
like everything, almost everything. But how did the police
find it at Anvil Lake?"

A hesitation, and she said: "I guess they must just have tried
everywhere and stumbled on the marks." There had been a
hesitation from the Kellys, and now Lorna. Dan or Bobby,
who else could it be? And if Dan, she would not say that. She
had said no critical word of Dan to him. He felt immensely sad
about what he had done, was doing, and would do. *Take what
you want*, he always had.

Nigel went over to one of the apple trees, the same early trans-
parents that were at the cabin. Some lay on the ground, and
deer had been eating them. "Let's have an apple," he said,
picking a pale apple from the tree. So they shared that apple.

> Thou saidest: I am sick of love
> Stay me with flagons, comfort me
> With apples for my pains thereof
> Till my hands gather in his tree
> That fruit wherein my lips would be.

"You do remember things," she said.

"Half-educated," he said. "Dibble-dabble, dilettante, well
not the flying, I was a pro at that."

"I think you're a pro at everything you set your mind to."
And she added: "Even loving."

"Love is many things," he said. But he saw something
scarlet in the boggy place where the well had been. "Do you see
what I see?"

"A Cardinal flower."

254

"Shall I pick it for you?"

"It will wither soon," she said. "Yes, please. I'll press it."

He picked that most beautiful of wild flowers for her. "Until tomorrow, then," she said.

"You seem so sure about tomorrow. You seem to feel the cabin is safe."

"Yes," he said. "I don't understand it, but I do. I wonder — would it be all right to tell Jake I'm here? I would like to see old Jake again."

"So would he. I couldn't begin to say how kind Jake has been to me in all this trouble."

This trouble that he had made. "Jake would be," he said. "You might ask him to announce himself, a buzz first or something." Ash picked up the gun from the grass where he had lain it.

"That hateful thing! Haven't you killed enough already? Couldn't you pocket your stupid pride and give yourself up and tell the truth and let me tell it? Oh no, you couldn't. That would never do for the arrogant Nigel Ash, or that crook Neil Arnott or whatever name you've condemned yourself to. So you'll force them to kill you, I know you will."

Lorna ran from there, and he was left with the hateful gun in the hidden place where men had struggled and had given up. But he would not give up.

Robert fell in behind again. It was hard going. They floundered on the boggy ground, struggling to get their boots out of it. They would come free with a suck, and go deep at every step.

McNaughton was going very slowly. "Don't leave the track," he grunted over his shoulder. "There's dangerous places."

It seemed interminable, that walk. McNaughton stopped often for breath, looking round to get his bearings.

But the last time he halted, it was abruptly. "That's him down there," he said.

Robert remembered the place well. It was safe enough in summer when the moor was dry, safe if you did not fall in. They called it the Peat Hole. No one cut peat nowadays, but the hags were still there, deep soggy erosions where nothing grew. The hole was seven feet deep, with overhanging walls. It was a dangerous place, an earthy dungeon that no man could escape without help.

The snow was deep in the hole. The man lay on it, face down, arms and legs spreadeagled. His very stillness spoke of death, and there was a loose finality in the lying of his limbs . . .

"I killed Tam in the end," he said. "My story killed him. So who was the killer?"

He got himself a drink, not to write with the deceiving aid of drink, but to encourage his worn mind to think about what must still be written so that he could escape from it. Seeking that end, he went back to the beginning, to the manuscript of the first chapter that he had written a time ago, and he read:

The old beast was uneasy. He rose, and stood with legs spread wide, nostrils thrust forward, head circling. Then the wind changed, and a wave of the man-stink struck him.

The White Stag was king of the bare deer forest. He had mastered many things, but this fear he had never mastered. He turned and fled. The blue was murky on the hills. The ground was indistinct. The White Stag ran blindly . . .

When he had sat another time through — a last time if God should spare him and give him strength — he rustled up scrambled eggs and bacon for his supper, not having much appetite.

It was curious that he should feel so safe here at the cabin. It would have been good to light the fire, but smoke would be too crass an advertisement, not his kind of folly. A single electric radiator was enough to take the edge off. Now that buzzer.

"Hullo."

"Sorry for my outburst. So unkind."

"Not unkind," he said. "And please don't be."

"Just to say that Jake is on his way down now. Goodnight."

256

The line went dead before he could reply. *Unkind*, she had said. *Unfair*, she might have said, but she had not.

He hid the unpopular gun, and went out to meet Jake, who was standing at the fallen spruce which Nigel had started limbing after the hurricane. "Now we got the jeep back, we can winch 'er over."

"Yes," he said. "Come in, Jake. Have a drink."

"No thanks," Jake said inside. "What the hell did you come back for?"

"I came back to finish it," he said, pointing to the yellow paper on the table.

"Couldn't you finish the darned thing some place else?"

"I don't know," he said.

"You don't know nothin' except what you want. You don't even think what Mrs. Ash has bin through. And who put her through it?"

"I did," he said.

"Yes, you did. And you came back totin' that goddam gun before her eyes. Well, I took a shine to you, just like we all did. I thought: *Here's a great guy*, and I guess you are too, a great crazy guy, and the shine's wore off."

In his lordly way, *I would like to see old Jake again.* "I'm sorry, Jake," he said. "I deserve everything you say. But the craziness . . ." He could not say it. How could he say it?

"I'm not all that blind," Jake said, with the wry kindliness which was his. Kindly now, but he did not relent. "Here you sit, Nigel, a sittin' duck if ever there was one . . ."

"I thought that, coming across the river. Not at the cabin, though. I only need tomorrow, and nobody's going to bother me. I'm sure of it, don't ask me why."

"Well, okay, let's say nobody's goin' to bother you. But who's gonna bother poor Mrs. Ash — she's twice the man you ever was or will be — who's gonna bother her, listening for the goddam gunfire up there to the house? You are."

"I know, Jake," he said.

"Just give me that gun, and she won't worry, not too much."

"I can't do that," he said. "I'm sorry, but I can't do that."

"It's your kind of kammerkarzee bastard that fucks the world up." Jake walked out.

They looked down into the Peat Hole, feeling the warmth of the sun on their backs, seeing the sharp ending of Diamond's life. The cap had fallen forward off his head. The hair was fair, a tawny gold against the snow and the dark blood.

"Is it safe to go down?" asked the inspector.

"Safe enough," McNaughton said. "I've a wee length of rope here." He opened his jacket and uncoiled the thin rope from his waist.

"How the devil did you think of that?"

McNaughton did not answer. "Who's going down?" he asked, showing no disposition to volunteer. Robert said nothing. Let the police do it, he thought.

One of the constables slid over the edge. He trampled the snow till it was packed hard. Then he unknotted the rope from himself and slipped it round Diamond's body.

They heaved on the rope. The body came up jerkily. Then they had it over the edge and laid out on the snow. The inspector bent over. He looked for a little at the pale face, and straightened again.

"That's Tam Diamond," he said. He began to speak, but hesitated as if he would say no more. But he did speak again. His face and his voice were compassionate. It was a moving thing to see the hard lines soften. "That's him," he said. "It's sad to see him this way after the long time. Even if he did a killing."

"He looks happy," Robert said. "As if someone had just told him good news." Diamond's face was peaceful. He was smiling a little. It was not the face of a man who had been hunted to his death. A carved-out, do-or-die face, Thoms had said, and it was that still, but smoothed of storms and trouble. A fine face, you would say; a strange face to find on a man who was a killer.

They turned back to help the policeman out of the Peat Hole. "It's a beast in here," he said, "a stag, a rare big head on him too."

Robert and McNaughton stood side by side. The man had cleared the snow from the antlers, but the rest of the beast was still hidden. Robert counted the points, six and six, and the left brow point was marked with blood. A Royal, a wonderful head, wide and symmetrical. He knew that head, surely he knew it.

258

"See if you can clear the snow a bit," said McNaughton sharply.

The policeman brushed away the snow with his hands. Then the top of the head was clear. He pulled on the antler, raising the head above the snow. It was pale gray except for the face, and that was white. The skin had deteriorated little.

"It's a bad way for the White Stag to finish," Robert said, "starved to death in the Peat Hole." The whole thing was painful to him, his own fault somehow that the great beast should have come to such a death.

McNaughton had taken off his hat. The gray hair was thick on his Viking's head.

"You're wrong, Master Robert," he said. "Mebbe the White Stag did die slowly in the hole, but that was not the end of him. Today was the ending."

McNaughton looked down at the stag and across to the fair-haired man who lay in the snow. Then he raised his eyes, turning to watch his hills; so cold now, so austerely clad; so warmly peaceful in the summer evenings; so bare and wild in autumn. He saw them, all the well-remembered places of his life, the steep hills and the glens, the hills of many legends. And he looked to the north where tall Schiehallion stood alone.

"The White Stag and the man," he said. "Yon's a right ending. Yon's a story they'll remember in the Highlands."

The bell of the old Kirk was pealing far away, calling to the people, telling of God's peace on a fine Sabbath morning.

And it was done. He read the ending of the story he had written, it was done.

But the cloak of safety, the certainty that God would spare him for this thing, was gone. Ash felt danger. Picking up Dan's gun, he toured the windows circumspectly, nothing. Then he went outside, still sensing danger, nobody and nothing at high water of the full moon tide. It was a cloudless day, and there was no wind. Nothing moved in the forest, at the shore, but still he felt it, a warning prickle in his neck, there had been something.

Something not dangerous was also here. "Oh, hullo," he said to the chipmunk, small striped beast, looking out from the cabin's underpinnings. "Fancy seeing you again. What about a cracker?"

He went for the soda cracker, crumpled it, and held his hand out. The chipmunk had various homes or storehouses — under the cabin, in a settler's rockpile wrested from the inhospitable earth, those and others — and it would come within about six inches, never quite to hand, and would fill its jowls until they bulged in aldermanic fashion, pop off to the store that it was using for the moment, and come back for more. But on this exceptional day it came without hesitation to Nigel Ash's hand, came, bulged, went and came again. He liked the demure chipmunk very much, and now that it fully trusted him, he liked it even more.

"What a simple sentimental cluck I am," he said, going in with his gun, sensing no danger. That would have been a fancy of his overworked imagination. He read it through once more at sherry time, and what was done was done, and nothing to be done. The burden had been taken from him. He felt light. He felt relief, not pleasure, just relief, and that eyelid fluttered.

He was going to buzz Lorna from the kitchen when there was a quick scuffle below the window, and soon a scratch at the cabin door.

In Congo's mouth was a golden black-striped offering that had been the chipmunk. Congo wagged his backside, managing a labrador smile despite the morsel in his mouth, so proud to be doing his duty bringing pleasure and good food, like the two ruffed grouse, the one spruce grouse, the one snowshoe rabbit, what's the difference?

"Oh, Congo," he said. The dog dropped the small body, which lay in the loose finality of death. Nigel took it outside, and up to the ledge where he used to watch the deer, forgetful of danger-prickles in his neck and all that bloody nonsense, and he threw the chipmunk as far as he could at high water of the full moon tide, and it would soon be ebbing. "That's what it's all about," he said, going back to be a decent chap to Congo, even pleased to see him, how about a bit of bully beef?

He buzzed Lorna. "Here I am," she said.

260

"Congo came to call. I finished it. Same place, same time?"

"Same place, same time."

He put the gun down at the edge of the clearing, and went across, Congo at heel. She was sitting on that granite block of the foundation, and she did not turn to watch him come. She had a pencil in her hand, and she tapped it, tapped it, tapped it lightly on the stone. One did not know what she was thinking of, a mystery, a magic, was it not? He kissed her cheek, brown in September from a summer's sun. "Here it is," he said.

Lorna read his chapter through, and when she had finished it, she said, "That name you printed out. How do you pronounce it?"

"Sha-hallion," he said, "as in medallion, vowels and emphasis the same."

"Could you read it for me, from 'then he raised his eyes'?"

" 'Then he raised his eyes, turning to watch his hills; so cold now, so austerely clad; so warmly peaceful in the summer evenings; so bare and wild in autumn. He saw them, all the well-remembered places of his life, the steep hills and the glens, the hills of many legends. And he looked to the north where tall Schiehallion stood alone.

"The White Stag and the man," he said. "Yon's a right ending. Yon's a story they'll remember in the Highlands."

" 'The bell of the old Kirk was pealing far away, calling to the people, telling of God's peace on a fine Sabbath morning.' "

"God's peace," she said. "That would be a right ending if ever it could be."

"Yes," he said.

"I'll bring it down later on. In the meanwhile will you do one thing for me?"

"Yes," he said.

"Will you hide this afternoon?"

He nodded, not well able now to speak.

"Heel, Congo," and she walked away.

Congo followed, and stopped, and whined in doubt between them. "Go on, Congo," he said. "Go with Mum."

"Even Mum's dog is hooked," she said with bitterness. "Oh, I am so sorry, Nigel."

27

THE BELL OF THE OLD KIRK WAS PEALING FAR AWAY, *calling to the people, telling of God's peace on a fine Sabbath morning.*

The last words of his story, simple words, he liked them, whatever they might mean. They came back to him as he lay in hiding on a fine Tuesday afternoon. They came back because he had lately made them, and one liked to taste again; and they came back because he did feel peace of a kind in this glade within the embracing forest, peace after what was done and gone, before what was to come. Was peace a nothingness in between? Or was peace a nothingness of finality? Was God? he meant. So evident, never to be fathomed.

Things happened, agreeable things. Nobody was killing much at the moment. What nonsense. Every worm and every grub that the parent robins brought to their belated brood in one of the apple trees was being killed, and a good thing too, make strong young robins to battle winter. All the world likes the amiable robin. Inaccurate again. The blueberry grower doesn't like him very much. He shoots robins by the thousand on his barren. Does he eat them? I bet blueberry-enriched robin would be good. *Do come for Sunday lunch and try,/My organo-phosphate robin pie.*

Another thing, or things, to watch were the bumblebees on the wild blue asters, which flowered in shades from pale to dark, and they favored the darker ones this afternoon, and so did he. If he said to Lorna: *Your eyes are like the wild blue asters, the darker ones, I mean,* she would probably blush in her most becoming way, a warmth to soft brown skin, but with exasperation, that kind of overt schmaltz not being her thing at all.

263

There were the robins and the bumblebees and so on, homely players in the simple, not the ugly sense. Best of all he would have liked to be lying here as quietly as any mouse, and to be seeing a deer come delicately, aware of him and unafraid, to eat a few juicy apples in a clearing where the doe and her fawn had lain together. But that did not happen.

The afternoon went on to early evening, and his mite of peace was over.

Nelson, square-jawed and implacable: *Don't you know what she's been through about all this, having to lie and lie and lie for you?*

Yes, he said. *I was wrong. I was trying to keep her out of it.*

We know that, Nelson said.

How is Lorna?

She's just great. Nelson scowled at him. *Do you want us to tell Lorna you've chickened out?*

That's a dirty crack, he said.

I know. I'm provoking you. Wouldn't she do the same?

I suppose she would . . .

Any other messages? Keith said.

Oh well, love and that sort of thing.

They both smiled about that sort of thing, his sort of trouble, which they seemed so well to understand.

And Jake yesterday: *I took a shine to you, just like we all did. I thought: here's a great guy, and I guess you are too, a great crazy guy, and the shine's wore off. — Well, okay, let's say nobody's goin' to bother you. But who's gonna bother poor Mrs. Ash — she's twice the man you ever was or will be — who's gonna bother her, listening for the goddam gunfire up there to the house? You are.*

"What should I do?" he said to himself, lost kammerkarzee bastard in the wilderness. But he was coming to know what he should do.

He went down by the trodden path, upon which one made no detectable sound, stopping often to listen and to look, and the woods were empty but for him and their native inhabitants, and

264

his prickle of danger grew. He put a four-ten shell between the third and fourth fingers of his trigger hand, a magnum twenty-two between the first and second fingers of his other hand.

Not now, he thought as he neared the log cabin at the shore. Please, not now.

"Mr. Ash!" said a voice from the left, from the green wall of cedars, a quiet voice but resonant. He swung to it instantly, to nobody.

A flicker of movement in his right eye, a flicker that he saw too late, and something smacked, loud as a pistol shot, something tore Dan's rifle-gun from his hands to clatter on a rock, and someone arrived. "Sorry," George Petrie said.

He saw the first punch coming a lead with the right, a feint with the right, and then things exploded.

Cold wetness on his face, and he was sitting in the armchair where he had been writing every, every, every day. He ached from his jaw to the top of his head. Soon his eyes cleared and blurred and cleared to observe Petrie standing, one hand on the table edge, the other, the left hand, holding a wet dishcloth. He wore a green high-necked sweater tucked into khaki trousers, no room for guns, unarmed in that respect. "Can you move your jaw all right?"

Ash tried that. "Creaks a bit," he said. "Christ, you socked me."

"A sock for a conk, all square, I would say, or had you forgotten?"

"I remembered at the bank."

"Same here," Petrie said. *"Have a nice day now, Mr. Arnott.* It clicked right back to Camford Point when I was coming round, and the doctor said: *Arnott, the pilot, brought you in, Arnott, the pilot,* it went on and on in my head, delirious, I guess." He gathered the dishcloth into a ball and flicked it across the living-room, neatly into the kitchen sink. "Showing off again," he said.

"That was a stone you threw, I suppose?"

"Yes," Petrie said.

"You must have been a fair good pitcher in your day."

"Fair," Petrie said. "I could throw straight. My curve ball wasn't much."

"And is ventriloquism another one of your accomplishments?"

"No. I came earlier to pay a call on you, and I happened to be standing at that spot you came to lately, and I distinctly heard a catbird mew from the cedars. But the catbird was not among the cedars. It was round the corner of the cabin on that apple tree. Quite a common trick of sound, it registered."

"What a clever chap you are."

"Thank you. One might even call you a clever chap, Mr. Ash, but that would not be a compliment. It never is."

"Am I under arrest?"

"Not noticeably for the moment yet." Petrie sat now on an upright chair. He was younger, stronger, quicker, tougher, in total command. There was no chance, and the word "arrest" was a figure of speech.

"You came unarmed?"

Petrie nodded. "I came off duty, in so far as one may be. And anyway, unlike you, I don't believe in pointing guns at people."

"I don't believe in pointing guns at people."

"Then you don't believe in what you do."

"Oh, God!" he said.

"First a question: Would you consider giving yourself up?"

"No," he said. "That's absolutely out."

"To appoint oneself Lord God Almighty, or in secular terms: Judge, jury and executioner is criminal, whatever extenuating circumstances there might me."

"There were no extenuating circumstances. And I told you: That is absolutely out."

"Very well, then, listen to me: When I ran into you by chance in Montreal, I had just arrived from overseas, and knew nothing about this. Right, so on Sunday I came down for the aquarium meeting, and by then, of course, I had heard the story. Now it happens that I was on a job in Gallery some time ago, and got to know a bit about the local ropes, so our man on the case phoned me here long distance to ask for my advice. He thought that your call from Kennedy Airport was feasibly genuine, and they're trying to check out Argentina, etcetera, not the easiest part of the world to plumb.

"But Sergeant Borton, a shrewd and assiduous officer if not the most appealing type, had a reserve suspicion that for two reasons you might sooner or later come back here, and he told me why."

"Yes," Ash said. "Lorna guessed that too. She hates your sergeant's guts."

"The feeling is mutual. I think she is the only person who ever got under the skin of that worthy cold fish Borton. So the fact is I am on a spot. I had to agree to meet him in Gallery at nine o'clock tomorrow morning. I am on leave, I have nothing to do with the case, but as has been before observed, the policeman's lot is not a happy one, least of all when his buddies regard him as persona non grata. But I will come to that.

"Well, here's my dilemma, Mr. Ash. On the one hand I have a bounden duty if my memory has served me right.

"On the other hand, you may have conked me, but you also saved me from the homicidal attentions of one McClintock, whom I caught up with later. Against that, I might mention that selling booze at vast profit to the dipsomaniacs tucked away up North to be safe from it emits the dirtiest stink I know, next to peddling drugs."

"Yes," Ash said. "How right you are."

"The remorse is somewhat belated," Petrie said coldly. "But to continue, I have to live with people, and my Trustee Chairman, the eminent S. K. Skafe, and my friends, the equally eminent Keith and Nelson, must have been tipped off about Borton's phone call — I am staying with Molly Becker, and I expect she spilled the beans, a secret society, this place — why else would all three of them treat me with positively glacial coolness?

"My guess is that they know something more about your crime than I was told by Sergeant Borton."

Petrie hesitated. He had been talking to the floor, but now he stared straight at Nigel and said: "Disregarding the deed itself, am I right in guessing at the sorest burden of your trouble?"

"Yes," he said.

"Memory," George Petrie said. "Such a fickle bitch. Sure, I remember — I think I remember — well vaguely, but I couldn't swear to it — no, that name doesn't ring a bell with me. What I am getting at is that under these peculiar, not to say confusing circumstances, and if one essential stipulation were to be met, the name Neil Arnott might not ring a bell with me."

"What is the stipulation?"

"That you never again carry an offensive weapon. I don't mean shooting for the pot. I mean: *Never never let your gun pointed be at anyone.* Didn't you learn that as a nipper?"

"I was taught it," he said. "And would you mind not being facetious?"

"Sorry. Under stress I utter inanities." Petrie stood and turned to look out of the window, his stance loose and limber, not a man to try to jump. "Yes or no?"

"You think you have me in a cleft stick."

"I not only think, I know. Call it blackmail, if you like."

"All right," he said.

"And it is clearly understood that I blow the Neil Arnott gaff instantly if you break your word?"

"Damn you, I never break my word."

"Damn you for making me break mine," said Petrie hardly. "Had that occurred to you?"

"I apologize," he said. "Will you have a drink?"

"Damn me, I believe I will."

That arranged for both of them, Nigel said: "I want you to make a second stipulation . . ." And he explained.

Petrie listened, frowning. When Ash had finished, he said: "Well, I suppose so, if you're sure it's best. Yes, I agree."

"Good, then," Nigel said.

268

"You're going to have to watch your step," said Petrie. "The FBI aren't bloody fools."

"I rather thought Cuba. I did a few jobs for Fidel in his salad days."

"H'mm," Petrie said, and the two fingers of his pitching hand wandered to bare the pointed peak of his ear, a mannerism, careful thought. He glanced intently at him and away. "That might be interesting."

"Fidel is my pal. And if you are having shady thoughts, you can forget about them."

"Shady thoughts in Public Relations?" Petrie said blandly. "Now, if I cop out altogether, as it were, may I ask you a thing or two about what happened?"

"Yes," he said.

"Borton mentioned the parallel of the White Stag in your story and the white-faced doe. Surely that wasn't the only reason you killed Dibble?"

"No," he said, and he told Petrie why.

"And one of the Dibble tribe witnessed it?"

"Yes," he said. "One certainly. Perhaps two."

"I wonder if Borton pursued that end of things."

"They have enough dim trouble in their lives without being grilled by the police about what they didn't do. The one who held the light even remonstrated with Dibble."

"They would not be grilled. They might be asked to explain in more detail just what happened."

"You've copped out. Now leave the poor sods alone."

"But I have to cop in tomorrow morning. Nothing can justify, but things can mitigate. I might suggest to Borton that people who knew you here thought highly of you, not a violent man at all in ordinary life, and might there not have been some additional provocation? That wouldn't harm anyone, and might possibly ease pressures in the hunt for you."

"I lost my bloody awful temper was what happened."

"Okay, you lost your bloody awful temper. Did you finish your book?"

"Yes," he said. "Lorna's typing that last chapter now."

"A labor of love," Petrie said, with a certain sadness. "And will she bring it down?"

"Yes," he said.

"You are safe here until tomorrow in the morning early, leaving no traces."

"Lorna has had a hellish time, entirely due to me."

"I would say that you have had a fairly rough time yourself."

"I asked for it and I got it," he said.

"More than one asks for is apt to be the case. May I go back a bit and pose a question?"

"Pose away," he said, much drawn to this diffident, formidable man.

"A chap like you — why did you get into the seamy side?"

"Boredom, I suppose. Disbelief, I suppose."

"And then you found it here?"

"Yes," he said. "I think I did, at the price of losing it."

"I rather question that. You were always strong in trouble, weren't you?"

"If you mean in emergency, I suppose I was."

"What about strong in truth?" George Petrie stood to go. "I looks toward you," he said with a small bow, shaking hands. Formal, relentless, gauche, laconic, Nigel Ash thought that the disparate components of George Petrie added up to what his own components never had: One man, whole. "Never trust a southpaw pitcher, he could hitchyer. How's that for corn?" He laughed heartily and left.

28

He gave her a buzz. "I've finished it," she said. "Just getting
things for supper."

"Are you coming soon?"

"Half an hour or so, but there's quite a lot to carry." Lorna
sounded fussed.

"Is the jeep back?"

"Yes."

"Bring that, then. It's quite safe. I don't mean hunches.
I mean guaranteed. I had a visitor."

"Oh, I see."

"I haven't got any vino here."

"There's a bottle in the fridge. But are you sure, dead certain
that it's safe?"

"I told you," he said. "Do take a pull, my dear good
woman." She giggled and hung up.

There were things to do, and things to think about. One set
the table, that was quickly done. One did various things quickly
without hurry, ever the enemy of good thought and action.
Then one sat on the red rocks at the shore, waiting for words to
put themselves together, wrote a few lines for what they were
worth, and waited, thinking. One had one's orders and one's
plans, and one would carry them out. The best way to do so was
the problem.

Nigel came to a decision about that, and he sat in quite contented melancholy, waiting for her. The tide was flooding, still
a long way out, but the living rim of it stole nearer, and it would
grow to be the great tide of this September moon. The sea was
flat calm beyond the shore, but farther out a roughness told of

light airs from the east. *Could mean fog before mornin'*, the pundit might have said to the kammerkarzee bastard.

The jeep was coming. It sounded healthy, if explosive, its leaking muffler none the better for immersion.

"You didn't bring Congo?"

"No," she said. "Jake's keeping him."

He took the basket and glanced into the back of the jeep. "Anything else to bring?"

"No," she said. "That's all for the moment." She carried the bottle of Riesling, beaded with moisture, and a big envelope under her arm, the manuscript of his opus, done, he couldn't care less about his opus.

"Who was your visitor?"

"George Petrie. He jumped me, and knocked me cold."

"And the gun?"

"Probably broken, confiscated, I don't know. He made me swear off guns."

"That's better," she said. "That's much more like it. But how did George Petrie prevail when us lesser mortals got the brush-off?"

"He threatened me with Neil Arnott and a Canadian passport. *Call it blackmail, if you like*, he said in his nonchalant way. He meant business too, a potent chap. So I gave my word." But the other thing about which a word had been given must wait, must wait. "Shall we have a drink?"

"My first today," she said. "I drank too much while you were on your holidays." When he brought their drinks, she took the manuscript from the envelope. "Here's another thing I did while you were on your holidays — I made a loose cover for it. The chapters are all punched and tied together. Blue, I thought. You do like blue?"

"I love blue," he said.

"Is there a title?"

"Yes," he said, and he wrote it with a black marker on the plain blue cover.

"I thought that was it, *The Storm and the Silence*, right for poor Tam. I was so afraid that it would be right for Nigel Ash." Lorna gulped half her whisky. "It hasn't been altogether funny," she said.

"You've been good to me. And look what I've done to you."

"You ain't done nothin' to me," she said, that enchanting smile, gamine. "Not yet. I'm shy of you, that's my trouble, shy."

"We always were, a bit," he said. "Could cold supper wait, or are you very hungry?"

"Not supper hungry," Lorna said. "Your eye is fluttering." And she put her hand across the kitchen table where they sat so decorously, shyly still, and she laid her finger on his eyelid, and she said: "Stop, flutter, I command you, stop!" She took her hand away, and the flutter had stopped, at her command, or at his desire.

"We waited so long," he said when waiting was past.

" 'Love me little, love me long/Is the burden of my song.' Good old words for Darby and Joan, I suppose, but not quite our thing. Love me deep and love me strong is more like the burden of my song."

"You're such good value," he said, and passion grew, and they loved one another.

But quiet again. God's peace, he thought. What else?

"God's peace," she said. It was uncanny. "I waited all my life to find it, scarlet woman on a bed of sin. What would the clergy say to that?"

"Good show, old girl." They laughed together.

"Shall we put some clothes on and have our supper?"

They had their supper, and drank the wine, and shared the armchair before the fire. It was driftwood, sparking orange, flaming green. "Do you have a song for me?"

> Vair me o ro van o
> Vair me o ro van ee
> Vair me o ru o ho
> Sad am I without thee.

"The Eriskay Love Lilt," Nigel said. "I don't have the Gaelic."

"Sad am I without thee. That's all over."

"Yes," he said. "That's over now."

"Let's go back to bed to slow and strong and deep and sleep."

When he woke the moon was high beyond the window. Lorna slept, her head on his shoulder, his hands on her breasts beneath the blanket and the sheet. He listened to her breathing, peacefully asleep. But then, not for the first or last time, he indulged his whim, and turned down the blanket and the sheet for a moment of the tide of time so that he might see her breasts, tipped hillocks in the wash of moon, and he covered her again.

"Mean beast," she said. "You woke me." And they watched the moon. "I used to fancy that old man until we took the giant stride."

"So did I," he said.

"But it did turn out to be your lucky moon."

"Yes," he said. *It has still to wane*, he might have said.

"When is departure time?"

"I think I should go about dawn," he said.

"I'm coming with you."

He told her rather well, that he was deeply fond of her, and was so grateful for everything that she had done for him and given him, but that he was a lone wolf, not a steady decent faithful chap, and in the fever of the book he had thought that he might have changed, but of course people do not change, you can't make a silk purse out of a sow's ear, and the fact was that he knew only too well that he would run true to form and tire of her. It had been so lovely while it lasted, while it grew, and now to this perfect climax, finish. He did his best to plant the seed to grow the tree of contempt for him. "Better now than let it wither," he said, arrogant four-flusher that he was.

"Like the Cardinal flower." Lorna had not stirred within his arms. "Have you finished?"

"Yes," he said.

274

"Don't give me that stuff," she said, his dear good woman, what a woman.

"I thought it would be easier for you."

"I'm coming with you, Nigel. My case is under the rug in the back of the jeep. I'm coming with you."

"No," he said. "They suspect you of being an accessory in a minor way; they know you covered up a bit. But if you came with me, you would be an accomplice to murder. And if you come with me, George Petrie splits on Arnott."

"George Petrie wouldn't."

"George Petrie would. I made him promise that in return for the promise I made him."

"Why, darling? Why?"

"Because . . ." he said. "Because I thought it would be best. I have to vanish. I have to be Neil Arnott for a while. First, I'll take the manuscript to Boston to that publisher."

"Your prison friend?"

"Yes," he said. "If they want it, okay. If not, I'll burn it."

"You want to burn every boat, including me."

"Dear love," he said. "Don't you understand?"

"Yes," she said. "I understand. Does it mean forever?"

"Petrie thinks it will die down. He thinks that in a year or two I could go back to Scotland, even. Not to Canada."

"And we could meet again?"

"If you still wanted that."

"It isn't utterly impossible." They laughed together. "The moon is dimmer now in fog, and love is many things, you told me."

"I told you what you taught me."

"Shall we be practical for a moment?"

"Okay, shoot."

"Is the dinghy gassed up?"

"I filled it last evening."

"So I take you across the river?"

"It's a risk for you."

275

"At six on a foggy morning? Don't be dumb. So then what?"

"Leave the rest of my clothes just as they are. Wash the dishes and the glasses, rub the door handles too. Get Jake to bring the jeep down early, and winch that tree over, make a mess of tracks all over the place. Okay, nothing to show that I've been back."

"And the manuscript, if that stinker asks?"

"Say I told you to burn it when I telephoned from Idlewild. So you burned it. But remember to hide the carbon copy of that last chapter."

"You think of everything. What else?"

"Nothing else except try to be your nicest self to Borton. Ask after his little ones or something."

"His little ones! Puzzle find the wherewithal to make any little Borton beasts."

"On the wander and alone," he said. "Not to have you to cheer me up."

"Dear Nigel," she said. "Now love me true before goodbye."

They thanked one another when peace came back.

"Can you manage two of Jake's eggs?"

"Yes," he said. "Tell him the kammerkarzee bastard managed two. Give Jake my best."

The fog would be called a mist in Scotland. One could see to the dinghy high and dry at the far end of the running line. So one squelched in rubber boots, Dan's boots, carrying one's small suitcase and one's shoes, one crunched a few clamshells on the mud, and one was pleased to see two spotted sandpipers, dipping and dabbling just as the six had done another time, and they called quite loudly and flew away.

"Such a low tide," she said. "Time is the tide, you said once."

"I said a lot of damned stupid things."

It was a short drag, and then a pole for depth, and put the motor down. He gave her the compass. "Keep the black end of the needle pointing thataways, square to us upriver. And I think it would be tactful to row the last bit in."

The motor started up first time, *quite a little rig*, as Jake would call it, a workhorse like the Micmac. Perhaps I will try to write about flying, he thought. She thought of that for me.

Lorna sat in the same way as she had sat before, facing the bow, a hand on each thwart but not wearing the scanty clothes of summer, wearing his windbreaker. *Swamps me a bit*, she had said another time. She pointed her right hand once to bring him on to course, and her left hand once to bring him on to course.

He timed it too. One could not be precise, but one could guess at a mile at eight miles an hour or so, say seven minutes. That elapsed, he stopped the motor, and they lost way in the fog. "I'll row us in," she said, turning, so that now they faced one another.

"I wrote a verse for you," he said. "I don't know whether it's any good," and he took the paper from a pocket of the dark pinstripe suit that she had admired.

"Please read it to me," Lorna said.

> There is no joy that knew no sorrow,
> Nor love that does not wait tomorrow,
> Nor any golden token
> To truth if truth be spoken.

The words, good or bad, were muted in the fog. She put the paper in his windbreaker, saying nothing, smiling, crying, smiling, as she rowed the short way in, his turn now to give direction, to bring them to the reef where he could land dryshod at this ebb tide.

"Goodbye," he said.

"Goodbye," she said in her soft sobless voice.

Lorna watched him climb the red rocks of the shore, no other living thing in sight. He turned and waved once and went into the mist.

She rowed a distance, and motored on for home, keeping the black end of the needle pointing thataways, square to them upriver.